THREE DAYS EARLIER

A PSYCHOLOGICAL THRILLER

THREE
A PSYCHOLOGICAL
DAYS
THRILLER
EARLIER

BESTSELLING AUTHOR OF *BREAKING MIDNIGHT*

LYNN WALKER

MZW
PUBLISHING
Washington
USA

Midnight Calling: A Memoir of a Drug Smuggler's Daughter

Breaking Midnight: A True Story

A Perfectly Good Fantasy: A Memoir

Trigger warning—This book contains scenes that may be disturbing to some readers, including sexual predation & abuse, abduction & one character's memory of childhood molestation.

For S.JW. ~

PART 1

VICTIMS

1

SEVEN MONTHS EARLIER

RACHEL HELD Kari's gaze a few seconds too long. That was her first mistake. She should have looked away. Like a jolt of electricity, a premonition zaps Rachel right in the solar plexus, and she knows something horrible is going to happen to her new boss. She has no idea *what* tragedy will strike Kari, only that it will not be good.

Rachel's mind starts churning, as it always does when she has a premonition. I bet Kari will be in a car accident. She has that forty-minute commute to and from work every day on a remote, hilly road, steep drop-offs, lots of deer. It would be a long time before another car passed by her crashed vehicle. A lot can go wrong in a car accident in a matter of minutes—

No! Don't even go there.

Even though a person might look fine after an accident, and may not be bleeding, their aorta could be ruptured from the steering wheel crushed against their chest. She could be gasping for air while you grope blindly through the shattered glass and crumpled metal for your phone.

Stop it! That was years ago. You're not in a car. You're sitting in an office. Focus on your job.

Desperately, Rachel tries to focus on work. She tries to unsee the final image of her mom in the car that day.

Rachel also tries to push away the sensation of Kari's impending doom. Taking slow, deep breaths—hopefully imperceptible ones so the other staff don't think she is hyperventilating during a routine, Monday morning staff meeting—Rachel tries to ignore her premonition that Kari is ... well, Kari is fucked.

The dark foreboding has moved up and formed a dense clot of dread in Rachel's throat.

"Why don't you come to the meeting with the Cedarbend Mayor tomorrow afternoon?" Kari says, looking right at Rachel. *I wish she'd stop doing that.* "Do you already know Mayor Shin?" Kari continues.

Rachel shakes her head, picking up her phone and tapping open the calendar app.

"Then I'll introduce you two tomorrow because you'll be working with her a lot on the city's land use rezoning."

"That's at one o'clock, right?" Rachel says, keeping her eyes glued to her phone while slowly entering the appointment into her calendar.

Kari nods and says eagerly, "You can drive over with me" —Uh-oh, Rachel thinks—"and I can give you some background on our work with the city and Mayor Shin. She's a bit of a ... handful—"

Rachel can barely pay attention as Kari prattles on about Mayor Shin and the city's contentious land use rezoning and how Rachel's expertise will be perfect for this case. Instead, Rachel envisions herself in Kari's car tomorrow, bracing herself against the dashboard as the car screeches underneath the back of a semi-truck. Or maybe Kari's car will careen off a bridge and sail through the air—Rachel can almost feel her heart flying into her throat—then smack into the river.

"So, we'll leave here at quarter to one?" Kari pauses, waiting for Rachel to respond.

The silence snaps Rachel back to the conference room. She glances at Kari, then back to her calendar app. "Ah ... sorry." Rachel swallows hard. "I've got a lunch appointment at noon tomorrow. I'll just meet you over there."

Rachel doesn't receive a premonition *every* time she locks eyes with someone. It can happen when she accidentally bumps into a person or is simply in close proximity. But avoiding eye contact, and relationships (with all but a few people), greatly reduces the risk of a premonition. She is an expert at such avoidance. This is why, until a few weeks ago, she was in private practice instead of working at a law firm. And why she is an environmental attorney and not a criminal attorney—no offenders, no victims, no juries, no need for extensive eye contact. This is also why she lives alone, will never get married and never, ever, under any conditions, have children.

At twenty-eight, Rachel has learned how to minimize premonitions so that, in a good year, she only receives a few. But this is the second one, and it's only April.

When she started working at Martin Law Office, one of the few firms in the small town of Cedarbend, Rachel was hopeful that she could maintain a normal job. Her first paycheck last week was very welcome since her three years as a private practice attorney required tight budgeting to get from one paid invoice to the next. And working with the City of Cedarbend was going to be a great opportunity to grow her career.

What Rachel wasn't prepared for were Monday morning meetings with the other four staff around a small table in a conference room with no windows. But she was managing to keep her lack of body contact natural and her eye contact light and breezy. She had the being-new excuse for steady note-taking in her laptop. Between her notes there was accessing information on her phone, glancing from one staff person to the next, staring at the ceiling or table with feigned concentration. With her hands always full, Rachel could avoid most handshakes. And there was always coffee—the paralegal and office manager, Meagan, makes wonderfully strong coffee—Rachel could add half-and half, stir it, take a sip, more half-and-half, get refills. These were all perfectly inconspicuous, professional ways to avoid a premonition.

But this morning, Rachel couldn't avoid looking at Kari as she discussed the very case for which Rachel was hired, not without seeming rude or disinterested. Rachel had no choice.

The worst part of her premonitions is not being able to help the person, but Rachel has gone around and around on this for over a decade. It isn't helpful to warn a person that something bad, not sure what, is coming their way so watch out. Or to suggest they drive super carefully. Or tell them to go get a full-body scan for tumors. Or to keep a super close eye on their kids. Rachel has analyzed, to death, all her options, and while most options would clear her conscience, none would help the person who is about to face some unknown calamity. All she can do is hope the catastrophe won't be too gruesome or painful then get the hell away from them so she doesn't find out what went wrong.

When Rachel was a teenager, she became consumed with finding out what happened after her premonitions came true, looking for some kind of pattern or hint or information that she could use to prevent the next injury or illness or death. She imagined herself becoming a superhero. But there was never any pattern, just vague, seemingly random bolts of impending doom; *someone else's* doom. Even when Rachel was far too young to understand doom, she once clung to her grandma, who was saying good-bye and heading back home. Her dad had to pry Rachel off her grandma, who was diagnosed two weeks later with late-stage breast cancer.

———

Rachel arrives at the office the next morning to find three of her co-workers—everyone but Kari—sitting in the conference room staring at the teleconference phone on the table. The two other attorneys, Jerry and Pete, look stunned. Meagan has puffy eyes and a shiny nose, which isn't too surprising. In the few weeks Rachel has worked there, she learned that Megan is quick to emotion, any emotion—crying with sadness, snorting with laughter, hugging with excitement. Rachel can think of very few workplace situations in which crying is warranted. Or hugging.

Popping her head through the open door, Rachel says, "Was there a meeting this morning? I must've—"

"No," Meagan shakes her head. "We just got off the phone with Kari."

Well, at least she isn't dead. Yet. Rachel perches on the chair nearest the door, briefcase on her lap.

Pete, the employment and labor law attorney (and

Rachel's favorite because he isn't a big-eye-contact kind of guy—too shy for that) starts talking. "While Kari and her family were asleep last night ... there was a fire."

A shiver runs down Rachel's spine, but she refrains from shimmying it off, holding her posture ramrod straight, her shoulders still. *Please don't let it be her kids.*

"Fire department says it looks like it was ... a frayed wire," Pete continues, "in the attic. Luckily, they all got out."

Thank god, Rachel thinks. A house fire though? Never would've thought of that one.

Meagan plucks a tissue out of the box and blows her nose.

It's all Rachel can do not to roll her eyes. *No one's dead. It's just a house.*

Jerry, the overly talkative, stands-too-close, corporate lawyer shakes his head, as if he can will away this calamity. "By the time the fire trucks arrived, the house was engulfed. The roof collapsed. House burned to the ground. Everything —gone."

A tear starts rolling down Meagan's cheek. Rachel finds herself focused on that single tear, wondering if it will make it all the way to Meagan's chin, maybe drip onto her lap. Rachel roots for that solitary tear. *Go! Go! You can make it! Uh-oh, here comes a tissue.*

"They saved the cats," Meagan adds, quietly.

That's good, Rachel thinks. She hates it when animals die.

Keeping a look of soft compassion on her face, Rachel is being pummeled by waves of emotion. Cold indifference hits first—*Enough with the tears; it could've been so much worse!* Next fury rolls over her—*Why must I be plagued with clairvoyance?* Then Rachel is slammed by a visceral desire—

felt mostly as tension cramping her legs—to race out of the office.

"I'm running a carload of stuff up to them," Jerry says. "They're staying with a neighbor but don't have anything but the pajamas on their backs. Even their credit cards are gone. Melted. I can't just sit here ... I have to do something."

Hah! Little late for that. Besides, if anyone could've done something, it was me, and I've never been able to stop a premonition from coming true.

Meagan says, "I'll go get those case files Kari mentioned" —she looks at Pete and Jerry—"and you two let me know who's going to cover what." She explains to Rachel that Kari won't be coming in for a couple of weeks. It is clear that no one expects Rachel to help cover Kari's workload since she hasn't met any of the clients or familiarized herself with any cases.

When they drift out of the conference room, Rachel goes into her office and leans against the closed door. She contemplates what to do, not about Kari but about the job. Turns out, taking this job was her first mistake. She should have just stayed in private practice: no co-workers up close and personal, no eyes to catch, no premonitions.

But that first paycheck was great. And taking this position gave Rachel a welcome break from her father's nagging for her to connect with more people, despite the risk of premonitions. He has a few variations of the same advice he has been giving her since she was a teenager: "Maybe your ESP is a gift," or "Sucks, but this is life," or "Sucks, but take a chance anyway," or "Sucks, but you can't live alone with your dog forever."

Ruby and I are just fine, thank you.

Rachel didn't cancel the month-to-month lease on her private practice office in case things didn't work out at Martin Law Office. Better safe than sorry was her thinking at the time. Sorry is exactly what she is, and safe is exactly what she needs.

Glancing around her office, Rachel feels stifled. Martin Law Office has no exterior windows anywhere. Rachel's other office has a big window by her desk. Just being able to see outside steadies Rachel—birds flitting in and out of the fountain outside her other office, the sun or clouds or a rain shower moving through the sky, leaves rustling in the breeze, the changing of the seasons. There is something about watching the world go on despite house fires and car crashes and human suffering that is reassuring. But being in Martin Law Office all day, without seeing the sky or a single blade of grass or a leaf, has been suffocating.

She stares at her spider plant, which is also not doing too well without a window. In only three weeks, its leaves have faded from vibrant to pallid green. If I stay, she thinks, I'll need to get a plant light.

No. No plant light. This thing deserves sunlight.

Rachel stuffs her few personal items into her briefcase: law diploma, a hilarious card from her boyfriend, Aaron, and the last photo taken of Rachel with her parents before her mom died. Then she scoops up her spider plant and hurries out of the office.

At the end of a long hallway, sunlight, at last, streams in through the building's glass exit door. A blinding, fiery explosion of light.

Pausing at the bathroom door, Rachel considers, again, if there is any reason to stay. Not for the day but for the job.

She really thought this job could last, maybe for a year or two. This is the only law firm in town that needs her type of expertise. Plus, the worst part's over now; rarely does she sense danger for several people at once or have premonitions one right after the other. It could be months before another one hits. And she got off easy—well, Kari did—with only a house fire.

Ducking into the bathroom, Rachel peeks under the stalls to ensure she is alone. Locking a stall door, she slumps onto the toilet lid and drops her head into her palms. She contemplates going back into the office and shouldering the burden of Kari's loss with Meagan, Jerry and Pete with their puffy eyes and sullen faces. Meagan would probably think Rachel, the only other female in the office for now, will offer hugs and comfort. Meagan would be wrong.

Damn it, Rachel thinks. I don't want to sense other people's tragedies; I didn't ask for this ... affliction. What the hell could I have done differently? Even if I warned Kari about every danger I could imagine, I never would've thought of a house fire. Then, with her house incinerated, Kari would've said, What the hell good was your ESP? Thanks for nothing!

This job was definitely a mistake. Rachel will stick with private practice. Later today, she will send an email to Martin Law Office and resign.

Straightening up, Rachel tucks the hair that has come loose back into her ponytail and stares at the metal stall door. There is a sign that reads: No feminine hygiene products in the toilet. Around the words there is a bright red circle with a slash through it. A big, red warning sign. Apparently, the toilet simply can't handle any more.

"I can relate," Rachel mutters. "I've had enough, too."

Outside the bathroom, Rachel takes one glance back towards Martin Law Office then looks at the exit where sunlight, bright and clear and simple, floods into the building.

Rummaging through her briefcase, she pulls out her sunglasses and heads into the blaze.

2

SIX MONTHS EARLIER

THERE HAVE ONLY BEEN a few men that Rachel took a chance on getting really close with and, so far, she has never had a premonition about any of these boyfriends. She always expected that would be the end of a relationship—a premonition, not a tragedy. Well, maybe a tragedy ... Fortunately, all her romantic relationships ended of natural causes: one boyfriend didn't like dogs, one wanted Rachel to be more open, one wanted to go out to bars, concerts and parties while she wanted to spend time in the woods. The normal incompatibilities.

But things are going so well with Aaron over the past few months that Rachel thinks the relationship might go somewhere. She even starts to let her guard down. Though she still feels like she is peering around the edge of her armor to see if any missiles are whistling towards Aaron.

That is when he shows up at her house for a Saturday morning hike with his hair freshly shaved to a three-day stubble length—a ruggedly handsome look, Rachel thinks—

and when she notices on his scalp an almost black, irregularly shaped mole.

Aaron was leaning over the breakfast bar watching with amusement as Rachel buzzed around her kitchen, pulling out dog treats and human snacks, chattering about different trails they could hike. When she bent down to stuff everything in her daypack, he could no longer resist.

Moving behind her, he looked down at her ass but didn't touch her. Not yet. He was good at waiting. "Can I help you with any of that?"

When she turned to face him, Aaron gave her a gently passionate kiss, hungry but not aggressive.

"This kind of help," Rachel murmured, kissing him again, "will not get us out the door. It might not even get us out of the kitchen."

"Fine with me," he said, his voice gruff with arousal.

He slowly walked her backwards to a barstool then lifted her onto it, his hands cupped around her ass. Pressing himself between her legs, he said, "Because your ass in these shorts is driving me crazy."

Kneeling in front of her, he gave her a seductive, half smile, then nuzzled her inner thigh. The sandpaper-scrape of his stubble against her skin, and the warmth of his mouth on her thigh, sent a surge of heat straight between Rachel's legs.

"If these shorts are driving you crazy," she murmured, "I better take them off."

That was precisely when Rachel looked down at Aaron and spotted the dark mole on his scalp.

Uh-oh. He needs to get that checked.

Her body stiffens, and Aaron pauses with his fingers on

Rachel's zipper. Looking up at her, his eyelids heavy with desire, he says, "You okay?"

She blinks. Staring into Aaron's unsuspecting eyes, Rachel's vision grows dark and all she can see is that damned mole. Her vision starts to tunnel and now, underneath that mole, Rachel sees a large, dark mass.

This is unlike any premonition she has ever had, way beyond a sense that something bad will happen. This is a visual image. Aaron has a mass, at least two centimeters wide, in his brain. Rachel is seeing things. An apparition. The ghost of a brain tumor.

Instantly, Rachel is filled with horror that this wickedly smart, very sexy, hilarious man, a man who is checking all her boxes, has brain cancer. He is only thirty.

Oh, I really adore this guy. Why won't the universe let me keep him? "I, uh ... I ... I think my period just started. Sorry. Be right back."

In her small, one-bedroom fixer-upper house that she hasn't had the money or time to fix up yet, the bathroom isn't that far from the kitchen. Rachel makes some noise in there, opens the draw, crinkles her hand around in the tampon box, runs some water. All the while, she tries to shake off this vision of cancer, telling herself this can't be right. Even if that mole is skin cancer, that doesn't mean he has a brain tumor. *I'm overreacting, freaking out about a little mole.*

Well, it isn't *that* little.

She considers marching out there and telling him about her premonition, but the only two people Rachel ever tells are her dad and Lorena, her friend since college. And her mom, before she died. But this isn't some vague impending doom; it is an explicit premonition. Aaron has brain cancer.

How can she ignore such an obvious forewarning? How can she withhold this information and maintain a clear conscience? Or a relationship?

Back in the kitchen, she flashes Aaron an apologetic cringe and says, "Bad timing." *Say something about the mole.*

He shrugs. "It happens. You get a raincheck. Anytime." Aaron gives her a wide, sexy, slow smile.

"So, where are we hiking today?" Aaron asks.

To the doctor's office. And soon. "Uh ... how about we go up Canyon Trail? Ruby can go off-leash up there."

At the sound of her name, Ruby's tail thumps happily against the floor.

Aaron and Rachel both look over at Ruby, a curly haired, Lagotto dog, all brown except for her long, white legs, currently sprawled out in front of her. The dog's soulful eyes track Aaron's every move.

That is another thing Rachel liked about Aaron: her usually cautious dog attached to him like glue. Only now, it occurs to her that, perhaps, Ruby wasn't attached to Aaron, maybe she was watchful. Or concerned. When researching working dog breeds, Rachel had learned that Lagotto dogs are notorious for their keen sense of smell, used for all kinds of nose work, including detection of diseases in people. People who aren't yet symptomatic.

Ruby also knows Aaron is sick, Rachel thinks.

Rachel reaches for Ruby's collar and leash, and the dog finally takes her gaze off Aaron to bound over and lunge into her collar.

At the door, Aaron asks Ruby, playfully, if she's ready. Ruby stands at his side, body tense, eyes glued to his.

"Okay ... Go!" He laughs and races her to the car, their regular routine and a race that Aaron will never win.

As they hike up the Canyon Trail, Aaron acts and looks so energetic that Rachel tries to talk herself off her internal cliff of doom. You're being paranoid, she tells herself. You're trying to sabotage what might become a relationship with a perfectly decent man. Just let it go.

Rachel takes in the mountain peaks in the distance still partially covered in snow, scans the dark, cool forest surrounding them. She inhales the pungent, citrus aroma of pine needles and sap. There is a stream gurgling alongside the trail and the occasional piercing call of a hawk. Up ahead is the steady *thump, thump* of Aaron's hiking boots. Ruby darts ahead then races back behind and between them, running circle eights around Rachel and Aaron.

The forest is her best place, her safe place. There are few people in the woods and no premonitions. Her senses are filled only with nature.

But not today.

Today, her mind returns, over and over, to that visceral awareness of Aaron's brain tumor. This is why I don't get close with men: potential premonitions. A few dates, fine. Sex, sure. Serious relationships, best avoided. What was I thinking?

Halfway through their hike, the sense of Aaron's cancer has ballooned inside her until she can't see or think or feel anything but this knowledge.

Rachel can't keep quiet any longer. Catching up with him, she says, "Hey, Aaron, you ought to get that mole on your head checked."

He waves his hand in the air dismissively. "It's been there for years."

Great. "So, you've had it checked?"

"Nah, I rarely go to doctors." He rubs his thumb and fingertips together. "Too expensive."

"Well ... what do you do if ... you're sick or something?"

He holds his hand up, his fingers crossed. His face scrunches up with a cringe, recognizing the risk in his approach to medical care. "Why? Does that mole look bad?"

What to say? That she occasionally, and randomly, senses harm coming to people? That she has, for years, but this one is a whopper, like a big, rapidly multiplying tumor that she is having massive trouble ignoring? She is certain that isn't helpful for anyone to hear. Besides, she could be wrong. This *is* the first time she has had such a specific foreboding. Since this wasn't a vague, lurking sense of something terrible, maybe it wasn't a premonition at all.

"Oh, I have no idea what a bad mole looks like," she says, "but it can't hurt to have a doctor look at it. Better safe than sorry." *She* is sorry because it might be too late.

He stops in the trail and turns, waiting for her to catch up. The late morning sun is behind him, and all Rachel can see is his silhouette. A very nice silhouette: chiseled legs and shoulders, lean and tall but not so tall that she needs to stand on tiptoe or strain her neck to reach his lips.

Wrapping her in his arms, he pulls her against him. This man smells good even when he is sweaty. Especially when he is sweaty.

"Rachel, don't worry about me, okay?"

Worry? That's putting it mildly. You have no idea how worried you should be. "I'm not worried just ... cautious."

She clasps her hands behind his neck. A cold shiver shoots down her arms and directly into her chest. Instantly, she has an impulse to recoil from the sensation of—what is that? Blackness? Sickness? Cancer? It feels like cancer.

Wait, you never had a premonition like this. He could be just fine. No, he is not fine. You have to stop seeing him. Soon. Before this premonition comes true.

You're crazy, just let it go. You adore this guy. Instead of stepping away, Rachel bravely reaches up and kisses him.

Breaking up now is better than later. It would be cruel to break up after he finds out he has cancer. Maybe he won't get cancer until he's, like, eighty.

Your premonitions always come true within weeks. Months max.

Aaron's mouth and lips always have the perfect amount of moisture. *You don't know that he has cancer. Your premonitions have never shown you what tragedy is about to strike.*

Tell him you have some personal issues to work on. That isn't a lie, that's an understatement.

As their lips part, she understands this might be one of their last kisses. Not because he is dying, though he may be, but because Rachel can't stay with this man. She can no longer gaze into his inquisitive eyes as they have deep conversations, or appreciate the spark in his eyes as they laugh together, or become aroused at the intense lust in his eyes that is always accompanied by self-control—sensing when she is ready, watching for her "yes," waiting for her to reach orgasm first. All that is gone. Now, all she will see in his eyes is a fucking brain tumor.

"I'm fine," he mutters, planting one more perfect kiss on her lips. "But I'll get it looked at."

She forces a smile but is sadder than she has been in a long time because in this mid-trail embrace with this terrific man, she can already feel herself pulling away, her armor clinking back together. Standing in the middle of the trail, inhaling Aaron's musky, salty perspiration aroma, Rachel knows she doesn't have what it takes to stick with Aaron through this tragedy. In this embrace, Rachel knows that she is already gone.

3

FIVE MONTHS EARLIER

A MONTH after Rachel extracts herself, as gently as possible, from her relationship with Aaron, he calls to tell her that she was right about the mole. He has stage-four metastatic melanoma. *Fuck me!* It has spread to his brain, his lungs and his liver. She can't help but wonder if all those metastases occurred in the last several weeks, if tumors grow and spread that fast. If only she had noticed that mole sooner ...

Of course, she doesn't say any of this. There is no point in voicing any of that now. Plus, her throat seems completely blocked, and her mouth has become so dry, she can't even swallow.

Dropping onto the couch, the phone pressed to her ear, Rachel listens to Aaron stoically relay his prognosis. The doctors have started him on an aggressive treatment regime, but the prognosis is bad. The worst kind of bad. Her body is suddenly cold, freezing. Ruby walks over and nudges Rachel with her nose, then sits at her feet. She strokes Ruby's head and back a few times, smiles at her reassuringly, but Ruby is locked onto Rachel's face. You can't fool a dog—they know when their owners are devastated.

As Rachel listens to the details of Aaron's spreading cancer and the tumor in his brain, her previously cold body now flushes with rage, white-hot rage. What damned good is it to sense someone's cancer if she can't do anything about it? And will she ever be able to have a normal relationship, one where she won't know when something horrible is about to happen to her partner. She is furious at herself, too, that she wasn't strong enough to stay with Aaron, to let herself fall in love with him while he began to die.

Bubbling up through Rachel's anger is something else. As Aaron describes the brain tumor, she becomes less angry and more frightened. It is two centimeters in size and exactly where she envisioned it to be.

By the time she hangs up, she is shaky with fear. Rachel is mortified because this is the first time a premonition has been so vivid and so accurate.

Maybe I didn't sense his cancer ... maybe I caused it.

As soon as Rachel gets off the phone with Aaron, she calls her father.

"Hey, Ricki Bear," he says, his long-standing nickname and his chipper voice render her speechless. Plus, she still can't clear the lump in her throat. "Rachel?"

She manages a grunt of acknowledgement so he knows she is still on the line.

"What's wrong?" He can read her like a book, even over the phone. If he was there and gave her a big hug, she would be sobbing. As it is, she refuses to cry so is still unable to talk for a few beats.

"I'm having a shit day," she finally gets out in a strained voice.

"Sounds like it."

"Aaron has melanoma. Really bad. Spread to his major organs ..."

"Ohhh, jeezus," he mutters.

The phone line is quiet for several seconds. "The worst part is, I had a premonition about it. I even told him."

"Whoa. You *never* tell people about your premonitions."

"I didn't tell him *that* ... just said, 'Hey, you ought to get that mole checked.' But, Dad, it's like what is happening to him is *exactly* what I sensed. This wasn't: Uh-oh, something bad is going to happen. It was: Oh, shit, he has a brain tumor."

"This isn't the first time your premonitions changed," he says. After the accident with her mom, Rachel's premonitions became more frequent.

A quiet sadness descends over their conversation, the memory of her mom palpable between them. Rachel clenches her eyes shut, willing away that last image of her mother's face growing pale. Her mother had turned to Rachel and gave her a feeble smile, the smile of a mother who knows she is dying.

"No, this was a huge shift. It wasn't like any premonition I ever had. It was *very* visual. When I first saw that dark mole on his scalp, I could see a brain tumor behind it. I didn't even know skin cancer caused tumors."

She starts pacing across the kitchen, not wanting to say what she is thinking, not wanting to *think* what she is thinking.

"Well, you told him. He got it checked. There's nothing

more you could do. It sucks that you have to deal with these." He lets out a heavy sigh. "Try not to let it screw with your head."

She stops pacing and stares out the window. It's a bright, blue-sky day, and the trees are thick with the green of summer, casting wide, cool shadows. Robins are tipping their heads, staring at the grass, plucking up worms. How cruel for Aaron to be staring death in the face while the world is pulsing with life.

"The thing is," Rachel says, "this one has me wondering ... what if I didn't *sense* his cancer? What if I ... *caused* it?"

"No. Don't do this to yourself. Lots of people get cancer. Every day. You can't stop it from happening. Doctors can't even stop it. You're just clairvoyant. Your intuition told you he was sick. That's all. There's no way you can *give* someone cancer."

When she hears him say this, she knows, intellectually, this is true. She couldn't give Aaron cancer. It's not like she poisoned him.

Except ... her premonitions always come true.

Before hanging up, Rachel's father encourages her, once again, not to let this set her back, not to keep missing out on life, not to hole up, alone, with Ruby. His usual lecture. Blah, blah, blah. She has heard it all before.

After her exacting vision of Aaron's cancer, living alone with Ruby is exactly what she intends to do.

———

In the three years since buying Ruby, Rachel has had zero premonitions that her dog will experience any harm or danger. And her radar has picked up on harm coming to animals, too, not only people. Rachel won't go anywhere near a zoo or a circus. But Ruby, she will live a long, healthy life. And Rachel will be her crazy, old dog lady.

For days after learning of Aaron's cancer, Rachel is completely shut down, physically and emotionally. Numb, she wanders, listlessly, around the house in sweatpants and a t-shirt. She keeps working, always, but does so from home and sometimes still in her pajamas. Though she has no appetite, she forces herself to eat each time she feeds Ruby, who never forgets a meal. Like a clock, Ruby shows up Rachel's side at precisely seven a.m. and seven p.m., wagging her tail and giving her a look that says, *Ahem. Excuse me, lady. It's chow time.*

When her dad or Lorena call, she texts them that she is in the middle of something and will call back soon. She doesn't call either of them back for over a week. The only person she calls, occasionally, is Aaron; she owes him that.

She is obliged to check on Aaron because she may have given him brain cancer with her twisted brain. Also, she cares about him and feels guilty for not being capable of remaining his girlfriend in the face of what was coming. Truly, Rachel has no idea why Aaron stays in touch with her. Maybe he cares about her, too. Or maybe she is the closest thing to the last girlfriend he will ever have.

Oh, god, she thinks, he better not hope we're having sex before he ... No. That is not happening.

Every couple of weeks, Rachel texts Aaron to see if he is up for a chat, then calls to hear how his treatment is going. Horribly, of course. He is sick from the meds and consumed with appointments for blood draws and radiation and immunotherapy infusions. When she asks if there is anything he needs, he mentions The Black Bird Café, which he says has great homemade soup and bread, two things he can keep down.

It seems like such a pathetic gesture, to take food to him and his parents, who are staying with him now, but it gives Rachel a blip of relief from her guilt. When she gets near his house, Ruby starts pacing in the back seat and eagerly looking out the car windows, whinnying with excitement. Ruby started this ecstatic routine after the first time they visited Aaron's house. She recognizes his house, probably by the smells, from several blocks away.

Before they get out of the car, Rachel tries to get ready for an onslaught of sensations from Aaron's body, and she isn't thinking about his great kisses. Those are long gone. Taking several deep breaths, she focuses on her breathing and imagines a buttery golden-colored light radiating from her, as if she were a glowing beeswax candle. This is a technique her nerdy therapist, Glen, taught her to use when she experiences social anxiety—his words and probably, also, her diagnoses. To Glen's credit, all Rachel has told him so far is that she is *really* uncomfortable around people, had a traumatic brain injury in a car accident and watched her mom die in that accident. He knows nothing about her clairvoyance.

Rachel is sure Glen's breathing technique works for social anxiety, but she hasn't found it too useful for dealing with an overwhelming intuition that someone around you is, basically, screwed. Unfortunately, her only other techniques are: avoid people all together; if people are unavoidable, don't make eye contact; and, if eye contact is unavoidable, keep it brief. Flitting eye contact is safe.

With a final, slow inhale and drawn-out exhale, Rachel envisions blankness. This is always her hope in any human interaction.

By the time she raps on Aaron's door, despite her continued slow and steady breathing, Rachel is pleading with the universe. *Please, please don't let me sense anything gruesome. I do not want to see the tumors riddling his major organs.*

Ruby and Aaron have a complete love-fest reunion, which involves a lot of licking, wiggling, chuckling and sweet-talking. Rachel is shocked at how gaunt he already looks, his cheekbones more prominent, his eyes more sunken. Underneath that ruggedly handsome face, she can clearly see the shape of his skull.

"Can I give you a hug?" he asks. That is another thing she adored about Aaron: he has so much emotional intelligence. She can count on one hand the number of men who asked for permission before wrapping their arms around her body.

Smiling, she opens her arms, forcing her body to remain supple as she braces herself for another malignant vision. Sometimes, Rachel receives premonitions when she touches a person or something they recently held or wore.

Under his previously muscly shoulders, she can feel his bones. She is hugging a skeleton. Somehow, he is still strong and gives her a solid, warm hug. And a blank one. Nothing. Just sadness. Mostly hers. She hates the universe for not letting her keep this great man.

When Aaron introduces Rachel to his parents, Rachel is relieved that they emit only overwhelmingly sad energy. Anyone who had an ounce of compassion could sense that. No premonition required.

All three of them insist that Rachel stay for lunch, during which no one pretends like everything is fine, like this is a normal luncheon. They talk about doctors and treatments and meds that counteract other meds and keeping food down. No one talks prognosis. The hearty soup and crusty sourdough bread is the first full, warm meal Rachel has eaten in days.

When Aaron and Rachel hug good-bye, she lets herself get teary-eyed because sometimes it feels good to let the tears out. He deserves my tears, she thinks. And it sucks that he has cancer and that I couldn't stay with him and that I came so very close to having a relationship.

There are some tears of relief there, too, because, with this hug, she can't discern his future. She is almost certain he is dying, but anyone can see that.

When they step away from each other, they both look down at Ruby. She is in her therapy-dog stance, body pressed against the side of Aaron's leg, watchful eyes locked onto his. Rachel is in awe at how Ruby can lock eyes with someone who is so sick, look right into the face of his disease and not look away.

Wish I could do that.

4

____

TWO MONTHS EARLIER

JUST SHY OF twelve weeks after his melanoma diagnosis, Aaron is dead. A seemingly healthy, virile man wasted away before Rachel's eyes and is now gone from this planet. Forever. Rachel is despondent, agonizing over the possibility that she killed him. The first visual premonition she ever had, where she saw exactly what was going to happen, and, just like that, he is gone. Things were going so well. Aaron was an ideal boyfriend. He might have become the love of her life.

In the end, he was my victim.

Rachel forces herself to go to the memorial, which is held in a park along one of his favorite rivers. The trees are aflame with autumn colors, and it seems fitting that the world is slowly, gorgeously dying all around. Clearly, Aaron was beloved in his job and community because there are more than a hundred people present. At this supposed celebration of his life, there is a lot of laughter among the tears, but all Rachel senses is fear and heartbreak and outrage.

After paying respects to Aaron's family, Rachel, as discreetly as possible, disappears.

On her drive home, Rachel ponders what *her* funeral might be like: I'm pretty sure the only people standing around my photo and urn of ashes would be Dad, Aunt Cherie, Uncle Lew and Lorena. Maybe my neighbor, Heidi. Hopefully, Lorena would bring Ruby, too, and that would make it six. How truly sad that would be for Dad to see five people and a dog at my funeral, proof that I never connected with people despite all his unsolicited advice about the dangers of a solitary life. Oh yeah, Lorena's husband, Fletcher, would come. Unfortunately. But, at least, that would make it seven.

Rachel wouldn't mind having another close friend like Lorena, though one not so exotically beautiful. Lorena looks like an Italian model, including a Roman nose—not hooked or witch-like but long. Somehow though, even her prominent nose is in perfect balance with her large, dark eyes and wide smile. Men are always checking Lorena out, which means more eyes roving in their direction when they're out together; a challenge when you trying *not* to catch anyone's eye.

As Rachel got to know Lorena during their first year at the University of Washington, Lorena remained a blank slate; never a hint of a premonition. Rachel was elated because she adored Lorena's dark sense of humor and her own brokenness. Lorena's father couldn't keep his hands off booze or women, and her mother was too dependent, financially and emotionally, to leave. Determined never to be anything like either of her parents, Lorena is brutally honest and fiercely independent. She wouldn't depend on someone else unless she was incapacitated, like she crushed her foot. Rachel wonders if, even then, Lorena wouldn't somehow just drive herself to the emergency room.

One of the problems with being twenty-eight and having only one close friend—besides low headcount at your funeral—is that if this one friend marries, you basically go from having one friend to having half of a friend. And making new friends at twenty-eight is tough because most people in this age bracket are either married, actively trying to become married, or overwhelmed with babies.

So, when Lorena started dating Fletcher in graduate school, Rachel was jealous about sharing Lorena and flabbergasted she liked him so much. He was so cocky and full of himself. Fletcher is the type of guy who is good-looking and knows it. In a yearbook, Rachel would have voted Fletcher the guy most likely to cheat on his partner. Rachel didn't need a premonition to know that—anyone could see Fletcher's roaming eye. Anyone except Lorena.

A surefire way to ruin a friendship: tell a best friend that she picked a man who is a lot like her own father.

———

For weeks following Aaron's death, Rachel buries herself in work and training Ruby. If working dogs don't receive *lots* of stimulation and challenge, they dig holes in the yard. Deep, muddy holes. At least that is what Rachel tells herself as she spends every evening and weekend practicing search and rescue with Ruby. Mostly, she trains her in the nearby forests where Rachel can also go for a run on the trails.

Several months ago, Ruby completed the most advanced scent training course: detective class. The overly enthusiastic trainer then talked Rachel into a nine-week course to get Ruby search and rescue certified so, if there was ever a natural disaster, she and Ruby could volunteer. Otherwise, the trainer said, Ruby would be held back from doing what might be the most important work of her life. Rachel thought that seemed a little dramatic, especially since there hasn't been a huge natural disaster in this area of Washington State since ... well, that she can remember. But the class only met twice a week, and, secretly, Rachel hoped to befriend another dog owner, maybe have some doggie playdates with a woman who also liked to trail run. After the premonition about Aaron's cancer, it was all Rachel could do just to show up for the classes; she was far too guarded and evasive to make a friend.

But at least Ruby and Rachel are both certified to conduct search and rescue during the next natural disaster. Ruby can find missing people on land, over snow and even if someone's scent is underwater, as in drowned. No avalanche search and rescue though; at twenty-four pounds, Ruby isn't big or tall enough.

After working long days and dog training and running each evening, Rachel keeps hoping she will fall asleep as soon as her head hits the pillow. She doesn't. No matter how exhausted she is, once her brain is no longer occupied, it starts churning about her graphic premonition of Aaron's cancer, his death and the fear that she might have killed him by "seeing" that damned tumor.

To help her sleep better, Glen prescribed hydroxyzine, which he said is basically an allergy medication that can be taken for insomnia. Coupled with melatonin, Rachel finds that she now falls asleep after only forty-five minutes of tossing and turning and brain churning. It does nothing to stop the nightmares.

Rachel never has premonitions while asleep. No, her dreams are not about future events, they seem reserved only for the past: vivid nightmares about the car accident in which her mom died and, now, nightmares in which she sees Aaron and his brain tumor. In this nightmare, Aaron is no longer handsome and rugged looking—he is skin clinging to bone.

5

─────────────

ONE MONTH EARLIER

RACHEL DECLINES an invitation to Lorena and Fletcher's house for a small dinner party, which, no question, will have some nice, single man in attendance. Instead, Rachel spends Friday evening in flip-flops and yoga pants (with no intention of doing yoga), perusing internet groups for people who have premonitions.

She has followed these online groups for years though never posts anything, just stalks the chat forums. Not surprisingly, there are only a handful of these online groups but some have posts by people who, legitimately, sound like they, too, have premonitions—or clairvoyance, ESP, precognition, whatever the hell this is. People call it different things; Rachel hates all the terms.

In the past, she always skipped over the groups that talked about paranormal this or psychic that. Those sounded a bit far-fetched, like people who read minds, see auras, talk to dead people or predict the future. This evening, Rachel sips on a beer and explores some of those groups she previously considered ludicrous. After all, she did *see* an explicit future for Aaron.

Surely someone else in the world, who isn't delusional, has genuinely seen images of other people's tragedies. What she really hopes to discover is how to eradicate, or at least weaken, this new version of her clairvoyance. At this point, Rachel would be happy to find a way to get back to nebulous premonitions of impending doom. Compared to her premonition about Aaron's cancer, those were manageable.

When her web searches lead her into the lunatic fringe—preventing natural disasters, prophesies for the human race and other rantings—Rachel pads into the kitchen for another beer.

Out on the back porch, she plays a few rounds of *Wordle*. Unfortunately, this word game stopped being fun, or occupying her brain, when she discovered that, if she doesn't think about it too hard and just follows her intuition, she can guess the word by the second try. If she really manages to not think about it, simply opens the game and, boom, enters a word, she sometimes gets it on the first guess. This surprised Rachel because, in college, she tried to intuit all kinds of things: winning lottery numbers, poker and blackjack hands, test answers. It never worked. After her recent success with *Wordle*, she tried the lottery again, to no avail.

After several mindless *Wordle* rounds, she mindlessly tosses a ball for Ruby, then goes back to the computer to scroll through the help wanted ads. She does this periodically to prove to herself that she *could* get a job if she wanted to. And to fantasize about a steady stream of income and support staff—she hates doing her own accounting. Plus, a job would be another good way to drum up a few more attendees for her eventual funeral. Martin Law Office is, once again, advertising for an attorney, which reminds Rachel that no matter how many pros there are for working at a law firm, there are always the big, glaring cons: co-workers, frequent engagement, eye contact, premonitions.

On Saturday morning, Rachel stops by her dad's house after a trail run. There is a red Chevy Bolt parked in his driveway. That isn't Aunt Cherie or Uncle Lew's car, she thinks. They don't own an electric vehicle; they're not that cool.

Knocking as she opens the door, Rachel hollers out a hello. Meanwhile, Ruby sprints to the living room then skids to a stop, tail down, cautious.

"Hey there, Ruby girl," Rachel's dad says. "It's okay, this is Margaret." With that, Ruby resumes her wags and wiggles, bouncing all around him and licking his hands.

Giving Rachel a peck on the cheek, her dad says, "Let me introduce you to my friend, Margaret."

Her father could have slapped Rachel in the face for how stunned she is to see, there on the couch, a lovely, athletic looking woman. In pajamas. A woman who owns an electric Chevy Bolt, which, suddenly, isn't so cool anymore. Of course, her dad has dated in the ten years since her mother died, and Rachel met a few of his girlfriends, she just hasn't seen one cozied up in PJs on their couch. The very same couch on which her mother once sat.

Margaret is more fit and trim than most women her age, which seems to be her late fifties, with some gray streaks in her shoulder-length hair and laugh lines around her mouth and the corners of her eyes.

With only a few strides—Margaret is strikingly tall—she

is in front of Rachel saying, "Finally, I get to meet the amazing daughter Phil's been telling me about."

Finally? How long has she been sitting on our couch? Rachel extends a hand, rather stiffly, readying herself for a zap.

Margaret smiles—those laugh lines really are attractive, like she spent more of her life smiling than frowning—and says, "Oh, I want to give you a hug. If that's okay?"

Her dad is grinning wider than he has in years, so Rachel opens her arms and tries loosen up for a hug. Thankfully, Margaret only envelops her lightly and briefly. And it's a blank hug. Rachel's shoulders relax.

When she steps away, Rachel silently and slowly releases the air in her lungs, as if holding her breath could have prevented a premonition.

Settling back in the living room, her dad explains how he met Margaret at the gym a few months ago. That would've been when Aaron was dying, Rachel calculates, so he probably didn't want to tell her about a new girlfriend.

Margaret tells her she is a school counselor.

Great. Hope she can't assess how screwed up I am.

As they chat, Rachel finds it difficult to dislike Margaret, though she is trying. Ruby, on the other hand, is sprawled out between Rachel's dad and Margaret with her head lolling over the edge of the cushion.

That is one happy dog. Shamelessly happy.

As if reading her mind, Ruby lets out a contented sigh. Rachel can't remember the last time she felt as relaxed as her dog looks. To make matters worse, Rachel's dad is practically glowing.

The traitors!

When Rachel sees her dad a few days later, she razzes him about holding out, not telling her about Margaret. "Guess I better stop showing up unannounced, huh?" she teases, but the words are like acid in her mouth.

"Nah, that's fine, Ricki Bear. But Margaret does spend a lot of time here." He pauses for a few seconds. "You really should do the same—"

"I do spend a lot of time here," she quips.

He rolls his eyes. "You should do the same and spend time with someone special." He says this as if she is a normal woman with nothing standing in her way.

Ughh, she thinks, it's pretty bad when your sixty-year-old father is probably—no, definitely—having more sex than you.

When he invites Rachel to join them for dinner Friday, Rachel's last shred of self-respect flies out the window. A third wheel on her father's date night? She will pass.

"And bring a date," he adds. She can think of no one she would ask out on a date. "It will be fun. We're going to Bucatini." Now, he is playing unfair. Bucatini is Rachel's favorite low-key restaurant: secluded booths, not crowded if they go for early or late dinners and authentic Italian food made in-house, even the pasta.

"Well, my social calendar is really packed," Rachel says, "but since it's Bucatini ... I can squeeze you and Margaret in for Friday." She flashes him a snarky smile. "But don't get your hopes up. It will just be me."

6

THREE WEEKS EARLIER

AT BUCATINI ON FRIDAY, Rachel and her dad peek at each other over the menus. They always order the tiramisu first. They have to—Bucatini has been known to run out, and that is just plain depressing. Tonight, with just a glance, they both act civilized in front of Margaret and only order entrees to start. This woman is already cramping Dad's style, Rachel thinks. Check mark in the negative column.

During the meal, Margaret suggests they pass their plates around and try each other's dishes. Rachel gives her a positive mark on that move. And during dinner, Margaret doesn't dote over Rachel's dad. Another positive mark for her; Rachel hates when women treat their partners like kids.

When they finish eating, Rachel can't wait to order tiramisu. They better have some left, otherwise she will be forced to eat crème brûlée, which she will blame on Margaret. Another mark for her in the negative column.

The three of them are all laughing about something—Margaret has a great sense of humor, for which Rachel gives her a grudging third positive mark—when the busser comes to the table with a water pitcher. With her head tipped back in laughter, Rachel looks at the busser, accidentally, and their eyes lock. He has icy, pale blue eyes.

Zap! Radiating from the busser is a desperate, hungry energy. He's hunting for something. Someone. A woman.

Instantly, Rachel looks down at the table. She can't bear to sense any more.

Oh, please don't let me see anything from his mind.

Frantically, she wants to escape, but he is standing right next to Rachel, reaching in front of her, refilling their water glasses. If she tries to slide out of the booth, she will be closer to him and might accidentally touch him. She sits rigid, frozen.

Please, go away. Please, please, please.

Quietly, not in a whisper but in a meek voice, the busser asks Margaret if she is done with her plate. As if carried on his breath, a sensation slams into Rachel's chest. He wants a woman. An older woman. He will stop at nothing to have her.

Margaret? He's going to prey on Margaret? No, no, no! Don't think this.

More waves roll off the busser. He can't let go of this woman. He is tortured by her. He doesn't *want* to hurt her, but ...

Bile rises into Rachel's throat. *Stop, stop, stop! What if I'm making this happen? Don't think this. Don't see this. Just stop!*

Trying to count down from one hundred in her head, all Rachel can do is repeat "one hundred" while the busser stacks their empty plates. One hundred, one hundred, one hundred. She can't remember what comes after one hundred. She is unable to breath for several beats until, mercifully, he leaves.

"Rachel? Are you okay?" Margaret asks. Her father is eyeing her, too. The concern in their faces makes Rachel want to race out of there. Only she can't move.

Her father stands and hooks Rachel's elbow. "Why don't we go get some fresh air, huh?"

Ushering Rachel from the table, he says over his shoulder to Margaret, "We will be back in a few."

On autopilot, Rachel stares at the space right in front of her as her dad, with his hand on her arm, steers her out of the restaurant.

The cool, evening air is bracing and snaps Rachel out of her stupor. Her pulse quickens. With every fiber of her being, she wants to bolt. Her legs are twitching with tension, ready to run down the street and not stop until she is miles from here.

"Was it that busboy?" her dad asks quietly.

At the mention of the man, adrenaline lights her up, all her nerves like spikes, ready for danger.

She whips her head around and looks back at Bucatini. No one is following them.

"It was *so* bad." Rachel's words come out shaky, and her heart is thumping in her chest. Continually checking up and down the street, she says, "He's some kind of ... predator—"

"Ah shit," her dad says, running his hands down his face and staring at the dark sky. She just laid this burden on her father, too. Now, they are both stuck.

"He is after a woman ... maybe stalking her. I've never

had a premonition about someone *doing* harm. So maybe this wasn't a premonition, maybe it was … I don't know, some fear of mine bubbling to the surface. Or he reminded me of someone from a scary movie, or …"

Rachel never watches scary movies. Real life is scary enough.

Tears start to roll down her cheeks and, at this point, she doesn't care. The pain that man could inflict is unfathomable. A little panic descends over her as she recalls how, a month after she envisioned Aaron's brain cancer, he was diagnosed with melanoma. And three months later, he was dead.

Rachel wills herself to stop feeling that busser's sensations, afraid that she will manifest this abduction, bringing it to life.

Her mind reels, thinking back to old premonitions, wondering if all these years, she was making these things come to pass. No, that doesn't make any sense, she reassures herself. *Until these last two, I only had vague intuitions that something bad would happen; I never knew what would happen.*

"I don't think there's anything you can do," her dad says. They stand there in silence for a minute.

"Nothing that won't make you crazy," he adds, "like going to the police."

Rachel shakes her head vehemently. "Yeah, that'd be a good way to get myself committed to an institution." *Probably exactly where I need to be.*

An evening breeze blows across her skin. The cool air, and the fear of what she may have set into motion, and the adrenaline dissipating, makes her start to shiver.

"I'll take you to the car," he says, digging his keys out of his pocket. "Then I'll go get Margaret and our jackets—"

"What are you going to tell her?"

"Hadn't thought about it. I'll just say you're not feeling well. But ... maybe you could tell her. Later. If you want."

Her mouth falls open in disbelief.

"What?" he says defensively. "She's a counselor—"

"I already have a shrink," she says adamantly.

"That's not what I mean. I'm just saying she understands people and ... I don't know what it's called ... the psyche. She understands that kind of stuff. Humans are complicated. She gets that." They stare at each other for a few moments. "I trust her. And so can you."

Hah! I've been in therapy with Glen for six months and still don't trust him.

But trust is not what Rachel needs. She needs someone who knows about ESP and can tell her why the hell she is not only sensing danger but is now, literally, seeing it. Rachel needs to know if, through some bizarre force, she manifested Aaron's brain cancer and this man stalking a woman. At this point, Rachel is no longer certain if she is clairvoyant, crazy or a criminal. Or all three.

Rachel is quiet in the backseat on the drive home. And cold, even wrapped up in her jacket. Silent and chilled to the bone. When she asks them to turn the heat up, Margaret looks over her shoulder and asks if she is getting sick.

No, I just turned the busser back there into a predator. Unleashed a monster. But thanks for asking. She mumbles something about having a hard day.

"Your dad told me about your friend who died a few

months ago," Margaret says. "I lost my husband to cancer several years ago. It's really tough."

"Yeah ... cancer sucks," Rachel says, staring out the window, headlights from passing cars washing over her—bright then dark, bright, dark—like a strobe light. The effect is hypnotic. She sinks into it, letting herself go numb.

7

———————————

TWO WEEKS EARLIER

THE PREMONITION from the busser drives Rachel deep into despondency and isolation. Being aware of someone's evil is bad enough, but what has Rachel sequestered is the way her premonitions are changing. Afraid that her ESP is spiraling out of control, evolving into something ominous, she is determined to avoid premonitions.

Morning runs with Ruby now start at six a.m. before the neighbors, or even the garbage collectors, are out and about. She goes into her office at odd times, ensuring that she won't cross paths with other building tenants. When she takes Ruby for a trail run or to practice scent work, it's on the lesser-used trails in the middle of the afternoon on a weekday. Since eating out has become dangerous, she occasionally orders carry-out or grabs something from the deli at the Third Avenue Food Co-Op, her favorite natural food store. Gone are Rachel's tiramisu-first dinners with her dad.

ESP is ruining her world, carved-out and small as it is.

Desperate to talk to her therapist about her mutating premonitions she rehearses the discussion. In these rehearsals, she imagines telling Glen, matter-of-factly, that what started decades ago as vague forebodings of danger have gone haywire. She would then explain how the precision of her intuition about Aaron's brain tumor pushed her over the edge, making her suspect that she caused his death. Glen probably won't believe her, so she will be compelled, attorney that she is, to provide some evidence. No problem, she has plenty of evidence. That's all, a quick dumping on her counselor's shoulders of a few facts. She could wrap it up by asking Glen if he has any experience helping clients with such matters?

Oh, she can picture Glen's face. And if she gets really bold, she could say, If you think causing cancer sounds horrific, there is also a possibility that I caused a man to prey on women. Then, with a grimace, she would ask if there are some meds, perhaps, to put an end to this?

There is one pro about getting honest in therapy (she has made multiple pro/con lists for spilling her guts to Glen). If she can tell him about her premonitions maybe he can help her get that busser's face out of her mind's eye.

Since her last premonition, Rachel is haunted by that busser. Over and over, she sees his vacant eyes and hears that boy-like voice. There was also something boyish about his appearance, with his hair parted far to one side and brushed over, like a boy scout, maybe trying to look innocent. His hair was a strange color, like a dusty blonde that looked covered with ... dust. Or ashes.

Driving to her counseling appointment, Rachel tells herself that this is the day. I'm ready to open up. It's time Glen understands exactly how messed up I am. How else can he help me?

She even researched under what conditions a therapist can have a client institutionalized against their wishes—better safe than sorry. He can only have her locked up if she is at risk of harming herself or others. Physically harming. There was, of course, no mention of telepathic harm.

Despite her practice conversations, when she settles into the chair in Glen's office, she can't quite get the words out, at least, not the words she rehearsed. Stage fright. Instead, they start off discussing grief over the car accident and her mother's death. So futile when Rachel's ESP is spinning out of control, and she is losing her grip on reality.

As they're discussing post-traumatic stress disorder, which seems to be Glen's favorite topic, Rachel tries to broach the *real* topic. "So, this PTSD you think I have, isn't that like what military vets have? Or kids who were abused?"

"There are all kinds of trauma." Glen pauses for long enough that Rachel feels fidgety. "Your car accident with your mom sounded very traumatic ..."

That gives her a cinch right around the heart. She looks away, then reaches for her tea cup. Takes a sip. "I really like this tea."

He smiles, ever so slightly, but doesn't even glance at her tea cup. No way he is falling for that distraction. They sit there without talking for several seconds. Several heavy, uncomfortable seconds.

"You were what, seventeen?" he asks. "The brain is very plastic—still developing—at that age. Kids and teens respond to trauma differently than adults."

"In what ways?"

He's being very still, not using much body language, talking quietly, as if he doesn't want to spook her. Good idea

—Rachel is good at bolting. "Hypervigilance. Their brains go into a continual state of fight-flight-or-freeze, prepared for danger. For years. Decades. Often, they don't even know it. They're not aware of the anxiety until it's triggered." He lets that sink in.

Oh, that is sinking in. Rachel reverts to attorney mode, analytical. *Maybe I don't have premonitions; maybe I'm just vigilantly looking for danger.* But wait, I was this way years before the car accident. Though my premonitions *did* increase in college, the year after Mom died.

"Could this hypervigilance allow people to …" She tries to discern if Glen is ready for this. Surely, he hears some weird-ass shit in this office. "I don't know … can it allow someone to sense things? About other people?"

"You mean, like being able to read people?" he says.

She shrugs and gives a more-or-less head bob.

"Probably. That could be a part of their vigilance."

"What about, say … knowing when something bad is about to happen? To someone else? Like having … ESP or something?" Oh man, did it feel good to say that. She can't believe those words came out of her mouth. Finally, she said it.

Without missing a beat, Glen gets all clinical—about, of course, PTSD. "People with PTSD are extremely sensitive to danger. It's a survival instinct. That could allow them to have perceptions that most people don't have. Or that most people aren't aware of. There's a lot about the mind and psyche we don't understand."

It seems to Rachel there is a lot that Glen doesn't understand. *I said, ESP! Forget PTSD. Let's talk about ESP.*

Just tell him the crux of the problem, she prods herself.

Something like, Well, since you asked, I've had ESP most of my life, but it's morphed recently and is scaring the shit out of me. That, or I'm insane.

Instead, Rachel lets Glen guide the conversation back to the frequent nightmares she has about the car accident with her mom, horrific, graphic nightmares that, mercifully, wake her up. After waking up from these nightmares, Rachel lies in bed, drenched, heart racing, wondering how many times she must relive that accident. The morning after a nightmare, she is completely leveled.

Okay, Rachel admits to herself, maybe I have a titch of PTSD.

Glen suggests that to lessen and, hopefully, alleviate her nightmares, they try something called EMDR: eye movement desensitization and reprocessing. He seems very eager about this acronym also, Rachel thinks. EMDR, PTSD ... my problem is ESP!

Glen practically geeks out as he describes EMDR, how he will guide Rachel through a relaxation exercise, then gently help her explore the nightmares, all while she watches a light that is streaking rapidly, left and right, across a light bar. And, if she would like—Glen nods eagerly—Rachel can hold in each of her hands little vibrating pods.

Rachel blinks at him.

Glen is smiling and his eyebrows are raised up in excitement; he is all but rubbing his hands together. This eye movement desensitization something or other seems to Rachel like a step up, or maybe down, from relaxation breathing and imagining light radiating from her body. But Glen said this technique is successful in helping war vets with *their* nightmares so ...

As Glen guides their first EMDR session to a close, he clicks the light bar off and Rachel hands him the no longer vibrating pods. Strangely, Rachel feels floaty, almost disembodied. Glen assures her this is a common feeling and that she should take her time, sit until she feels grounded again. As she gradually settles back into her body, she feels lighter and somehow more detached from her memories of the car accident.

That week, Rachel has only one dream about her mom's death, and it isn't nearly as vivid as previous nightmares.

When Glen and Rachel complete another round of EMDR the following week, she has not one single dream about the accident. Sleep is, finally, giving her the break from her mind that she always longed for, the mental break she assumed everybody but her received during the night.

That Glen, he is on to something with this EMDR, Rachel thinks. She is eager to try, once more, to talk to him about *her* acronym because maybe this technique could get rid of her premonitions, too. Her eyes are so much at the root of her premonitions, the zaps almost always coming when she catches someone's eyes. Maybe this light bar thingy can fix her, fix the strangely broken connection between her brain, her eyes and other people's eyes.

No matter what, Rachel promises herself, I'm telling Glen about my clairvoyance. She is elated with hope. EMDR hope. Eye movement desensitization and—what does that "R" stand for? She will call it "rewiring." Next week, with any luck, her brain and eyes will be rewired.

8

THREE DAYS EARLIER

PATRICK JUST CLOCKED out and is leaving work when his eyes land on her. Instantly, he gets a hard-on. It's her hair that does him in, the way it's a little messed up—strands hanging loose around her face. So fucking sexy, like she ran there just in time to see him. He imagines her running, then imagines reaching out and grabbing her by the hair. A jolt of excitement shoots down his chest and lands right between his legs. Shifting his jacket to cover his erection, he keeps moving towards the door. His mind is racing. Oh, man, she wants me, bad. Wants me to catch her—

God dammit! This bitch triggered me. Patrick snaps his gaze away from her, shoves the door open and hurries out. Without daring another glance.

That's the first step, knowing he is triggered, which his shrink says is the most important part. The first step to freedom. One: know your triggers. Patrick has a little saying to remind himself of this: one is a gun, as in a trigger. As in, might as well shoot himself because if he gets triggered and acts on it, he is going back to prison. For a long time. And he would rather shoot himself than go back to prison.

Knowing he is triggered is supposed to make it easier to walk away. *Okay, I'm walkin' away. Now what?*

Fuck if he can remember. Yes, he is triggered but can't remember what to do next.

Keep walkin', just keep walkin'.

The woman's face is blazed into his mind. Her eyes were a striking green—not greenish blue, not hazel, but dark green, like jade. And with those heavy eyelids, those were bedroom eyes. Her hair was an unusual color, light brown, almost golden, like the flaxen-colored mane of Tilly, a horse he takes care of at Mountain Home Ranch. That woman had an edgy look, like something troubles or torments her. He can tell, saw it in her gaze, the way she took in everything around her without really looking at anyone.

Images and sensations seize him, pulsing like a strobe light. Her running. Him getting closer. Her shoes pounding on the road, calf muscles straining. Him close enough to smell her deodorant mingled with sweat. Her running faster, gasping, lungs sucking air, looking over her shoulder, hair in her face, face full of fear—

You idiot. This is a goddam trigger. You wanna go back to prison? One is a goddam GUN!

Patrick can't remember the next step, is racking his brain but coming up blank. What is the next part? Step two? What is step two? Two? Two? Is it true! Yes, a fact check. Ask yourself if your thoughts are true. Two: is it true? Then third is to refocus. Right, he thinks, I can do this.

He starts repeating the words in his head, like a mantra, One: gun. Two: true? Three: re-see.

He runs a fact check. *Is it true that bitch wants me? She don't know me. Might think I'm hot, but that ain't the same. Maybe she didn't even notice me. Fact: I have scared women. I have hurt women. Another fact: women don't wanna be chased.*

Patrick hates that fact, clenches his jaw.

Maybe he can just pretend this time. Find somewhere to jerk off and just pretend he catches her.

Three: re-see. See somethin' else. Do somethin' else.

His shrink always says exercise is a good way to refocus. Patrick picks up his pace, weaving around people, almost jogging to the bus stop.

Ain't gotta act on my thoughts. They're just thoughts. Focus on somethin' else. Keep runnin'.

In prison, Patrick worked out every day. It was a great release; one of the few. Every once in a while, when he was out in the prison yard, way off in the distance he saw horses grazing on a ridge. That was a rare and priceless sight, one he looked for every day. Some days, those horses would come running over the ridge—not galloping but running, full speed —looking so powerful and free.

Stepping off the sidewalk into the bike lane, Patrick breaks into a full-on run, not stopping until he reaches the bus stop.

As he waits for the bus, other riders congregate at the stop. *Women* congregate there. It starts spitting rain and everyone huddles into the bus stop shelter. No longer running, no longer distracted, women squeezing in close, Patrick is aroused again.

Stepping out of the shelter, he needs someplace safe and neutral where he can wait for the bus. Wiping the rain splatters from his glasses with his shirt, he scans the nearby shops. His eyes have grown dark, his pupils dilated and wide with his arousal.

Maybe a shop that has a bathroom—jerking off is a good diversion. Just gonna pretend, he thinks. The images flood into his mind again. Her ass pumping as she runs. Grabbing a handful of her thick, unruly hair. He can almost feel her hair, soft and tangled around his fingers. The excitement in her face—

You're doin' it again, man. Two: is it true? He does another fact check. Being chased scares women. He would see fear, not excitement, in her eyes. More images. She cries. Pleads. Pisses her pants.

Walking away from the bus stop, and the women there, he sees a bar. No booze, Patrick reminds himself, my PO can piss test me anytime. I'll just have a Coke.

Pushing through the door, the place stinks of stale beer and greasy, deep-fried food. Once his eyes adjust to the gloomy bar, he sees two women sitting at the bar. They sound like they have been there for hours, talking over each other and laughing too loud.

I shouldn't be in here, he thinks. Drunk women. Too much temptation.

Moving away from the women, a dim, blue glow at the end of a dark hallway catches his eye. The sign for the men's restroom. It calls to him, practically pulsing blue.

Blue. Two. A new little poem—two: is it blue? Second step is to find a men's room and jack off. Patrick lets out a snort. The drunk women glance in his direction then go back to their cackling. The bartender peers at him then returns to wiping down the bar.

Moving towards the back hallway, the men's room sign is reeling him in like a sultry bitch. Nervous and excited, he licks his lips then presses his lower lip over the bottom of his mustache, enjoying the tickle of it.

Then, uninvited, comes the image of his shrink at last week's group therapy session. Patrick can picture Dr. Levitsky as clear as if he were sitting at the bar, though Patrick knows his shrink wouldn't be caught dead with the likes of those women. Hell, he wouldn't be caught dead in a dive bar like this. He sees Dr. Levitsky with his heavy, black-rimmed glasses and his serious face, holding up two fingers and saying, Two. Ask yourself, is this true?

No, Dr. Levitsky, it ain't true. Jackin' off back there won't help. It'll feel good as hell for five minutes but won't help.

Pretending never satisfies Patrick. In fact, fantasizing about having his way with a woman always makes him want the real thing. It sets off a craving so intense he can't resist.

I gotta get the hell outta this bar, Patrick thinks. Gotta keep runnin'.

Hurrying out the door, Patrick crosses the street and runs into Derby Park. He can jog home from there, cut through the park, and it's only two miles. No bathrooms to slink into. No alcohol. No women. Women don't walk through the park this late in the evening. Unless they're looking for trouble.

A cold drizzle is now falling. He stares at his feet pounding on the sidewalk, carrying him to his apartment, to safety. This is good, running. And he plans to do sit-ups and push-ups when he gets to his apartment. Lifting weights in prison, Patrick got pretty ripped and has kept those muscles. For being thirty-eight, he figures he is in damn good shape. That is the one good thing that came from prison because, when he went in nine years ago, he was a wiry punk.

The rain comes harder now, a downpour.

Just my fuckin' luck, he thinks. Forget the damn bus. Tomorrow's payday. I'm gettin' new tires and fillin' the tank in my car.

Tomorrow's my day off, too. That gives him a quick thrill, followed by a twinge of fear. Days off can be dangerous—nothing to refocus on, no distractions.

He brushes aside the fear. *Gonna get my car goin' and get some boots at the thrift store. Work boots* and *a pair of cowboy boots.*

His feet splash through puddles, cold water soaking through his tennis shoes, saturating his socks until his toes are freezing. He hates that. Reminds him of prison where it was always freezing.

Least I'm not in prison anymore, he thinks. I'm a free man.

Making sure no one is in earshot, Patrick starts listing, out loud, what else is good in his life. He needs to hear, actually hear, something good. Still running and panting, between heavy breaths, he says. "The horses. Good job. Discount on the food. Good pay. For a felon. PO's stayin' off my ass."

Course, I ain't tellin' my PO about this little slip. Wasn't even a slip. Didn't do a thing. Didn't even pretend to hurt that woman.

Back at his apartment, Patrick cranks up the wall heater and, standing in front of it, changes into dry clothes. He props his only pair of shoes, soaking wet now, in front of the heater. He is warm and dry, but, suddenly, his apartment isn't so safe. There is no accountability. And no way to escape—

what did his shrink call them?—devious sexual fantasies. Or was it deviant?

Patrick starts pacing, back and forth, like a caged animal, like a hungry, caged animal. Don't dare turn on the computer, too much temptation on the internet. Can't take a hot shower, too risky to get naked now that he is triggered by the woman he saw at work. The desire to sink into a fantasy about her is fierce, like it is clawing up his legs, threatening to consume him. His heart is beating so fast, he is afraid he is about to have a stroke.

Taking a sharp inhale, he then releases the air in a long, slow exhale. "One: gun. No shit, I was triggered. Two: is it true? No, she doesn't want to be chased and fucked. Three: re-see ..." He tries to think of something *really* good about his life, but all he comes up with are the horses.

Those horses are basically his only friends. There are a few guys from the sex offender program who he banters with, but they aren't friends. His mom—tyrant that she is—hasn't spoken to him since his rape trial.

Something keeps nagging at the back of his brain, something else he can do to get relief.

I can take out some lady. After I get tires tomorrow and some cowboy boots ... "Date night," he says, cackling bitterly.

Then it hits him: there is a support group at his shrink's clinic at five thirty every weekday. Some of the guys from his group therapy said the meetings help. Supposed to be like a sex addicts meeting or some shit like that. He stops pacing and looks at his clock.

The five-twenty bus will get him there ten minutes late. Or he can just risk driving there on bald tires.

Glancing at his shoes in front of the heater, he hates the

idea of putting on wet shoes. Or having a tire blowout while driving.

For several beats, he stares at the door. This isn't a prison. He can walk right out the door. Anytime. Go anywhere he wants. Anywhere. That begins to slow his pulse.

I'm a free man.

He puts on his wet shoes and grabs his car keys. *I gotta find some kind of escape cuz I can't sit here alone and battle these demons.*

That is a battle he knows he will lose.

PART 2

____

MISSING

9

DAY ONE

COMMITTED to telling Glen next week about her premonitions, Rachel celebrates by eating dinner on the couch while streaming a movie. *Woo-hoo!* Also, she eats her Black Bird Café dinner straight out of the to-go containers; washing dishes is not celebrating. Sadly, the Café has no tiramisu, so she was forced to order the chocolate lava cake, which is served warm. And that is why she *had* to eat the cake first.

Ruby is lazily sprawled out on the couch next to her, not begging. She knows better. Her chin resting on her paws, head unmoving, Ruby's bushy eyebrows give her away: perking up as her eyes follow Rachel's fork to her mouth, doggie eyebrows lowering as the fork sinks back into the food.

"Give it up, girl," Rachel says. "It's human food." Scooping up another mouthful, she smiles at Ruby then thinks, You're celebrating with a dog.

Picking up the phone to talk to a human, maybe even invite Lorena—and Fletcher, no choice in that matter—for dinner, Rachel sees a notification from her King County news app. She taps it and a middle-aged woman's face pops onto the screen. The woman might be about fifty. It's hard to tell because she has a youthful look with a slightly crooked smile—ticked up higher on one side—and a scattering of freckles across her nose and cheeks. Her thick, strawberry blond hair is graying, and it must have been breezy when the photo was taken because her hair is blowing slightly across her forehead.

Above the woman's picture, the notification reads: MISSING WOMAN. SHERIFF'S OFFICE SEEKING INFORMATION IN CONNECTION WITH ALICIA MEYERS, LAST SEEN LEAVING BUCATINI RESTAURANT YESTERDAY, OCTOBER 27TH, AT 9:00 P.M.

Oh, hell no! This can't be happening.

Three weeks after getting zapped by the busser's premonition—or did Rachel zap him?—a woman is missing. This can't be a coincidence.

The phone rings, and Rachel flinches, dropping it. Scrambling to pick it up, she sees her dad's name on the caller ID.

"Did you see the news?" he says.

"Just saw it. I can't believe it. Really, I—I don't know what to do."

"Well, if you want to do something, I can go with you."

She *could* go back to Bucatini, follow the busser. Maybe he has the woman locked up at his house. And if Rachel made the busser abduct this woman through some kind of telepathy, then she must find her before he hurts or kills her. If he hasn't already.

Then again, she never had a premonition about someone

hurting others. Maybe it was inaccurate, some kind of misfiring, ESP gone awry. That busser could be completely innocent.

"Go where?" she asks.

"To the police. If you wanted to do that."

"Oh ... you think I should? They're not going to do anything because I have a *hunch* that the busser abducted—" she glances back at the missing woman post "—Alicia Meyers. They will think I'm nuts." Rachel learned that lesson in elementary school when she told a teacher that something bad was going to happen to a girl in the class, and the teacher freaked out. Mostly because of Rachel's demeanor: wide-eyed with concern, but matter-of-fact, even apathetic. At age nine, Rachel was already shielding herself against the onslaught of intuitions. The teacher immediately called Rachel's parents into a conference with the principal and expressed concern that Rachel was having delusions of harming the girl. After the girl fell off the swing a week later and dislocated her shoulder, the teacher never said another word about it.

"Well, you've got more than a hunch," her dad says.

"Pretty sure that distinction will be lost on the cops. Hunch, clairvoyance. Same thing to them."

"Maybe just call anonymously. Or I can call for you."

"Even worse—crazy lady has father call police. I don't think I want to do anything right now." The phone line hums for a few beats. "Is that terrible?"

"It's fine. I support whatever you do. Or don't do."

How about following a psycho criminal? Will you help me do that? But she doesn't dare ask. No question about it, he will draw the line at supporting her in that effort. She wonders if Lorena will go for it.

For the next hour, Rachel searches everything she can about Alicia Meyers. It's a common name, so she doesn't find much. The most she can glean from the internet is that she is a teacher, is married and has what looks like a teen-aged daughter.

Trying to find something about a local restaurant busser whose name she doesn't know is impossible. Searching the registered sex offender database for guys living in a three-mile radius around Bucatini turns up nothing. Not surprising since that is more of a commercial area. She contemplates widening the search, but the thought of scrolling through the faces of offenders looking for the busser causes her stomach to knot up.

If only she knew his name.

Closing her eyes, Rachel thinks back to seeing the busser, trying to recall if he wore a name tag, but her memory of the man is shrouded, dark, almost black. There is only one option: she has to go back and try to get his name. Or follow him. More stomach knots.

The next morning, Rachel's plan to go back to Bucatini to discover the busser's name seems sketchy. For one, he might not be there. Two, he might not wear a name tag. And, three, stalking a sexual predator can't be a good idea. Rachel gets a little shudder. The last thing she wants is to have an encounter with this icy, ashen man. And to think that she even considered enlisting Lorena's help sickens her. Lorena encountering this predator could be horrendous; she would most certainly catch his eye. Men are always drawn to Lorena's striking beauty.

Screw these premonitions! Besides, I could be wrong. The guy could be harmless.

In her head, she hears a vaguely familiar voice, almost like her mom's, say very steadily and quietly, Trust your instincts.

No! Screw my instincts.

10

———————————

DAY TWO, 7:30 AM

ON THE WAY TO WORK, Rachel keeps the radio off. Outside her office door, she snaps up the newspaper without looking at it, stuffing it in the recycling bin. Her dad would have called if there was any news on the missing woman.

Rachel spends the day buried in work, extensively reviewing a complicated engineering project permit that keeps her face, and her thoughts, glued to the documents. She loves paperwork; no eyes there. And no missing woman.

Whenever she takes a break, her mind starts niggling over the busser and Alicia Meyers. As she takes a sip of coffee, the busser's eyes flash in Rachel's mind: cold and vacant. Clenching her eyes shut, she wills away this image but can't clear it from her thoughts.

That's it. Break time is over.

Not wanting to spend the evening alone with the busser's eyes, or avoiding news of Alicia Meyers, Rachel invites Lorena for a late afternoon hike. Lorena refuses trail running —hiking only.

Not long into their hike, Lorena says, "You seem really out of it. Is it ... Aaron—"

"No, no. I mean, I *am* sad about him being gone, but that's not it."

"Did you get another bad premonition?" Having learned of Rachel's premonitions coming true over the past decade, Lorena knows how she can be tormented.

Rachel gives Lorena a sideways glance but they keep walking for a minute, neither one of them talking. They watch Ruby exploring the trail and forest, oblivious to the unspoken heaviness hanging between the humans behind her.

Finally, Rachel spits it out. "It was the worst one. Really. Worse than Aaron's cancer. This one, like Aaron's, was visual. Nothing vague. And so graphic ... I can't get it out of my head. I need some meds or something before I lose my mind. I can't live this way."

Lorena is brooding, brows creased, mouth frowning.

"Don't worry, I'm not going to kill myself or anything." Rachel hates to burden her one close friend with all this angst, probably destroying their friendship.

"Do you want to tell me about this one?"

Ruby bounds ahead, pausing only to stare down birds who dare to flit near her. There isn't anybody around them, or Ruby would be at Rachel's side. So, as they huff uphill, the trail switching back and forth, Rachel lays it all on the line: the busser, the premonition and now the missing woman.

At the ridgetop, they pause to catch their breath, drink some water, and take in the view of the distant mountains. There is a dusting of snow on the few peaks that are higher than five thousand feet. The sky above the peaks is tinged orange as the sun drops closer to the mountains.

Heading back down the ridge, Rachel confesses the worst part—that because her ESP is changing, she is afraid that she isn't just sensing harm but is, in fact, causing it. That somehow, she is hurting people with her brain.

Lorena throws her head back in laughter. "That is the dumbest thing you've ever said. Are you still seeing that counselor because you *are* going to make yourself nuts."

"Yeah, I was going to tell hi—"

"You haven't told him yet? You've been seeing him for, what, seven, eight months? Before Aaron, right?"

"I *know*. I started to, but ... it's too bizarre. I've never had a premonition about a person hurting someone. And the one about Aaron happened *exactly* as I envisioned it. So, if this one comes true ..." Rachel pauses for a few beats. "You know, a therapist can commit you if they think you're going to hurt someone."

Lorena rolls her eyes. "Sensing this man abducted a woman isn't you hurting someone."

"What if Glen thinks I'm projecting ... or deflecting or ... whatever the psychobabble term is. That *I'm* really the one who abducted Alicia Meyers."

"Okay, now *that* is the dumbest thing you've ever said. First, you had nothing to do with this woman going missing. So, get that out of your head. And, I don't think they can lock you up"—she snaps her fingers—"just like that. You have to actually hurt someone."

They stop and stare at each other.

Lorena throws her hands up in the air. "What?"

"That's exactly what I might be doing."

She waves that statement away. "I'm pretty sure there has to be some evidence. You're not hurting people, Rachel. You have ESP."

"Yeah, but it's changing. These last two are very different from any I've ever had. And you know, my premonitions always come true—something bad always *does* happen to the person."

They walk for a few minutes, then Lorena says, "I don't know how you've coped with it this long. Maybe there's a counselor who specializes in ESP."

"Ha-ha."

Several moments later, Lorena says, "I wasn't kidding."

They hike in silence for a long while, and Rachel's mood lightens, partly for having unloaded all this on Lorena, the one person with whom she speaks most candidly about her premonitions. Lighter, too, because in the woods her mind can unwind and stop being in overdrive or—what did Glen call it?—hypervigilant. Here, the tall pine trees and rugged hills shroud Rachel from the rest of the world. Sinking into her surroundings, Rachel notices the birdsong is becoming more sporadic as the birds settle in for the evening. Under her shoes, dried up, brown maple leaves crunch and release an earthy, musty smell of decay.

In one of Ruby's many doggie loops around them, she skids to a stop and shoves her nose into Lorena's hand. Ruby has a glove in her mouth.

Checking her pockets, Lorena says, "Hey, when did I drop that?"

"Good girl, Ruby," Rachel says. "It's that search and

rescue training we've been doing. She can find anything with that nose."

As Lorena takes her glove from Ruby's mouth, a thought sprouts in Rachel's mind. Ruby can find *anything* with her nose. Rachel wouldn't need to follow the busser and risk getting close to him; she could have Ruby track his scent. All she needs is to get ahold of something with the busser's scent.

As the forest darkens and the sky becomes streaked with purple, Rachel talks Lorena into, at least, jogging before they run out of daylight. Ruby seems happy the humans have, finally, picked up the pace and barks excitedly, perhaps pretending the slowpokes are trying to catch her.

Navigating over and around roots and rocks, they don't talk during this last stretch of the trail. Rachel's brain starts niggling over how Ruby could track the busser. The hard part would be getting a scent cue: something with his smell on it. That would require going back to Bucatini and interacting with the busser again.

What am I going to do, snatch an apron off a predator? Ask him for his shirt?

She ponders ordering carry-out from Bucatini. No, the containers would smell too much like food for Ruby to detect the busser's scent. Sneak out some silverware or a water glass the busser sets on the table? No, his scent wouldn't be very strong on something hard and nonporous.

Okay, she thinks, what if I did, somehow, get his scent? Then what? They'd start outside Bucatini, and Ruby could track where he goes after work. To his house? No, only if he walks, which isn't likely. To the nearest bus stop? Still, not very helpful. To his car? Still no good; only cops can get personal information from a license plate number.

Deflated, Rachel realizes none of these great ideas will lead to Alicia's location. The busser can't be holding her captive somewhere within walking distance, or scent tracking distance, of Bucatini. These are all dead ends.

What Rachel really needs is a scent from Alicia. Then Ruby could search from outside the restaurant, where Alicia was last seen, to wherever her scent ends. Unless the busser, or whoever, abducted Alicia in a car. Then Ruby would lose the scent at the spot where the car was.

Or maybe Alicia wasn't even abducted, Rachel thinks. What if Alicia just left her husband—couldn't stand him anymore, had her boyfriend pick her up down the street, and they split?

That's ludicrous, Rachel thinks. Surely, the Sheriff wouldn't have a missing person campaign if they suspected that Alicia was simply a dissatisfied wife. Plus, she has a teenager; she wouldn't just walk away from her daughter.

Catching a glimpse of the parking lot at the trail's end, Rachel abandons her best laid plans. Rachel can't think her way out of this situation. Or *into* it; she isn't even sure which direction she is headed. The situation is hopeless, and Rachel feels cursed with her clairvoyance and this damned predator.

Just like all her other premonitions, she should just let it go. Mind her own business. Walk away.

Rachel and Lorena pace around the empty parking lot until their breathing slows. "So," Lorena says, "what are you going to do about this premonition?"

"Probably nothing. Dad said he'll go to the police with me, but ... I don't want to involve him. And I'm sure the police won't do anything based on a premonition."

"There's a faculty member in Fletch's department who

works with the Sheriff. Brett. You could talk to him. He does some kind of research on law enforcement investigative techniques … something like that. Hey—" Lorena's eyes go mischievous, and she gives Rachel's arm a playful swat. "He's single, too."

"Uh-uh. No. Absolutely not." She waves her hands at this disastrous idea. "No blind dates. With your husband's friend? I could think of a few ways that could go so wrong."

She shrugs. "Okay, but when you're forty and still sitting around with just a dog, don't say I didn't try. You could at least talk to Brett, see if he—"

"No way. I don't want you involved in this … mess. Besides, I don't want Fletcher knowing about my things." Rachel circles her finger around her temple, realizing her symbol for ESP is also the classic symbol for being cuckoo. *Exactly.*

"Why not? Fletch is very open-minded. He's a poli-sci professor, for god's sake. He'll just wonder if you can predict if he's going to get tenure." They both chuckle then go quiet.

After a few minutes, Lorena says, "How long are you going to avoid us? Since I married Fletch, you sort of … disappeared on me."

That gives Rachel a stab of guilt. When Lorena married Fletcher, Rachel was full of mixed emotions. She was glad Lorena found someone who she, apparently, trusted and loved, but Rachel couldn't stand the guy. Conversations with Fletcher always feel like a debate, in which he needs to prove his point about, well, everything. His need to be right exhausts Rachel; he should have gone to law school. Fletcher's only redeeming quality is that Ruby likes him, but that is because he will play fetch with her endlessly. That dog will play fetch with *anyone*.

To further complicate matters, Rachel dreads that she will have a premonition about Fletcher. Another surefire way to ruin a friendship: tell a best friend that something dreadful —you aren't sure what—is about to happen to her husband.

While distancing herself from Fletcher, and thus from Lorena, it never crossed Rachel's mind that Lorena—all cozied up with her verbally combative, arrogant husband—missed her, too.

Finally, Rachel says, "You know why I ... backed away."

"Not really. At first, I thought you were just giving us space, newlyweds and all. But when you stayed away, I figured you were worried about premonitions."

Rachel nods.

"But maybe you won't have one about Fletch. You never had one with me."

"I just don't want to risk it, Lorena. It would screw up our friendship. Then I really will be sitting around, completely alone, at forty."

"At this rate, you're going to anyway." She smiles. "Why don't we just agree that if you have one, we will just ... deal with it?"

"What does *that* mean?"

"Well ... you'll just tell me, like you always—"

Rachel glances away.

Lorena glares at her. "Really? You don't always tell me about your premonitions?"

Rachel shakes her head.

"Like how many?"

"Why does it matter?"

"Why? Why? Because you're lying to me!" Her voice is getting shrill.

"I'm not lying. I just … it's a lot to ask of a friend. To hear all this negative crap all the time."

"Shit!" Lorena turns away, hands on her hips, pacing a small path and staring at the ground.

"You know about most of them. I've probably told you about, I don't know … two-thirds of them. Since you got married, maybe half." Suddenly, Rachel feels like they are talking about affairs instead of premonitions. "I don't want to burn you out or drive you away."

Several moments later, Rachel says, "Besides, I have a therapist to help with this shit."

Lorena jerks around to face Rachel, her eyes wide with anger, her jaw hanging open. "You just said you haven't told your shrink about your premonitions."

Touché, Rachel thinks. Lorena isn't a hot-headed person, so this flare of anger makes Rachel feel guilty. And the glimpse she is catching of herself through Lorena's eyes—withholding to the point of dishonesty—leaves her feeling like a rotten friend. This is not the friend Rachel wants to be or that she used to be.

Lorena's face softens. "You don't have to carry all this around. Alone. I want to go back to telling each other whatever. Whenever. And I can handle hearing about your premonitions. All of them."

Rachel gives a half-hearted nod.

"You are so full of shit," she says, scowling at Rachel. "Can we at least agree if you have one about—wait, have you had one about Fletch already?"

"No, I haven't."

They stare at each other for a few seconds. "Honestly?" Lorena says.

"I haven't."

"Okay, can we just agree that if you do, you'll tell me? Just like you said you would if you ever had one about me."

Rachel nods, but none of this is going to happen. She already said way more than she wanted to.

DAY TWO, 2:00 PM

SITTING ON AN OVERTURNED BUCKET, Patrick is taking a smoke break out back when a cop cruises by, real slow. The officer takes a good, long look at Patrick, even cranes his neck around as he drives past. Patrick breaks out in a cold sweat.

Only thing he hates more than his mother, more than women, are cops. They're always looking for trouble where there isn't any. Since this missing woman, cops are driving by his work, parking down the street, watching who knows. Probably him and all the other registered sex offenders in a fifty-mile radius.

Retracing his every move over the past couple days, he mulls over whether anything he did or said will make him a suspect. No way, he thinks. I'm clean.

Taking one last draw off his cigarette, he flicks the butt in the direction of the cop car.

In his session with Dr. Levitsky, Patrick decides to talk about the deputy who drove by him, rubbernecking, trying to intimidate him. This will get it documented that he don't know jack shit about that woman, in case someone starts asking around, talking to Dr. Levitsky about the offenders in the program. Maybe confidentiality doesn't apply to shrinks who work with sex offenders on parole.

"You heard about that missin' woman, yeah?"

Dr. Levitsky nods, calmly folding his hands in his lap.

Of course he has, Patrick thinks. Cops probably called all the sex offender shrinks in the area, first thing.

"I ain't had nothin' to do with that woman. But them cops are drivin' by all the time now. Had one starin' me down today."

Dr. Levitsky nudges his glasses higher up on his nose. "Sounds uncomfortable."

"Hell yeah. Since I got a prior, these sons-a-bitches are gonna be all over me. And I ain't done shit! I do everything my parole officer tells me to do."

"Then you don't have to worry about the police. Just go on about your bus—"

"*Ah man*, you know how this works. Innocent 'til proven guilty, my ass." Patrick is agitated, talking loudly. Too loud. He doesn't want to sound so angry that he seems guilty. Talking to his shrink about this might backfire on him.

Dr. Levitsky gazes at Patrick steadily, without any reaction. "Have you been questioned by the police?"

"Not yet," Patrick says.

"I imagine police will be looking for evidence of Alicia Meyers in many places. That doesn't mean they're watching you."

Patrick likes how Dr. Levitsky used her name, didn't just call her "the missing woman." It's makes her seem so— familiar and real, not just a face on a poster or a newscast. He daydreams about her so much that it's like he *does* know her.

"Anyways," Patrick says, "the whole thing makes me sick."

"Feeling like the police are wa—"

"Nah. I mean, it's sick that she was kidnapped ... or whatever."

"Ah. Yes, it's really sad. Her family must be very scared."

Patrick never thought about her family. Yeah, her husband must be feeling ... helpless and weak. "But you're right, I don't gotta worry about cops. I worked that evening. I'm cool ... I got an alibi."

12

____

DAY TWO, 5:00 PM

AS SOON AS Rachel gets home, she feeds Ruby then settles in front of the computer, still unable to shake the idea of using Ruby to help find the missing woman. Ruby could, at least, find the last place this woman walked after leaving Bucatini. Who knows? That could lead to another clue. If a drop of Alicia Meyers' blood dripped somewhere outside the restaurant, Ruby will find it. And using Ruby to track Alicia is better than Rachel burying herself in work, skirting around the daily news and tormenting herself about whether she set this abduction into motion.

First, Rachel looks up how long a person's scent remains detectable by a dog. Several days, maybe one week. In some cases, up to two weeks, especially with a dog trained in ground and water scent work—exactly how she trained Ruby. Scents last longer on moist, vegetated areas than on hard surfaces because the smells settle among and cling to the vegetation and soil, as opposed to being easily blown off hard, flat surfaces.

Leaning back in the chair, she tries to picture the area

around Bucatini. There is a sidewalk out front and other businesses up and down the street. There is curbside parking in front of those businesses. Closing her eyes, she visualizes exiting the restaurant. She and her dad have walked in and out that door many times. She imagines walking to the curb. There are shade trees in that part of town, arching over the streets, and a grassy strip—*Yes!*—between the sidewalk and road where the trees are growing.

Excitement bubbles up in her chest. For seven days that woman's scent could remain detectable. That isn't long. This is day two. Five more days for her scent to be detectable. But how would they do it?

All Ruby needs is some article that has Alicia's scent on it, but she can't exactly go talk to Alicia's husband and ask for one of her dirty socks. Though he would probably cooperate. He wouldn't have anything to lose, and he is likely desperate for any clues.

Wait, maybe the Sheriff has dogs and tried this. I could call them and ask if they have a canine unit.

If they don't have dogs, then Rachel would offer Ruby's services. She wouldn't have to say anything about her premonition, just that she read the news, wants to help and has a dog that is search and rescue certified.

This has to happen right away, like tomorrow. The Sheriff's office probably won't go for this or, at least, not that quickly. There are probably liability issues if Rachel gets hurt. Or potential legal issues if Ruby can't find Alicia and, later, the Sheriff finds her body. Alicia's husband could claim that if they had a better trained dog, Alicia might have been saved ...

Just what I need heaped onto my already full shoulders, Rachel thinks—that I *almost* saved a life.

Stop overthinking this. Just call and offer a dog for search and rescue.

"Ahhh," she groans, turning away from the computer.

Ruby prances over, nuzzles Rachel's hand then gives her the smiley dog face—mouth parted slightly, row of little bottom teeth showing.

Apparently, I'm fine, Rachel thinks. Good to know.

She doesn't feel fine. She is mentally drained and ravenous. Rachel snarfs down some dinner while reviewing her search and rescue dog handler certification paperwork, seeing if there is anything in there about liability. There isn't.

Criminal law is not her specialty, but she settles back in front of the computer and reviews some of her go-to sites for legal information. Volunteers can be used by police departments for anything that doesn't require a search warrant. Of course. Search and rescue operations are the most common situation in which police use volunteers, mostly during natural disasters.

At that, Rachel snorts. "Well, Ruby and I are ready when the next tornado or hurricane hits Washington."

Next, she finds the Sheriff's website. There is no mention of a K-9 unit. Clicking around, she finds at the bottom of their public information page a phone number and email address to contact about volunteering for the Sheriff's office.

Her stomach flutters with tension. This is how she can help without telling anyone about her premonition: volunteer to search for Alicia Meyers. After all, she could be wrong about the busser; sometimes *husbands* kill their wives ...

That quiet, still voice from the back of her mind, says, again, Trust. Your. Instincts.

At eleven p.m., Rachel watches the nightly news to see if she can discern anything more about Alicia Meyers. When Alicia's face comes on the screen, Rachel moves in close, staring right into her eyes. No intuition whatsoever. Blank. Rachel doesn't know why she bothered; she has never received a premonition from someone's photo.

The Sheriff's office is still seeking any information that could lead to her whereabouts. Rachel scribbles down the hotline number. Now, she has two numbers at the Sheriff's office to call and volunteer Ruby's services. Alicia's scent will only remain detectable by Ruby for a matter of days.

There is no time for anything else.

13

———————————

DAY THREE, 8:00 AM

THE NEXT MORNING, Rachel dials the Sheriff's hotline for the missing woman. If she is going to, just this once, stop minding her own business, she might as well dive in.

She introduces herself, adding that she is a local attorney —since *everyone* knows all attorneys are law-abiding, upstanding citizens—says she has a search and rescue certified dog and wants to help search for Alicia Meyers.

There are a few seconds of silence over the phone line from Sergeant Hagen. Clearly, he doesn't know dogs, Rachel thinks. Or scent work. She knew it was a smallish Sheriff's office but figured that all police knew about dogs doing search and rescue.

Rachel continues. "I wasn't sure if you had a canine unit or already did a dog search—"

"We don't have a canine unit. We requested help from King County. They should be able to get a dog over here in a couple of days."

"Well, it's best if the scent is no more than a few days old." She strains to keep the urgency out of her voice.

"Yeah, that's what King County said ... but they've got their dogs and handlers on other cases. Hadn't thought about a volunteer dog search. Has your dog done this before?"

"Only in trainings, but she has her detective dog certification." There is a beat of silence over the phone. "That's the same certification police dogs have. My dog can follow the scent of a person anywhere. She can even find scents that are buried under dirt or water. And we can do a search as soon as you're ready."

"Well ... let me email a volunteer application and an authorization for a background check. You okay with a background check?"

"No problem. Ruby doesn't have any priors," she says, chuckling.

Sergeant Hagen doesn't laugh. Not even a slight chuckle.

Fifteen minutes go by, then thirty, and still no email with the forms. Sergeant Hagen's lukewarm attitude about a volunteer detective dog leaves Rachel feeling discouraged and indignant. For over a decade, the best strategy she found for dealing with her clairvoyance is to mind her own damned business, so that is exactly what she does: goes to her office and gets busy.

She meets with two clients, navigating them with her usuals: sorry, no time for a lunch meeting (too much eye contact); and please come to my office (set up for side-by-side seating with enough space to avoid brushing against someone).

Rachel usually loves work and can easily get lost in a complicated environmental planning document, but today, her nagging self-talk keeps interrupting her. This premonition is different. The busser could kill that woman, if he hasn't already. This premonition is one you might, actually, be able to use to help someone. Why the hell hasn't that detective emailed me back?

At lunch, Rachel goes home and takes a fast run with Ruby—something about the lungs trying to breathe really shuts up her nagging brain. Usually.

On her run, Rachel can't shake her growing animosity toward this deputy—or Sergeant or detective or … whatever— who is either lazy, doesn't understand the importance of follow through or has no intention of following through.

After her run, she gulps down a glass of water, wipes the perspiration from her forehead and is poised to call this Sergeant Hagen back and remind him that for a detective dog, time is of the fucking essence. This is when her phone pings with an email notification.

It's from the Sheriff's office. Quickly, she fills out the forms and returns them, attaching her search and rescue dog handler certification, as well as Ruby's detective class certification.

Two hours later, Sergeant Hagen calls and asks if they can meet for her to demonstrate how a detective dog search would work. He is available later today, he offers, if that works for her.

She envisions hauling Ruby into the Sheriff's office, walking past a bunch of deputies, then sitting across a desk from this guy. No doubt, cops experience some gruesome stuff, about which Rachel doesn't want to have any intuitions. And Ruby would be distracted in a busy office.

"We can meet at the Sheriff's office," he says. "Or is it easier if I come to where you and your dog are?"

Both options put her on guard. Rachel lets few people

into her house. It is a challenge to welcome a visitor while avoiding handshakes and prolonged eye contact, especially in her tiny house.

Either place, the Sheriff's office or her house are vulnerable situations.

Rachel suggests five thirty, after she gets off work, and rattles off the address for her dad's house. More spacious and, at least, there will be one other person to share the normal contacts. Her dad is an expert on diversionary handshakes and greetings on Rachel's behalf.

14

DAY THREE, 9:15 AM

THE KNOCK on his door sends a jolt of anxiety through Patrick. Probably my fuckin' PO, he thinks. No one else comes here. Automatically, he glances around. "Comin'," he hollers, scanning the kitchen on his way to the door. Nothing to worry about. Doesn't even have a brewski in the fridge.

Peeking through the chained door, it is Daniel, his parole officer—and a cop. Patrick thinks it might be the same cop who drove by him the other day. His underarms sting with perspiration.

"Hey, man, lemme unlock this." As he slips the chain out, he takes one last peek over his shoulder. Ain't nothin' in here can get me in trouble, he tells himself. Just be cool.

"Hey Patrick, this is Sergeant Hagen," Daniel says. "He wants to ask you a few questions."

Patrick looks at Hagen then back to Daniel. "About what?"

Hagen bobs his head, like that is a fair enough question. "We're talking to sex offender parolees about Alicia Meyers."

He opens a folder and tries to hand Patrick a missing woman flyer.

Patrick stares at the flyer, at her beautiful face and her sweet name printed there: ALICIA MEYERS. He looked up what her name means: princess. So perfect for that face. He doesn't take the flyer from Sergeant Hagen, doesn't dare touch her in front of these men. But then Patrick becomes aware of his hands hanging at his sides, uselessly.

They're gonna try to pin this on me. No way I'm goin' back to prison. Didn't do shit to Alicia.

Jiggling the flyer at Patrick, Hagen says, "Have you seen this woman?"

Pulling his eyes away from his creamy-skinned princess, Patrick is aware that both men are watching him. Real close. Especially Hagen, doing that thing cops do, assessing whether a person is guilty by how they react. I should ask for an attorney, Patrick thinks, but that always makes you sound guilty. Besides, he isn't sure if he can ask for an attorney, since he *was* found guilty before and his parole officer is standing right there.

Shit, I was only found guilty cuz that bitch lied. She wanted me. She was askin' for it.

Forcing his face to relax, Patrick looks at the two men. Then, trying to appear unfazed, he shakes his head. "Just seen her on posters like that one." He ticks his chin at the princess without taking his eyes off Hagen. Shifty eyes make people seem guilty.

Out of the corner of his eyes, Patrick notices that Daniel is scanning the apartment. Patrick takes what he hopes isn't a noticeable swallow; he doesn't want to clear his throat, that will sound guilty.

"Y'all wanna come in—" Patrick sweeps his arm towards his tiny apartment "—and look around?" No guilty person is going to invite a cop to take a look around. *Please, please say no. Say no, and I promise, I'll never look at another woman.*

Daniel looks over at Hagen, who shakes his head and says, "That's not necessary."

Hagen slides the poster back into the folder. "One more thing," he says to Patrick. "Do you recall where you were Monday evening?"

Glancing at Daniel, Patrick says, cool as a cucumber, despite his heart pounding in his chest, "Should I have an attorney here?"

"If you want." Daniel shrugs. "But, I'm your PO, and I ask you that shit all the time. So, why don't you tell me. Where you were Monday evening?"

Hagen is watching Patrick like a hawk, like a bloodhound on a trail, all but sniffing him for clues. Patrick can tell this cop thinks he took Alicia.

"Let's see ..." Patrick purses his lips, like he is contemplating his whereabouts last Monday. "That was that, three nights ago?"

Hagen nods.

Fuckin' pig. Thinks I don't know when Monday was. "I worked the late shift that day. Clocked out, oh ... probly around eight forty-five. Drove straight home."

"Boss can confirm you worked that night?" Hagen says.

"Sure can." Patrick can't tell if they believe him, but he sure as hell hopes they don't go talking to his boss. That will get him fired, and it took months to find a place that would hire a felon.

15

DAY THREE, 5:00 PM

WHEN RACHEL ARRIVES at her dad's house, she is dismayed to see Margaret's car in the driveway. The realization that she needs to stop arriving, unannounced, at her dad's house makes Rachel more than a little lonely. She suspects it's time to expand her social life beyond her father being one of her few, regular human contacts. Sitting in her car, Rachel stares at the house and thinks, What if Dad and Margaret are ... busy? Like, sitting together on Mom's couch. Or lying on Mom's bed.

Since Rachel is already out front and Sergeant Hagen will be there shortly, she dials her dad's number. He doesn't answer her call but texts: WITH CLIENT. CALL U BACK?

Rachel forgot that he is getting into year-end accounting stuff so working later than usual. She dreads going in and making conversation with Margaret while her dad is still at work. At least she won't be alone with Sergeant Hagen. Nothing like trying to have a normal conversation with one other person while stealthily evading extended eye contact. Rachel does not want to have a premonition about a cop.

Rachel texts her dad: At the house. Margaret's here. ok if I go in?

He responds: She'll love it! I'll be home in 30 mins.

She sends a thumbs-up emoji. Then adds: fyi don't freak out. I'm meeting cop here. Volunteering Ruby to search for missing woman.

He texts back a head-exploding emoji. She chuckles because she recently showed him how to add emojis to texts, and it seems the exploding head is his favorite.

On her way up to the house, Rachel rehearses what to tell Margaret without revealing anything about her premonition. She is volunteering with the Sheriff so Ruby can get some real-life search experience. And because she wants to be of service, what with the missing woman. The thought of Alicia being missing for three days grinds her rehearsal to a halt. Does she really need an excuse to search for a missing woman?

Margaret envelops Rachel in a light hug. Trying to relax her shoulders, Rachel returns the hug and, this time, even breathes while doing so. Margaret smells faintly of lavender from her lotion or deodorant. The motherly affection Margaret exudes makes Rachel feel both revulsion and hunger; disloyal to her mom and starved for mothering. After Rachel's mom died, Aunt Cherie tried to mother her, but Rachel was reeling from grief and the trauma of the car accident and recovering from a bad head injury. She pushed Cherie away like only a seventeen-year-old girl can—with disdain and simmering anger and lots of walking away and door slamming.

Rachel can't help but wonder what her relationship

would be like with her mother if she was still alive. She wonders what it would be like, as an adult, to have a mother.

Clearing her throat, Rachel says, "Hope I'm not interrupting your guy's plans for the evening"—Margaret waves away her statement—"but I need to meet a cop here."

A slight frown of concern falls over Margaret's face.

"Oh, it's nothing bad," Rachel clarifies. "I'm just seeing if Ruby and I can do some search and rescue."

"Right," Margaret says, nodding enthusiastically. "Phil told me about that training you do with Ruby. Sounds like that dog has quite the nose."

"She does." There is an awkward pause between them. "And I didn't want a cop, who I don't know, in my house. Not that I know *any* cops. But you know, alone, with a man, at the house ... but I forgot Dad works late this time of year."

"It's fine," Margaret says. "Well ... of course it is. This is *your* house. Besides, Phil—I mean, your dad—should be home soon."

Out of politeness, Rachel waits to be invited into her own living room. Margaret hesitates before finally moving in that direction and saying, "Should we ... wait in there?"

Just when Rachel isn't sure how much longer she can tolerate being a stranger in her own home, the home she grew up in, Ruby barks and races to the front door.

Opening the door, Rachel is disconcerted to see a very fit, strikingly handsome cop; a paunchy, older one would have been preferable. Catching his eye briefly, he remains blank to Rachel, so she hazards another passing glance. Still nothing. Great eyebrows though: dark, long and straight but not bushy or a unibrow. They give his eyes a penetrating, almost brooding look, very Theo James-like. His facial expression is intense, all business, probably from years of being a cop.

"Ms. Sharpe?" he says over Ruby's barking. "I'm Sergeant Hagen. We talked a couple of hours ago." He extends his hand.

Rachel avoids his handshake by looking down at Ruby and saying, "No bark." She points at a dog bed. Ruby sulks over to the bed but keeps her eyes on the man.

"Come on in." Rachel closes the door behind him as Margaret walks up and introduces herself.

"If you don't mind," Rachel says, "I'll release my dog now. She's not aggressive or anything, just *very* vocal. And a little cautious. She'll just run over and check you out."

He glances at Ruby and shrugs.

"Okay, Ruby," Rachel coaxes. "Come over and say hi."

With that, Ruby skitters over to Sergeant Hagen, sniffs his boots, his knees, his hand and, thankfully, skips the always embarrassing crotch sniff. Uncharacteristically, she does all this with her tail up and wagging, and a doggie grin showing her bottom pearly whites.

Sergeant Hagen squats down to give her a vigorous *thump, thump, thump* on her side. "You call this cautious?" He looks up, also grinning. Geez, Rachel thinks, those two make a happy couple, and they hardly know each other.

Margaret invites them to come and sit—on Mom's couch, of course. Rachel wonders if she will ever get used to this woman occupying her mother's house. Doesn't she have her own place?

"So, we don't have any deputies trained to use canines," Sergeant Hagen says, "so I'm not sure how, or if, we can use your dog. Can you tell me about this"—he shuffles through some papers in a folder—"detective dog certification?"

"Sure. I've been training Ruby in scent work for two years," Rachel says. "Detective Dog is what they call the highest level of this training. Then we just finished search and rescue training. Basically, she's had the same training police dogs go through."

He purses his lips, looking unconvinced or intrigued—Rachel really can't tell. For all she knows, he is doing face yoga. Also, no cop should have lips that sumptuous.

Rachel continues. "So, Ruby can search for someone, like that missing woman, if she can smell something with her scent on it. Their scent leaves a trail that she can follow." She pauses, not wanting to sound urgent, though Ruby only has a few days left. "If the scent is still fresh."

"And you would direct the dog? Because I don't—"

"I would do that. A lot of the training is really for the handler." She gestures at the folder that he laid on the coffee table. "I emailed my rescue dog handler certification, too."

"Can you ... somehow demonstrate how this works?"

"Hmm, let's see ... I need something that smells like you," Rachel says, pointing at his watch. It is one of those beefy watches with a rugged, webbed band.

As he unhooks it, Rachel begs the universe not to give her a premonition if she accidentally touches him. She isn't about to pluck the watch from him like it's contaminated, using her thumb and index finger like tweezers.

No zing. Silent exhale.

"Go outside and walk somewhere from here," she says. "It doesn't matter how far or where. Go, at least, say, several blocks. Half a mile. Then text me when you're in your hiding place."

While awaiting Sergeant Hagen's text, Rachel's dad comes home, and she and Margaret fill him in on what's happening. The three sit around chatting for several minutes, including about the possibility of Ruby searching for the missing woman. Her dad gives Rachel an eyes-wide nod, a discreet message of support. Rachel mutters that it's the least she can do to help the Sheriff's office.

When Rachel gets the text that Sergeant Hagen is ready, she tells her dad and Margaret not to follow along—less distraction for Ruby.

Outside, Rachel hooks a leash onto Ruby's collar and says, "You ready for some real work?" Placing the Sergeant's watch at the dog's nose level, Rachel says, "Find him."

The dog takes one sniff of the watch and takes Rachel straight to Sergeant Hagen's cruiser.

Praising Ruby, Rachel lets her smell the watch again and commands her again to find him.

Eagerly, she starts sniffing, and Rachel jogs so as not to hold her back. When she is on a scent trail, Ruby is hyperfocused, almost obsessed.

Ruby leads Rachel out of the neighborhood and into an area, several blocks away, that has some small shops and restaurants. Pausing often to sniff the air, Ruby eventually makes a bee line straight to an old house that has been converted to a Thai restaurant. Rachel's favorite Thai—another restaurant with good spacing between tables and never crowded. Five stars for low risk of catching people's eyes.

Ruby sits at the steps in front of Bahn Thai and stares at Rachel. A perfect alert signal.

Must've lost his scent, Rachel thinks, or was sidetracked by the food aromas. "You sure, Ruby?" Putting the watch to Ruby's nose again, she commands her again. "Find him."

Ruby bounds up the stairs to the outdoor dining porch on the side of the restaurant. There, at one of the tables, sits Sergeant Hagen.

Staring at him for a moment, Rachel can't believe Ruby found him. This was the longest search Ruby's ever completed. In classes, the dog trainers never hid this far away.

Sergeant Hagen nods his head in amazement. "That's impressive."

Ruby prances over to him and nudges his wrist, right where his skin is pale from always being underneath a watchband.

"Okay, *that* is actually scary," he says.

Rachel sits down across from him. "*That* is tracking. It's amazing what their noses can find."

She notices then that he has a pot of hot tea. How odd, she thinks. I must have some stereotype about cops. Coffee, of course. Beer, yes. Whiskey, certainly. But jasmine tea? Very strange.

"How does she do that?" he asks, sliding the teapot towards Rachel.

Rachel pours herself a cup. "Hundreds of millions of olfactory receptors. Humans have six million, but dogs have three *hundred* million. You basically left a scent trail behind you, and she could smell it."

Rachel reaches down and gives Ruby a proud head rub. "When she started pulling me in this direction, I was worried the food smells through her off your trail. I figured you'd hiding down one of the side streets by my house."

"Nah, people don't like to see a cop wandering around the neighborhood. Freaks 'em out. Plus, I love this place. Got some dinner to go."

As they walk back to her dad's house, she says, "So, Sergeant Ha—"

"It's Chris. Chris Hagen."

"What do you think? Want Ruby to search for the missing woman?"

"Can't see that the Sheriff's office has anything to lose. Suppose the worst that could happen is your dog doesn't find any ... evidence. I got all the paperwork I need from you. What does she need?" He ticks his chin towards Ruby.

Rachel explains that she will need a scent cue, a personal article of Alicia's. It needs to be something that hasn't been washed but also hasn't been mingled up in a hamper with her family's clothes. A watch or a shoe is good if she wore it often and recently. A perfect scent cue would be one of her bras because women don't wash them every time they are worn. Whatever item he picks, her husband shouldn't touch it. Just use a new plastic bag to pick it up, then seal it.

Chris says he will contact Alicia's husband tomorrow, then suggests they search the morning after that.

Rachel shakes her head. "That will be day five."

"Don't see how we can do it any—"

"The fresher the scent trail, the better."

"Yeah, but I want to go to the PLS—"

"The what?"

"Sorry. Place last seen. Bucatini restaurant. I'd like to go there in the morning. Before they open."

The image of the busser watching them search for Alicia gives Rachel a chill. That could tip him off and make him nervous, maybe nervous enough that he moves Alicia to another hiding location.

Wait, this busser might not even be the one who abducted her.

"Yeah, morning would be best ..." Rachel says. "I don't want to draw attention, get a bunch of onlookers. The more people around, the more disruptions for Ruby. Is there any chance we could go tomorrow morning?"

Chris glances at his watch. "I'll call her husband this evening and see if I can pick up a ..."

"Scent cue."

"Right. I'll see if I can get one from her husband tonight."

Two hours later, Chris texts that he has a scent cue. They agree to meet at the restaurant at six thirty the next morning.

Rachel hits the sack early, wanting to be well-rested, but can't shut off her mind. She worries that Ruby won't be able to track Alicia; this *is* her first real search. Not a practice, not a training, a live search, for a live person. Well, hopefully Alicia is still alive.

What if Ruby only tracks the scent for a short distance, to where Alicia was thrown into a van or hopped into her lover's car or whatever made her vanish?

So much for getting a good night's sleep.

Focusing on her breathing, she begins counting down from one hundred, but her mind keeps intruding, very rudely, about Chris. And Ruby. And Alicia. And the busser. Repeatedly, Rachel resumes the countdown. Eighty, seventy-nine. Now, she sees an image of the busser's face. Inhale. Seventy-eight, seventy-seven. The busser's eyes. Exhale. Where was

I? Seventy-five, seventy-four. The busser's craving for that woman. Shit! Inhale. Seventy-three, seventy-two, seventy-one. Exhale. Seventy.

Then that internal voice says, Ruby needs to track the busser.

With that, Rachel throws off the covers, stomps into the kitchen and reads the label on the hydroxyzine bottle. The prescription reads, "1 tablet at bedtime as needed for insomnia." She swallows a second tablet. Hey, she tells herself, this *is* needed. I need to be knocked out. And it's only an allergy pill.

16

———————

DAY FOUR, 6:15 AM

ON THE WAY TO BUCATINI, Rachel considers, again, all the ways she could use Ruby to track the busser, in addition to Alicia, but hits the same dead end as before: to his car or a bus stop. After that, Rachel still needs to follow him to find out where he lives and, more importantly, where he has Alicia. She doesn't need Ruby for that. It would be simpler to park outside the restaurant and simply follow him when he gets off work.

The police must have questioned Bucatini staff already, ran background checks. Maybe the busser *is* a key suspect, has already been questioned, is even being watched by the police.

What she really has to do is tell Chris about her premonition and the need to track the busser. That is the simplest option and, likely, the most useful. But, no matter how she rehearses saying this, she imagines some variation of the same response from Chris. Throat clearing. Extracting himself from the conversation as quickly as possible. Or, the best case, him explaining that, even if he did believe her, a premonition doesn't constitute probable cause. They can't arrest someone based on intuition.

The convolutions in her thinking always lead her back to the same conclusion: if searching for Alicia's scent this morning doesn't lead to anything significant, she will go back to Bucatini, lock eyes with or bump into the busser, and hope for another premonition. A specific one. The thought sends a cold shiver down her back.

At this hour, the several blocks of downtown Cedarbend are a sleepy village. As she nears Bucatini, there is a faint brightening in the eastern sky through the bare branches of the trees. The streets are empty and the stores all closed.

A couple of blocks before Bucatini, she passes the Third Avenue Food Co-op, which is still dark inside. Then up ahead there is a Sheriff's car and a second one right across the street from Bucatini.

Even in the dusky morning light, Rachel can tell it is Chris standing outside the patrol car closest to Bucatini. He is tall, but it's more his posture, the way he carries himself, that she recognizes.

Pulling up behind Chris' car, Rachel watches him walk towards her. He must be over six feet, she thinks, and such long legs.

Hooking Ruby's leash onto her collar, Rachel talks calmly to Ruby in hopes she won't pick up on her nervousness. But she knows you can't fool dogs—talk about extrasensory perception.

Chris hands Rachel a plastic bag containing a sports bra, hopefully one Alicia worked out in recently. Then, looking from Rachel to the bra, then back, he says, "So, what should I do?"

"For starters, just stay in your car. That will be less distracting for Ruby. Then, if she leads me out of your sights, you can follow in the car. But stay back. When she's taken us as far as she can, I'll wave you over."

Walking Ruby across the street, Rachel kneels in front of the restaurant. "Let's do some work, Ruby. You ready to do some sniff-sniff?" Hearing those words, Ruby sits and stares at Rachel, intense and focused. "Good girl."

Rachel slips on medical gloves so as not to get her scent on the bra, then opens the plastic bag and places it in front of Ruby. "Find her."

Ruby nudges her nose into the bag, then her nose goes in the air. She is trailing, looking for the scent. *Please let this work.* Eagerly, she works her way back and forth outside the door of the restaurant, then makes a larger circumference, nose in the air and on the ground. Rachel lets her sniff the bra again. Ruby begins to root around in the grass and dirt and trees along the sidewalk then, with a jerk of her head, makes an about-face. She sniffs her way along the grass strip in the direction of Marsh Street, occasionally, smelling the air.

Ruby takes a hard right—a definitive right—onto Marsh Street, her nose still in the grass strip. She tracks the scent past an alley, across Third Avenue, then to the intersection with a second alley. There, she seems to lose the scent.

Moving all around the intersection of the alley and Marsh Street, Ruby's nose is in the air, back to the grass, in the air again, back to the sidewalk. At one point, she starts sniffing at a streetlight post, which Rachel assumes is dog pee, so she instructs Ruby to leave it. Leaning down, Rachel puts the bra in front of her and commands her, again, to find it.

Briefly, Ruby puts her mouth on the bra, looking at Rachel excitedly and wagging her tail, then gets back to work

A car is parked on the street at the intersection, and Ruby nudges her nose under it. There isn't any traffic and no one in the car, so Rachel lets her walk around the car. Ruby sniffs frantically, trying to find the trail. Her nose in the air again, she suddenly swings her head towards the alley.

She locks onto the scent again, solidly. Down the narrow alley Ruby goes. Fast. She is tugging on the leash to go faster. Without any streetlights, the alley is dim, so Rachel watches her step. When Chris slowly turns into the alley, his headlights lighting up the alley. Able to see better, Rachel breaks into a jog so as not to restrain Ruby.

Ruby mostly keeps her nose in the edge where the backs of buildings meet the asphalt, occasionally moving over to smell a pothole. All places that scents would settle. At the end of the alley, where it runs into Clark Street, Ruby leads Rachel through a walkway into a three-story, open-air parking garage. Chris pulls over in the alley next to the garage, and Rachel motions for him to stay put.

Ruby takes her to a corner of the garage where there are a few empty parking spots squeezed between an elevator and the outside wall of the garage. Stopping at the parking space closest to the elevator, Ruby sits in her definitive alert stance, eyes locked onto Rachel's.

In front of Ruby's curly haired, white paws, right where the trunk would be if a car was parked in that spot, nose in, lays a teardrop shaped, silver earring.

Staying in her exact position, Rachel signals for Chris, who has entered the garage and clicked on a flashlight, to come over to them.

As he walks over to them, slower than Rachel would prefer, he scans the parking garage. The light from his flashlight flits in every direction: left, right, up, down. Cops must get so tired of being hyperaware, Rachel thinks. Then, as if he has nothing better to do, Chris stops several car spots away from Rachel and stares at the ceiling for a moment, his flashlight aimed at something up there.

What the hell is he looking at? Ruby found an earring over here!

When Chris gets near, Ruby goes all waggy and wiggly but stays put. Rachel starts talking. "She tracked her scent to this location"—she points at the earring—"and alerted on that."

Directing his flashlight at the earring, they both stare at it. Even Ruby seems to be staring at it. Rachel imagines what could have happened to Alicia to cause her earring to be pulled out. Shoved into a trunk, she figures. She hopes Chris is figuring that out, too.

Chris goes to his cruiser and comes back with evidence bags. He squats and places the earring in an evidence bag, then examines the concrete all around, sweeping his flashlight left and right.

When he stands, Rachel says, "Maybe the woman parked here?" *Yeah, then climbed into her trunk.* It takes several beats before Rachel realizes she is looking directly into Chris' eyes. She glances down at Ruby and the empty parking spot.

"No, we found her car," he says walking back toward his cruiser, "parked on Marsh Street. At the corner with the alley."

"Where Ruby was sniffing around the car there?"

"Yep."

"That was her car?"

"No, we towed her car from that location a few days ago."

"Ahh. That's why Ruby got confused there. But she definitely found Alicia's scent again in the alley. She was on the scent, hard, all the way down the alley."

He puts the evidence bag with the earring in his patrol car, then whips out his phone and opens a mapping app, holding it where Rachel can also see it.

Pointing at the map on his phone, Chris says, "So, according to your dog, Alicia walked from the restaurant, turned right on Marsh Street, got in her car—"

"She didn't, necessarily, get *in* her car. She may have, but Ruby would've picked up her scent just from the car being parked there."

"Okay, hold on a sec," Chris says, pocketing his phone and pulling out a notepad. He turns to catch the morning light and starts jotting notes.

Now we're getting somewhere, Rachel thinks.

Chris continues. "Then she walked down the alley into this garage?"

"Uhhh ... she might not have walked."

"What do you mean?"

"Ruby followed the trail of Alicia's scent."

He stares at her blankly.

"Her scent would be in the alley if she was ..." Rachel doesn't want to put any ideas in his head. There have been enough images—cancer, men hunting women—firing between her and other people's brains lately. "If she was ... I don't know ... inside a vehicle or ... if she was carried." *Or dragged.*

Rachel pauses while Chris jots something else down.

"Then, for some reason," Rachel says, "one of her earrings fell off in that parking spot by the elevator."

"Well ... *someone* lost an earring there."

Doing her best to conceal her frustration, Rachel says, "That is *Alicia's* earring. Ruby alerted on that earring, not that parking space, not anywhere else in the garage. She detected Alicia's scent on that earring."

His eyebrows shoot up doubtfully.

"You saw how quickly she found you the other day," she says.

"Yeah, but I was sitting right there, probably releasing a much stronger smell than a tiny earring that may have been laying here for weeks. Or months."

Now Rachel looks at him skeptically. There was barely a scuff on that earring; the silver hook wasn't even bent.

"Ruby is telling me that earring is Alicia's," Rachel says.

"How accurate is all this?"

"Well, this dog breed is used to detect stuff like Parkinson's and cancer"—Rachel gets a pang of sadness remembering how closely Ruby watched Aaron—"with about ninety percent accuracy."

More scribbling in his notepad. Either he thinks this is a bunch of BS, or he is collecting evidence. Rachel is hoping it is the latter.

When Chris appears to be done taking notes, Rachel points at the parking garage and asks why he was checking out the ceiling inside there.

"Security camera lens up there's been blasted with spray paint."

17

DAY FOUR, 6:45 AM

A SPRAY-PAINTED camera in the very garage where Ruby just tracked Alicia? That can't be a coincidence, Rachel thinks, as a hard knot of fear forms in her gut.

"If that"—Rachel ticks her head towards the security camera—"was spray painted recently, Ruby can track it. See if it leads anywhere near the earring. No guarantees, but ... I'm happy to try."

With his lips pursed in concentration, Chris saunters back into the garage. Rachel follows. He stares at the camera for a moment. The camera is higher off the ground than Rachel expected.

"Guess it can't hurt," Chris says, "just to see if there's any possible connection ..."

"I can't get her up that high," she says. "Do you think you can?" He is certainly tall enough, Rachel thinks. And looks strong enough. "She weighs twenty-four pounds."

"Oh, yeah. That's no problem."

"Okay, you have to get her nose close so she can get a good whiff of the paint. If possible, close enough she can touch it if she wants to. Don't shove her face against it, just as close as possible."

"Alright. How long do I hold her up there?"

"Just until I give her the"—she spells out the word—"F-I-N-D command."

Chris holds Ruby up to the camera for a few seconds, then Rachel says, "Find it," and Ruby's feet hit the ground running, literally.

Ruby pays no attention to Chris, or anything else, so Rachel scoops her hand at Chris, indicating he should follow. Whispering to him, she explains that this scent trail is either really fresh or really strong from the chemicals.

Rachel's mind is racing, and so is her heart, expecting Ruby to take them straight to where the earring was. The busser must have had spray paint in his car, sprayed the camera earlier that day, went to work, then abducted Alicia.

Instead, Ruby leads them out of the garage and back into the alley she tracked Alicia's scent through. The sun is rising, so the alley, while still in shadow, isn't as dark as it was earlier.

Several feet before the back door of a shop, Ruby stops abruptly and alerts. Maybe it *wasn't* the busser who spray painted the camera lens, Rachel thinks, somewhat relieved and very perplexed.

They scan the asphalt, shop door and wall all around Ruby but can't figure out her alert. There isn't spray paint anywhere. Stepping back to take a broader look at the wall, Rachel says, "Maybe it was just kids doing graff—" They both see it: a camera directly above Ruby. The lens is spray painted black.

Uh-oh.

Chris whips out his phone and takes a photo of the security camera.

"Good alert," Rachel says, tousling the curlicues on Ruby's head and slipping her a treat.

He walks up and down the alley, takes another photo aiming towards the parking garage and one aiming towards Marsh Street, where Alicia's car had been parked.

When he seems to be done Rachel says, "Ruby, can you find any more?"

Ruby prances back in the direction of the garage, nose to the ground, but, instead of heading into the garage, she turns the other direction and trails the scent to the side of the Third Avenue Co-Op. She alerts at the dumpster.

"Huh," Chris mutters, scanning the area for cameras or spray paint, then he lifts the lid of the dumpster. Hoping Chris won't ask for Ruby to search through trash for the spray paint can, Rachel peers over the edge. It's mostly empty: two crushed beer cans, a crumpled pack of cigarettes, an empty potato chip bag.

Someone had a lovely picnic dinner out here last night.

"Must've been emptied yesterday," Chris says.

"Yeah, but the can had to be tossed in there. Very recently."

"With all those other smells? Food and garbage and ... whatever, she could smell the spray paint in there?"

"Definitely."

His face twists up with doubt. "Well, I can at least find out when they picked up here."

Undeterred, Rachel says, "Let's see if this is the end of the scent trail." She slips Ruby a treat and says excitedly, "Good alert, Ruby. Good girl. Let's find some more!"

Off Ruby goes, sniffing all the way. She tracks for another block then turns into the alley behind Bucatini.

Holy shit!

Without averting her nose even slightly, Ruby leads them directly to the back door of Bucatini. Rachel's mouth drops open, and her armpits prick with sweat. Ruby noses frenetically around the base of the door, scratches at it, then sits and stares at Rachel.

"Alert," Rachel says numbly, in case Chris missed it.

On the contrary, Chris is poking around the employee's coffee-can ashtray, the recycling bin, the dumpster, the drum of waste cooking oil. He walks up and down this alley, too, looking for spray paint or cameras or doing other cop-like things, all the while checking his mapping app and taking photos.

Still standing near the back door of Bucatini, a panicky feeling descends over Rachel. Recalling the sense of the busser preying on a woman, her stomach goes tight. For all her scheming about seeing him again in hopes of getting another premonition, she isn't ready to face him, not here, not now, standing in the dimly lit alley with her dog and a cop rooting around for evidence.

Pulling out her phone, she feels a beat of relief to see it isn't even seven thirty a.m. Bucatini doesn't open for hours. Still, she wants to get away from there. The stench of fermenty-smelling, empty wine bottles, used cooking oil and cigarette butts is making her stomach go sour. Or maybe the proximity to the busser is souring her.

Chris comes back and says, "Lens on the camera down this alley isn't sprayed ... what do you make of all this?"

She blinks. *Tell him exactly what you make of all this: the busser spray painted the cameras and abducted Alicia!*

Rachel assumes the Sheriff already searched Bucatini and talked to staff. But they haven't arrested anyone, she thinks, so the busser covered his tracks. So to speak. He didn't cover his scent tracks—

"Not about that camera being unsprayed," Chris says, thumbing over his shoulder. "I mean, what is your dog telling us?"

Yes, that is a good start. Rachel coaxes Ruby a few steps away from the back door. Someone, the busser, *could* be in there early, cleaning or prepping or ... making tiramisu.

"Okay ... she's telling us that a spray paint can—no, let me restate that. The *scent of the spray paint* traveled between the camera in the garage to the camera in the other alley, to the Co-Op dumpster, then through this door. I'm not sure how, or in what order."

His brows are furrowed. "Maybe the person who sprayed the cameras chucked the can in the other alley or somewhere around here, then someone brought it here"—he points at the back door of Bucatini—"to throw away. An employee who hates litter?"

"Wouldn't they just toss it in there?" She looks over at Bucatini's dumpster.

"Maybe they did."

"No. She would've alerted at this dumpster like she did at the other one."

"C'mon," he says, holding his hands out in question. "You mean she can tell the difference between trash smells?"

"She can detect the scent of the spray paint. If that spray paint can was in *this* dumpster in the past week, she would've alerted at *it*, not the *back door*." Rachel pauses, wondering how to convince him. "Three hundred million olfactory receptors," she says adamantly.

He shakes his head in disbelief.

"My guess is someone sprayed the two cameras, tossed the can in the Co-Op dumpster, then went through this door. The scent was strong, it would've been on their hands and clothes, even after they tossed it at the Co-Op."

Glancing at the Bucatini's back door, Rachel lowers her voice. "Someone who works here and didn't want to be seen with the can. There must be a suspect who—"

He gives her a glare that says, You're not getting that info, then looks away.

"Well ... someone who works here could've easily done that."

Ruby has grown bored and is sniffing around the milky, sticky pavement in front of the dumpster. *Blech. Over a thousand bucks I paid for this purebred working dog, and she's still just a scavenger.* Rachel clicks her tongue for Ruby to come to her side, then takes a few more steps away from Bucatini.

"I'm just saying," Rachel tries again, though she is dismayed with Chris' skepticism, "Ruby was following the paint smell intensely and made a beeline there." She stabs her finger at the back door. "The scent trail went through that door."

"Ninety percent accuracy?"

He wants me to quantify this? "What do you mean?"

"Earlier, you said they can find cancer in pe—"

"Right. Yes. The way she locked onto the scent in the garage—you saw her take off as soon as you put her down—

then alerted at the other places ... I'm confident she tracked the smell of the spray paint to that door."

Rachel is jittery about the possibility of the busser appearing. Checking the time again, she heads in the direction of her car. Chris follows.

The further they get from the restaurant, the easier it is for Rachel to breathe, not just because the dumpster stench is gone, so is the risk of an alley encounter with the busser.

As they walk, the pressure to say something about the busser gives Rachel nervous flutters in her gut. Worrying her teeth over a tag of skin on her chapped lip, she is just about to speak up when she notices Chris scrutinizing every single thing in the alley. All he wants is hard, cold evidence, something he can take a picture of and write down in his notepad. If she tells him about her premonition, she can just see his note: WOMAN HAS "SENSATION" THE BUSSER DID IT.

The only logical option here is for her to point Chris in the direction of the busser, and the spray paint trail into Bucatini seems like her best chance.

"Would you need a warrant for Ruby to search Bucatini for the spray paint smell?" Rachel asks.

"Depends," Chris mutters, focused on the map on his phone, zooming in and out, checking his surroundings. "Not if the owner agrees to a search. First, I need to scout around for other cameras and see when those two were painted over." He shrugs. "They might've been that way for years."

Really? Has Ruby taught you nothing? "Ruby wouldn't have tracked that fast, or given those strong alerts, if the paint was years old. Just like finding you yesterday ... and the earring."

"Hey, I'm just ... thinking out loud. Sometimes these

cameras aren't working anymore but are left up as a deterrent. Then I won't know exactly what day they were sprayed."

Clearly, a dog's sniff test with ninety percent accuracy isn't enough proof for Chris that a camera was recently painted. She hopes that camera is still working so he gets the proof he needs. And soon.

"Okay, well ... let me know if Ruby can do any more work. Track the paint scent inside Bucatini or ... any other searches. This is what she's trained to do."

"I'll let you know. Like I said, the nearest canine unit can't get over here to help us for days."

"That's all you have left before Alicia's scent is gone," Rachel says. "And, if you find out those cameras *were* sprayed in the past several days ... that smell is getting stale, too."

"Does the restaurant have to be closed? For her to smell for spray paint inside?"

"Right. There can't be"—*psychotic bussers*—"a bunch of commotion, like people talking, loud noises, food being cooked." She smiles. "Especially Italian food."

"Got it," he says, without a smile.

Cops are *so* hilarious, she thinks. Must be all that hypervigilance.

18

───────────────

DAY FIVE, 8:00 AM

PATRICK FEELS like he is walking on a tightrope since Sergeant Hagen questioned him about Alicia. At work yesterday, Patrick swore that his boss, Giselle, who usually doesn't pay him much attention, had her eyes on him, watching his every move, breathing down his neck. That got Patrick paranoid that the cops talked to her, except he still has a job, so they must not have talked to Giselle.

When he got hired there—filling out a bunch of paperwork for a program that hooks up ex-cons with companies willing to give parolees a second chance—his boss warned him that if there was so much as an inkling of trouble, she would let him go.

Being on the cops' radar and being paranoid about losing his job should scare Patrick straight, but he can't keep his mind off Alicia Meyers. Not wanting to be triggered, he avoids all TVs, radios, newspapers, anything with news of Alicia being missing. But she is unavoidable. Posters with her face are plastered everywhere: light posts, bulletin boards, fences. Patrick walks around staring at the ground.

Every time he catches a glimpse of her face, it's like he is being slapped around, like when he was a kid. First, he gets a sick stab in his gut about the woman being abducted—the look on her face is so happy and ... carefree. Then comes a jolt of arousal, imagining what might be happening to her. This is followed, instantly, by a hard stab of guilt about his arousal. It is despicable—that is exactly what landed him in prison—but he can't help it. His arousal is involuntary.

This is his mother's fault, the fuckin' whore. Couldn't keep her goddam hands to herself.

19

DAY FIVE, 10:30 AM

CHRIS CALLS LATE the next morning to say that he has the green light from the owner for Ruby to search Bucatini for spray paint this evening.

"Did you find out when the cameras were spray painted?" she asks. "Is it pretty fresh?"

"Camera in the garage hasn't been working for months. The one in the alley was hit with paint seven days ago. At night. They had a flashlight shining right into the camera before they blasted it so no clue who it was."

Counting back, that is the day before Alicia went missing. Rachel grimaces. That sounds like more than a coincidence; it sounds premeditated. And more than a little creepy.

He also tells her Alicia's husband confirmed that she had a pair of earrings just like the one Ruby found. Rachel's vindication quickly dissipates when she imagines how sickening it must have been for the poor man to see his missing wife's earring. Urgently, Rachel wants to blurt out the details of her premonition about the busser but keeps her mouth shut. For the moment. She will see how this next search goes.

Chris explains that Bucatini's owner and a second deputy will be inside the restaurant, but he assures her that all other employees will be gone. As they discuss logistics, Rachel peruses the restaurant's website to make sure the busser isn't, by some weird chance, also the owner. There aren't pictures of any staff, but under CONTACTS the owner's name is listed as Adriana Piretti. That is certainly not the busser.

Rachel suggests they start Ruby in the parking garage at the spray-painted camera to see if she follows the same path again tonight. Assuming she does, Rachel asks for the back door to the restaurant, and any interior doors, be open so Ruby can follow the scent without any obstructions. She tells him to instruct the other deputy and the owner to sit quietly in the front of the restaurant and, if Ruby follows the trail in there, they shouldn't interact with her.

"Great. So, tonight at, say, ten?" Chris says.

This man must never sleep, Rachel thinks. That, or he is a workaholic. "Do you ever go home?"

"Deputies don't exactly have thriving social lives. Except with other deputies. Cops put people on edge."

So do people with ESP.

"One last thing," Chris says. "I'm going to email you another form. Would you mind signing it real quick and shooting it back to me?"

"Real quick? Did I mention I have a specialty in permitting law? As in, contracts, legal docs ..."

"It's a confidentiality agreement. Because you'll be searching inside someone's property. I've got to have it on file."

"Will it be part of the public record? I don't want

anything seen by a future suspect." *Especially a psychotic busser.*

"Nope. These are treated like personnel files, they're not public. Just ensures that you won't tell anyone what we find or reveal any names or identities ... that kind of stuff."

The irony. The police want Rachel to agree not to tell anyone what happens there tonight. Meanwhile, she may know who abducted Alicia but isn't telling the police.

———

By the time Rachel pulls up next to the parking garage just before ten p.m., she dreads going back into Bucatini, but, at the same time, hopes this will lead to the busser somehow. Then she can go back to minding her own business and let the Sheriff handle this.

Shortly after ten p.m., Ruby follows the spray paint scent from the parking garage camera to the back door of Bucatini again.

With the door propped open tonight, she trots straight through it, nose to the floor.

Rachel tries to keep her breathing steady as she recalls the sensation from the busser. There's a cop right behind you, she reassures herself, wearing all kinds of weapons. You're fine. Then Alicia Meyers' face from the news flashes in her mind. Alicia is *not* fine. Stay focused.

They follow Ruby into a wide hallway with the kitchen on the left and two open doors on the right: one to a storeroom and one to small break room.

Ruby pauses in the hallway, nose up off the floor and into

the air. Her nose aims towards the front of the restaurant, wiggling, working, then she looks back at Rachel. Ruby has caught the scent of the owner and the deputy up front, so Rachel says, reassuringly, "They're okay. Let's keep working. Can you find it?"

Back to work she goes, happily nosing the floor again. Sniffing right past the kitchen—plenty of food smells there but she is undeterred—she moves into the break room. Along the back wall is a row of four lockers with no names, numbers or locks on them. In the corner is a small table with two chairs, and mounted on the wall is a time-clock machine and several coat hooks with a sweatshirt, an apron and a baseball cap hanging on them. Rachel's heart is pounding. The room is claustrophobic, too close to the busser for her liking. He could have been in this very room twenty minutes ago. That could be his sweatshirt dangling on the coat hook. The hairs on the back of her neck bristle.

After sniffing along the row of lockers, Ruby leaves the break room. Rachel is stunned. She was certain Ruby would alert at one of those lockers, that inside they'd find a spray paint can and ... maybe something of Alicia's. Her other earring. Or a long strand of grayish, strawberry blond hair. They could DNA test it to prove it was her hair. Then it would all be over. The Sheriff would be onto the busser without her ever needing to mention her premonition.

Instead, Ruby heads into the storeroom. Just inside the storeroom there is a metal desk cluttered with papers, a well-seasoned coffee mug, a computer monitor and a landline phone. Along one wall there is a large, stainless steel commercial refrigerator and, next to it, a narrower freezer. On another wall, there are floor to ceiling shelves full of flours, sugar, tomatoes and cases of wine. In the corner, next to the shelves, are two large, cardboard boxes sitting on a handcart.

Ruby begins sniffing intensely, swinging her head left and right, nose to the floor, zeroing in on the scent. Rachel is scanning the shelves for spray paint cans but sees none. Ruby sniffs noisily around the boxes that are sitting on the handcart. She then gets up on her hind legs and puts her front paws on top of the boxes.

It is then that Rachel notices a pair of lightweight work gloves laying on the boxes. Ruby touches her nose to the gloves, then pops off the boxes and sharply sits down in front of them. She stares at Rachel.

"Alert," Rachel says.

"She's alerting about these gloves?" he asks.

Rachel hesitates, licks her lips. "I'm pretty sure."

Without averting her gaze from the gloves, Rachel feeds Ruby a treat while Chris slips on a pair of medical gloves. When he picks up the work gloves, Ruby wags her tail excitedly then nudges her nose against Chris' leg.

"That's a big-time alert on the gloves," Rachel says.

Carefully, Chris separates the pair and rotates each one, examining them. On the right-hand glove, on the tip that would cover the index finger, there are splotches of black spray paint.

Rachel and Chris stare at each other for a moment.

In his mic, Chris asks Deputy Morrissey to bring an evidence bag.

Chris heads up front to talk with the restaurant owner while Deputy Morrissey puts the gloves in an evidence bag and labels it. Rachel is no criminal attorney, but she knows there is nothing incriminating here, even with Ruby's great nose work. So what? Someone who works here spray painted a couple of cameras? Could be a teenaged boy who is a dishwasher.

A wave of urgency hits Rachel. She has to find out if the gloves belong to the busser.

Sauntering towards the front of the restaurant, pretending as if she is texting, Rachel tries to make out what Chris and Adriana are saying. Rachel hears Adriana asking Chris what this search is all about.

Deputy Morrissey, who is still in the storeroom, can see Rachel in the hallway, so she can't stand there and eavesdrop. There are restrooms at the other end of the dining area, past where Chris and Adriana are talking, so Rachel heads in that direction.

When Chris looks over at Rachel, she points to the restrooms and he nods. Passing by, she doesn't recognize Adriana—either she spends all her time in the kitchen or has a manager who runs the place.

Once out of their sights, Rachel pauses at the bathroom door to listen.

Adriana has no idea whose gloves they are; could be anyone's. Yes, an employee who took them off when they got work or wore them to dig around in the freezer. Could belong to someone who delivered food or wine. Adriana says she can ask around. No, not yet, Chris says. Doesn't want to alarm anyone.

Rachel can't make out much more, except that Chris sounds like a decent cop. No obnoxious intimidation or manipulation. That's good, she thinks.

When Rachel passes back through the dining area, she says to Chris, "You still need me?"

"Yeah, I'd like to talk before you go. Can you wait—" he checks his watch "—five more minutes?"

"Sure. I'm going to take Ruby out back in case she needs to pee."

Walking past the storeroom, the gloves in an evidence bag are sitting on the desk right by the door. Deputy Morrissey has his back to the door.

Silently, Rachel pauses and rests a hand on the gloves. Inhaling deeply, she even imagines the busser's icy blue eyes, willing herself to receive a premonition, though she has never received one from an inanimate object before. Nothing. Figures. The one time she *wants* a premonition.

The thought crosses her mind to snatch the gloves, or to let Ruby get a good snort of them, but to what end? A dead end. The same one to which her brain keeps dragging her. Her best hope of locating Alicia Meyers—or her body—is looking, again, into the busser's eyes for another premonition.

Out in the cold, stinking, dark alley, Rachel sees things in a different light—that of a single, bare lightbulb over the back door. *What am I thinking, trying to face the busser again? I don't know if the spray-painted cameras have anything to do with Alicia going missing or if those are busser's gloves or if he abducted Alicia.*

Waiting for Chris and trying to shut up her racing thoughts, Rachel paces up and down the alley, far enough from the dumpster but not too far from the door, in case someone comes down the alley.

When Chris walks up behind her, she practically jumps out of her skin.

"Hey, sorry to make you wait," he says. Then he leans down and rubs Ruby. "And *you*—" he chuckles softly—"did a great job!" Rachel gets a pang of jealousy, about what, she isn't sure. Because Chris will chuckle for her dog but not her? Because he didn't acknowledge *her* part in this search?

"Hey, thanks for doing this," he says, standing back up. "I'll walk you back to your car."

Thank god. "That's really not necessary."

He starts walking alongside her anyway, clicking on his flashlight. "So that I'm clear, your dog's nose says the paint on the gloves is the same paint on the camera?"

"Well, I'm no paint expert. I don't know if Ruby could distinguish between two separate types of spray paint, side-by-side, but her nose definitely followed the smell from the paint on the camera to the storeroom and right to those gloves."

He rubs his jaw thoughtfully, and Rachel can hear the coarseness of his five-o'clock shadow—well, now it is his ten-o'clock shadow. *I bet he's got quite a scruffy jaw in the morning.*

"Does the owner know whose gloves they are?" she asks, feeling guilty for asking when she knows the answer.

"No. All the staff are in and out of the storeroom. We could, maybe, get DNA samples from the gloves, but ..." He lets out an exasperated sigh.

"You still have no evidence linking any of this to the missing woman."

"You sound like a defense attorney."

"Hah! Never."

She wants to yell, Search the busser's house. Let Ruby search for Alicia's scent in his car, in his trunk!

But Rachel gets it: they can't search him, his car or his house because they still have no probable cause to link the busser to Alicia's abduction. Even if Rachel tells Chris about her premonition, they still have no probable cause.

"Well, those gloves would be great scent cues," she says. "I mean, if they end up—" she pauses for a few beats "—being somehow related to the missing woman."

20

———

DAY SIX

AFTER THE TWO SEARCH EFFORTS, all the while withholding information about her premonition, Rachel is rattled. She can't analyze her way out of this predicament, and analyzing is what she does best. On top of all this, or probably because of all this, her insomnia is at its worst ever, her nights spent lying awake, thinking, dissecting, her stomach churning. She resorts to taking two hydroxyzine pills every night, even with the morning grogginess. The three cups of coffee she drank this morning have cleared her head but made her jittery and her stomach burn with acidity.

I would make a pathetic drug addict, she thinks.

Trying to reestablish some normalcy, she spends a long, busy day at work, emailing documents to several clients, submitting a few invoices and setting up some meetings for late next week—she doesn't have the energy for professional eye avoidance this week. Plus, she wants to keep the next several days open in case—in hopes—the Sheriff's department needs Ruby to do another search before Alicia's scent vanishes. Or in case she gets the courage to go to Bucatini and face the busser again.

Busy days typically keep her focused, but today Rachel continually finds herself staring out the window. The window overlooks a courtyard where the trees have dropped all their leaves, the stark, gray branches appearing bleak. The outdoor fountain has been shut off for the winter months, so there are no birds swooping around it. No signs of life.

She schemes about lunch at Bucatini, but the thought of looking into the busser's eyes leaves her anything but hungry.

By eleven thirty, she convinces herself to go to Bucatini anyway.

At noon, the thought of waltzing into Bucatini and staring right into the busser's stone-cold eyes has her glued to the office chair.

If she knew, for certain, that another premonition would lead to Alicia Meyers' location, she would be at that restaurant every day, looking for the busser, hunting him. But she has so many doubts, not the least of which is, if she is somehow causing these things to happen, another premonition could conjure this psycho to do more harm. She can't handle another premonition like this coming true.

Back at home, Rachel watches the news, hoping to hear the Sheriff's department has new information on the whereabouts of Alicia Meyers. They don't.

Contemplating how some missing persons are never found, Rachel imagines Alicia's teenage daughter being motherless, imagines the agony that would cause Alicia's parents and husband, never knowing what happened to her. The agony of never finding any sign of life ... or death.

Once more, the twentieth time, Rachel checks her phone

to see if she, somehow, missed a text from Chris. She didn't. Stretching out on the sofa, Ruby at her feet all warm and twitching to some dream (probably one that involves sniffing), Rachel dozes. In that state between awake and asleep, still conscious of the drone of TV talking heads but not comprehending what they're saying, she hears that soft, steady voice from deep in her mind. Trust your instincts.

"Trying," she mumbles.

When she is almost asleep, drifting, finally, into oblivion, she hears these words, clear and bright, in her head: Tell Chris.

Rachel bolts up, startling Ruby off the sofa. Ruby glares at her with what looks like indignation, then plops down in her dog bed.

Swinging her feet to the floor, Rachel drops her head into her hands, wishing she could ring the neck of that inner voice. Anything to shut it up.

After a few minutes, Rachel drags herself into the kitchen for another hydroxyzine pill. Tossing her head back to swallow the pill, the wall calendar catches her eye. Walking over to it, she rests her finger on today then, counting backwards, taps each day leading back to when Alicia Meyers went missing. It has been six days. She has been missing for six days. Her scent is likely, or soon will be, undetectable by Ruby.

Today is over. An entire day gone. Lost.

21

———————

DAY SEVEN, 7:00 AM

IN THE MORNING, Rachel can't shake that message to tell Chris the truth. It's like a huge, un-ignorable mass in her psyche. It won't budge. She even considers having a few beers, but her so-called "drinking days" in college never did anything to squelch her premonitions or her anxiety about them (though she didn't drink very hard). There is no reason to think now would be any different, especially as both, her premonitions and her anxiety, are becoming more acute.

Maybe something stronger than beer. A few gin and tonics? That was the only drink her mom ever ordered, a handful of times that Rachel can recall, always with a wedge of lime. Such a refreshing drink soured by the memory of her mom.

Also, she hasn't even had breakfast. The last thing Rachel needs to become is an alcoholic clairvoyant.

Instead, she takes Ruby for a long run. The "Tell Chris" message remains in her head. She runs faster, hoping to pound the message out of her brain. By the time they return home, Rachel is heaving for air. Despite her brain being occupied with getting more oxygen to its partnering major organs, another internal suggestion surfaces: Tell Glen about your premonition.

Rachel does have a counseling appointment this afternoon, and, a week ago, she was committed to telling Glen. But her ESP completely changed in the past week: a premonition about a predator, then a woman goes missing. Her world has been flipped upside down. The stakes, and Rachel's apprehension, are much higher.

Checking her phone again, there are no missed calls or texts from Chris. He must not have any more leads for Ruby. It doesn't matter because, by now, the scent trail for Alicia Meyers would be getting pretty faint.

Unless I go to Bucatini, Rachel thinks, and try for another premonition about Alicia's location. Before it's too late.

No. You've gone round and round on that one. Forget it.

"Who am I even talking to?" Rachel mutters.

Checking her calendar, there is nothing at work that can't wait, so she texts Lorena to see if she can meet for lunch. Lorena always calls Rachel on her bullshit, and, at this point, Rachel isn't sure what is a good idea and what is bullshit.

———

Rachel arrives at Black Bird Café before Lorena and snags her favorite booth in the back. This place has become her new favorite restaurant—secluded tables, uncrowded. They don't have tiramisu, but their homemade sourdough bread can't be beat.

As soon as they order, Rachel updates Lorena. She already told her about the searches with Ruby, in general terms, so as not to violate the confidentiality agreement with the Sheriff's office, but enough that Lorena understands Rachel has been tormented not telling the Sheriff's department about her premonition.

"My gut tells me it's time to tell the cops," Rachel says. "Before it's too late. Even if they can't do anything with the information, at least I tried."

"I agree. It's past time you tell the cops. Really, what do you have to lose?"

"My reputation—"

"Your reputation? For what—future dates with a cop? You think it's going to affect getting clients?"

"I don't want people to think I'm looney." As soon as she says that, Rachel realizes that isn't why she is keeping her mouth shut.

"No," Rachel starts shaking her head. "It's just that ... I've spent my whole life not getting involved, you know? And that's worked fine. Well, for me. And there was never any reason to tell anyone"—she lowers her voice—"about a premonition. But I don't think that's true for this one."

"Exactly. So quit mind-fucking yourself and go tell the cops. You can talk to Fletch's friend—"

"No. If I talk to anyone, it will be the deputy I did the searches with. He's the lead on this case."

———

Once Rachel settles in the chair at Glen's office, she is already losing her nerve. "I've had a tough week," she says.

He has his pen in hand, notepad on his lap, but doesn't

scribble, just tilts his head ever so slightly. "I'm sorry to hear that."

It's a good thing Glen knows how to gaze softly at a client, Rachel thinks, because his dark eyes could be piercing. Reminding herself the purpose in telling Glen is that he might be able to help her get rid of her premonitions, she recalls Lorena's question: What do I have to lose? My world can't get any smaller.

"So, I've been wanting to tell you something." Best to dive in, but then she hesitates for several beats. "For a long time."

"Okay." He lays his pen on the pad, an offer of his full attention.

They must train counselors to do that, Rachel thinks—make sure a client can "read" them, like an open book, then exude neutrality.

She breathes out a big exhale. "Well ... I see things. Actually, I sense things. Or, lately, I am ... kind of seeing them."

He rolls his pen under his finger, a very slight up and back motion. Rachel wonders if he is forgetting his neutrality training. Or maybe he is itching to write that down: PATIENT SEEING THINGS.

"What kind of things?" he asks.

"They're not hallucinations," Rachel says. "Remember when we talked about hypervigilance and ... being able to sense harm that people will experience?"

"I remember you wondered if that could come from PTSD."

"Right. Well—" deep breath "—I do that. Always have." It feels better to say that than she imagined. "I've had this ESP —or clairvoyance, whatever we want to call it—long before the accident with Mom, so I don't think it's PTSD or from my brain injury." Bolstered, the words are flowing now. "These premonitions are the real reason I'm uncomfortable around people because they're always about other people. About something bad happening to them. Usually, they come to me when I lock eyes with them. Sometimes when I touch them ... or am just near them."

Rachel releases a sigh of relief, then continues. "I can't take it anymore. I walk around like I'm antisocial, avoiding eyes, avoiding people ... avoiding the world."

Glen is looking less neutral than he has ever looked, a little crease knitted between his brows. The gentle pen rolling continues though. Rachel figures he is itching to write: ASSESS FOR HALLUCINATIONS.

"So ... I was wondering if the EMDR gizmo"—Rachel points at the light bar and dangling pods—"might be able to help me stop ... sensing things." She specifically avoids repeating the phrase, "seeing things," in hopes she won't fit the criteria for a complete nutcase. Besides, she only had two premonitions where she truly saw the pending tragedy. "You know, the EMDR completely got rid of my nightmares. And this ESP is—kicking—my—ass."

Unfortunately, Glen does not grab the EMDR light bar and say, Yes, let's get rid of that pesky ESP. Though, he has stopped rolling his pen.

"Can you tell me about some of your extrasensory perceptions?" he says.

Of course, that *would* be a therapist's first response. But must she go into the gory details?

Instinctively, Rachel reverts to eye contact avoidance, at which she is a pro, but this is a small office. She takes a sip of tea, stares out the window, peruses his artwork for the hundredth time. Then she glances at the clock. Fifty minutes remaining!

Fifty minutes. Can she condense a lifetime of ESP—and, now, maybe killing people—into fifty minutes? She has had way more than fifty premonitions. Hundreds. Thirty seconds to describe every one? No way. She could focus on some of the worst ones. Then a few that were devastating. And she would want to tell him about the intuition before the car accident. That gives her a few minutes to describe each one.

Impossible.

Setting her tea down, Rachel takes a deep breath, a sharp exhale, and looks at Glen. Directly into his eyes. Yes, she can tell, he needs the details. Then her gaze drifts down to his nose, his chin, his neck. He has a large freckle there, near his jugular. Or is that a mole?

Glen says, "Just an example or two so I can better understand what you're experiencing ..."

How else can he tell if I'm crazy or really am clairvoyant?

Rachel starts with a few early ones, like telling her parents that something was wrong with Aunt Cherie's baby, but this was before she knew Cherie was even pregnant, and long before Rachel could comprehend a miscarriage. Next, she sprinkles in some sad ones, like her high school friend, Kaitlyn, being raped at a party that Rachel pleaded with her to skip. In college, hurrying out of a bank near campus, her stomach knotted up with anxiety, then two weeks later, hearing the bank had an armed robbery.

She describes to Glen a lifetime of sensing darkness emanating off people, dozens of them over the years. Complete strangers and people she knew—people next to her on airplanes, in stores, walking down the street.

Then, Rachel discusses in detail the worst premonition of all, how she could barely get in the car the morning of the accident.

Glen knows about the accident, but now she explains how a tidal wave of fear hit her that morning so that, by the time she and her mom got to the car, Rachel was paralyzed. It was the most intense, foreboding sense of doom she ever experienced. Before or since. Rachel's hand was on the driver's door handle, but she was unable to move.

By that time in her life, Rachel's parents knew the signs, knew when she had a premonition. They had long since stopped dismissing her vague fears and were really good at letting her talk about them. Sometimes they brainstormed with Rachel what she could do, which was usually nothing. Rachel wasn't aware, until she moved out for college, just how much her parents helped her cope with the ESP so that it didn't destroy her life. Or her sanity.

"The morning of the accident," Rachel tells Glen, "Mom and I decided the best thing would be for her to drive, drop me at school and go on to work. Usually, I dropped her at work. But she had way more experience driving, so I thought ... we thought ... Plus, I was in no condition to drive after my premonition." Tears start flowing down Rachel's face. "You know, I never had a premonition about me or my parents before then. Or after. And I never knew what was going to happen ... or when. I couldn't just hole up in my house and never leave, never go to school."

The loss of that day is grievous, but what torments Rachel are the what-ifs. Would they still have gotten in the accident if Rachel had driven? Would it have been her aorta, instead of her mom's, that ruptured under the force of the steering wheel impact? If the cops had gotten there one minute earlier, could they have saved her mom?

Rachel pauses to snatch another tissue and blow her nose. Glen jots quickly on his notepad then returns his attention to her. He is looking, if not perturbed, at least, challenged.

Pressing on, Rachel explains how the ESP has recently evolved, such that she had one very vivid and very accurate premonition about Aaron's cancer. Glen couldn't resist jotting a note about that one. Glen knows about Aaron dying because Rachel was already in counseling when she and Aaron started dating. In fact, it was through counseling that Rachel dared to take a chance with Aaron. Yes, dating him was *such* a healthy growth opportunity.

Rachel's grand finale is the premonition about the busser abducting a woman, the first intuition about someone hurting others, and how, two weeks later, Alicia Meyers went missing. Well, the actual grand finale is when she explains her latest fear: that all this time, she hasn't been sensing bad things—she chokes back a sob to get this one out—but has been causing them.

That one gets a reaction from Glen, one eyebrow arching up and his pen goes completely still. No scribbling. No rolling. His pen is stymied.

An overwhelming lightness fills Rachel, like one of those helium balloons, she could float away. Right out of this room, which would be lovely because she is unable to continue looking at Glen. Snatching another tissue, she busies herself with wiping her eyes and blowing her nose.

Peeking at the clock, she is shocked to see they still have fifteen minutes left. The sum of her life's anguish can be described in a mere thirty-five minutes? Staring at her hands, she fiddles with the tissues accumulating in her lap. The sum of her life's anguish can be contained in a few wadded-up tissues?

Glen clears his throat and says, "Thank you for trusting me with all this. I'm sorry to hear how much you've been suffering."

Suffering? That word breaks something open inside her, and she starts crying again. She held herself together for years, was a straight-A student, a mostly helpful teenager, tried not to burden her father after her mom died, graduated law school magna cum laude, maintains a law practice by herself, yet, all the while, inside, she has been suffering?

Yes. She *has* been suffering.

This simple truth makes her want to run out of Glen's office, go hide in the restroom and let it all out, allow great, big, heaving sobs to choke out of her chest. For some reason, though, she stays. Somehow, she manages to stay in her chair and sob with some dignity.

While Rachel adds those final tissues to the damp pile of her life's anguish, Glen seems to have regained his neutral, open composure. "We have ten minutes left," he says. "What would be most helpful for you?"

What does she need in the remaining time with Glen? Confirmation that she isn't insane? Assurance that her brain isn't using telepathy to kill or harm people? A plan to put an end to her premonitions? Suddenly, her reliably analytical, attorney mind is cotton. She has no idea what she needs.

Luckily, Glen has some ideas. "We can do a guided imagery exercise—with or without the light bar—to calm your system down a little. Or we can talk about some ideas moving forward to cope with these extrasensory perceptions." He says that so matter-of-factly, like her ESP is a fact.

"So ... you believe that I have ESP? You don't think I'm just hallucinating?"

"You are not hallucinating." He shakes his head and flashes a dismissive smile, lips pressed together. "You don't fit the clinical picture."

"Why not?"

He lifts his hand in the air, elbow on the armrest, pen pointing at the ceiling. "Well ... for one, people who hallucinate typically don't function very well."

Functional, huh? I'm high functioning. At least, in my job.

"And hallucinations involve seeing or hearing things that aren't there. Things no one else sees or hears."

Uh-oh.

"Like people's faces on the wall ..." he continues, "or hearing orders to shoot someone. Stuff like that. What you've told me is that these things you see or ... perceive always come true. That's not a hallucination."

She is stunned, and her mouth falls open. She snaps it shut. A therapist, a mental health professional, just validated her premonitions. Just like that. With a hand propped casually in mid-air—always with that pen—Glen confirmed that she has ESP.

"Do you think I'm—" Rachel swallows then gravely continues "—causing these things?"

He hesitates for a moment and looks at Rachel with some concern. "I don't see how it is possible for you to cause these things, but ... we need to work on *you* believing that."

Rachel's relief is immense and profound. Not only about Glen believing she has clairvoyance but that she isn't causing these events. Intellectually, Rachel could often reason her way to this same conclusion, but deep down inside, in a place far more primal than her intellect, Rachel was caged by this fear.

Sitting there in the quiet of Glen's office, she understands —accepts, in her gut—that her premonitions have undergone a metamorphosis over the past several months, but they're still only a form of ESP. She has no supernatural powers, no evil. Rachel is liberated.

For a moment.

"Can you help me get rid of the them?" she asks.

"Hmm. I think we need to explore them first, to learn what we can. How your ..."

"Premonitions."

"Learn how your premonitions get triggered. I know they started before your mom's death, but that trauma could've have heightened your senses, made the receptors—in your brain—even more hyperaware of any danger. Then the slightest stimulation, that you're not even aware of, could be activating those receptors, alerting you to danger. We can work on calming your system, calming down those brain receptors. And see if that makes them ... the premonitions ... be triggered less frequently."

Rachel leaves Glen's office feeling spent, but with the tug of a smile on her face. Today, Glen's nerd-talk sounds good: a calmer brain, fewer triggers. This sounds better than the image she now has of an exposed wire dangling in her brain, sparking every time she locks eyes with someone for more than a second.

22

DAY SEVEN, 5:30 PM

PATRICK STARTED ATTENDING the sex offender support group this week and plans to go every Tuesday and Thursday. He prefers these evenings because they are the nights his shrink runs the group. Plus, Monday, Wednesday and Friday are the evenings he volunteers at Mountain Home Ranch.

Part of the offender rehab program is participants are required to develop a Good Living Plan, which Patrick figured would be some lame shit like in high school where he could pick which corny class he wanted to take: woodworking, auto mechanics or welding. So, he was really surprised when Dr. Levitsky said he got to pick *any* healthy hobbies and the program staff would help Patrick find a way to access those hobbies. He picked weightlifting and working with horses. Within a week, he had a membership at a local men's gym and, two weeks later, a volunteer position at a therapeutic horse ranch for men with addiction. Patrick is even on the waitlist for one of the six rooms they have available for men to live at Mountain Home Ranch, which would be a dream come true.

At tonight's support group, Patrick wishes he was at the ranch instead. Mitch is blathering about the missing woman. None of the guys can stand Mitch, who is almost too stupid to be in the offender program. He was definitely too stupid for prison; he would have got himself killed within a month. Lucky for Mitch, he got sent, instead, to the state hospital for ten years after fooling around with a fifteen-year-old. Mitch is a real sick fuck.

Before the group starts, while everyone mills around grabbing coffee and a seat, Mitch starts in. "Okay, guys," he says, grinning around the room, "which ... which one of y'all ... uh —" He starts to snicker, then puts his hands over his mouth. Mitch tries again, and a couple of men are already shaking their heads. "Who ... who took that pretty lady?" he finally says, snorting with laughter. It's all Patrick can do to keep from punching the smirk right off Mitch's face.

Dr. Levitsky says firmly, "Mitch, that woman's name is Alicia Meyers. And a missing person is no laughing matter." The room is now hushed, and he stares at Mitch for several seconds. "Do you understand?"

Mitch forces a frown on his face, something he, no doubt, learned to do in the state hospital: act remorseful.

"And it's inappropriate to blame your peers like that," Dr. Levitsky adds, eyes staying on Mitch.

Looking down at the floor, Mitch mumbles, "Sorry."

Patrick likes how his shrink doesn't take shit from no one. And how he always calls Alicia by her name. *That's showin' these jerk-offs how to treat a woman.*

Patrick always calls Alicia by her name, too, or sometimes he calls her Princess. And he knows how to treat a woman.

23

———————

DAY EIGHT, 9:00 AM

FEELING LEGITIMIZED by yesterday's session with Glen, Rachel is determined to trust her instincts and tell Chris about the busser. It's too weird and intimate to invite him to her house, so she heads into her office and texts him to see if he can stop by to discuss something more about the searches. She wants to have the I-know-who-abducted-Alicia conversation in person so she can discern if Chris believes her or is dismissing her. Besides, talking to a cop over the phone is probably on a recorded line—she doesn't want this conversation recorded.

That gets her wondering if he wears a body camera; she never noticed a camera amongst all the other cop paraphernalia on his body. Quickly, before Chris arrives, she checks the internet for what a police body camera looks like.

Gesturing for Chris to have a seat, Rachel checks his chest and belt: no body camera. Good because she really didn't want to start the discussion by asking him to turn off his camera.

Sitting down across from him, Rachel doesn't waste any

time. "I have something really strange to tell you about this missing woman case," she starts in. "It's the reason I volunteered Ruby and ... well ... it's going to sound really weird—"

His police radio crackles. "Oops, sorry." He turns down the volume.

She sits up straighter, steeling herself. "I'm not sure if you found out whose gloves those were in Bucatini but"—her stomach flip-flops—"I wonder if they were one of the bussers."

"Didn't run DNA because ... there was nothing really ... incriminating there. Pair of gloves someone left on a stack of boxes ... Anybody could've left them there. Why do you ask?"

Glancing down at the table, she worries her finger back and forth over a scratch there. "Okay, this is the weird part. See, I sometimes have these, um ... premonitions. They're always about dangerous things that are about to happen. To someone else. And I had one the other day, well, a few weeks ago now—before Alicia went missing. It was coming from one of the bussers at Bucatini."

His seat squeaks, and she glances up. He is leaning back in his chair, seemingly unconcerned, or uninterested. Probably trying to get as far away from me as possible, Rachel thinks.

"Which one?" he asks.

"Uh, I don't know his name." *Is this happening? Is he glossing right over the premonition part?* "He's tall. Short hair, kind of ashy blond color, parted far to one side. Really pale blue eyes."

"Hmm." He stares at the ceiling for a moment. Rachel watches his adam's apple slide down and back up. "Anything else?" he asks.

Yeah, I have fucking premonitions. I see things. Did you hear that part? "It gets worse. The sense I had, it was very strong, was that, basically, he's … a predator." Rachel is surprised at how good it feels to say that. To a cop. The cop who is on this case. Now, she can let the Sheriff handle it from here on out.

Rachel isn't sure if it is because Chris is sitting in the office of an attorney—everyone knows they *never* lie—or if this cop is good at hiding when he thinks someone is full of shit, but he takes out his notepad and starts jotting notes. He scribbles as if this is one more piece of information, something worth documenting. That, or he is pretending to take notes because he doesn't know what to say to the whacko lady sitting across from him. Maybe he is just writing a grocery list.

"I know this sounds crazy," Rachel forges on, "and this kind of information may not be evidence, but it was eating me up not telling you. Especially when Ruby's search led us straight to Bucatini."

He stops scribbling. "You get these—things a lot?"

She nods. "All my life."

They don't say anything for several long moments. Then he says, "That must really suck."

She lets out a scoffing grunt. "You have no idea."

"Oh, I don't know … cops see some pretty twisted shit."

She never thought of that. Cops see, up close and personal, way worse pain and suffering and evil than she will ever sense. And cops can't avoid it. Day after day, they clock in and trudge straight into the worst of humanity. That is almost as bad as being a criminal defense attorney.

"Do they ever … you know … come true?" He looks her

straight in the eyes, trying to read her, to see if she is telling the truth.

Returning his gaze, coolly, Rachel says, "Always."

"Well, I'm not ruling anything out in this case, but you're right. This isn't exactly evidence, so .... not sure what I can do with this kind of ... information."

They sit there for a minute, neither one of them speaking. Rachel contemplates how to tell Chris what *she* can do: try for another premonition about Alicia's location. What does she have to lose, besides feeling that busser's disturbed energy again? She cringes inside to think of what Alicia has to lose.

Deciding on a nonchalant approach, Rachel gets up to pour herself a cup of coffee. "Want some?" she asks.

"Nah, I can't sleep if I drink coffee."

With her back to Chris, Rachel says, "My dad and I are regulars at Bucatini, so I was thinking we'd have dinner there tomorrow night." Shrugging, she adds, "To see if I can get a sense of where Alicia might be. You know, see if I can get another premonition."

She peeks over her shoulder. There is a deep crease between his brows. He doesn't support her idea, or he is calculating the risk of her going there again, or he is recalling another item to add to his grocery list.

When she sits back down, Chris says, "I don't like it. I can't get a warrant to record any conversation you—"

"These aren't auditory premonitions. They're more like— visions or physical sensations. There's nothing to hear or record."

"Still. You should stay away from there. I mean, we appreciate you doing the searches with your dog but ... we can't have civilians interfering with an ongoing investigation. You know what I mean."

"So, you *are* investigating that busser?"

He stares at her.

"Ohh—right, you can't say. Of course. Well, I don't plan on interfering with anything. Like I said, I'm a regular at the restaurant. Just like the food."

"Well, I can't stop you from going, but I don't think you should. And if you do, I can't be in there."

"I'm not asking you to be there." Though Rachel would feel safer if he was. And she loathes the idea of talking her dad into going. She and Chris could have pretended to be on a date, Chris out of uniform. Just pretending, of course ... "Nothing bad will happen. The guy won't know a thing. I'll be eating dinner with my dad, like I was a few weeks ago. The busser will keep our water glasses full, clear our plates, and either I'll get a premonition or I won't."

"Still don't like it," Chris says, tossing his hands in the air.

Too bad, Rachel thinks.

"And now that you've told me about your ... plan, if I'm involved while you in there, it's ... kind of like entrapment." He shakes his head. "And I don't want to make this man untouchable. In case he turns out to be a suspect."

"Okay, okay," Rachel says, her hands up defensively. "I get it."

Chris opens his mouth to say something but pauses for a moment. "What time do you guys usually eat dinner? I occasionally cruise that area ..."

24

DAY EIGHT, 5:30 PM

BEFORE ASKING her dad to meet her over at Bucatini this evening, Rachel fills him in on everything, including the fact that she told the lead detective about her premonition.

Her father is unconvinced. "You're going to try to force yourself to have a premonition? This could be traumatic. Who knows what you might sense!"

She doesn't have time for this, but she isn't going there alone. "Dad, for once, I'll be prepared for a premonition. It won't be such a shock because I won't ... you know ... be blindsided by it."

"I don't know, Rachel ..." *Uh-oh, he rarely calls me that.* "This sounds ... this is getting a bit ... obsessive."

Rachel looks at the clock. Maybe she is going to Bucatini alone. She could ask Lorena to go but wouldn't feel right doing that without Fletcher knowing, and she doesn't have time to explain everything to Fletcher. Plus, she doesn't want Lorena anywhere near the busser. She could never forgive herself if Lorena ended up one of his victims.

"Let the cops deal with this," her dad says adamantly.

"You told them about the guy. Isn't that enough? The ball's in their court now."

"They can't use my premonition for anything—an arrest, a search warrant, they probably won't even question him. But if I get a premonition about Alicia's location, then they can search for her there. Ruby could search for her. This might help the police find Alicia."

"So, you're going to, willingly, expose yourself to this ... predator? What if he starts following you?"

She swallows hard. That is a scenario she is trying very hard not to imagine.

"Detective Hagen will be nearby," she says, stretching the truth because she doesn't know, for sure, if or when he will be nearby. "Besides," Rachel pauses for a few seconds, "what choice do I have? If Alicia Meyers is never found, or is found dead, *that* will traumatize me. Forever."

———

At seven p.m., Rachel and her father stroll into Bucatini as casually as possible, given their tension, and she scans the restaurant for the busser. There are only a few tables occupied and no bussers in sight. After they're seated, a different busser, a young woman, comes to their table with menus.

Rachel and her father stare at each other as the female busser fills their water glasses and asks if she can get them any drinks. Rachel orders a diet soda and he says water is fine.

Casually glancing around, Rachel spots the busser across the room with his back to them. She would recognize that ashy hair anywhere. Her stomach goes queasy with anxiety.

She clears her throat to get her dad's attention, then subtly flicks her eyes in the busser's direction.

Her father's gaze roams around the room, then he looks back at Rachel with a look of concern on his face. "Are you sure you want to do this?"

Rachel is sure that she does *not* want to do this; she *must* do this. "It will be okay." Leaning forward, she mumbles, "I have to get closer to him—you know—to get something."

"How?"

Feeling discouraged, her shoulders slump. Her throat is parched, and she takes a few gulps of water. She could go to the restroom, which is over on the side of the restaurant where the busser is working. She could even hang out in that hallway—the same one she used to eavesdrop on Chris and the owner a few days ago—until the busser is in sight, then catch his eyes on the way back to her table.

"C'mon, let's just get out of here," her dad says. "We can always try another time."

Alicia's scent is eight days old. "I don't think we have any more time."

When their waitress comes to take their order, her dad smiles apologetically and says they're just having dessert. They order two tiramisu and two decafs.

"I'm going to the restroom," Rachel says, tipping her head in that direction. Her dad starts rubbing his temples as if he has a splitting headache. *I* am his splitting headache, Rachel thinks.

"Well ... you're too old for me to go with you," he says. "Please—be careful."

Rachel takes a long, slow breath in, then out, before casually heading to the restroom. In her peripheral vision, she sees the busser coming into the dining area from the kitchen. A cold prickle runs straight down her back. She looks at him but his eyes are down, looking into his apron. Still, she keeps her eyes on his face. He remains a blank slate. But he won't look at her.

In the restroom, she locks the door and paces back and forth, breathing slowly, then counting down from one hundred. She even tries Glen's technique and imagines a warm, golden light, like a beeswax candle, glowing inside her, radiating from her. Oh man, nothing is calming her down—that beeswax candle has been snuffed right out. The only thing that is going to alleviate her anxiety is to get this over with.

Having not heard anyone else jiggle the doorknob or go into the adjacent men's room, Rachel peers out the restroom door. The hallway is empty. Inching into the hallway, she lingers there for a moment, watching for the busser. Stalling, she rummages through her purse, all the while watching for him.

There he is.

Out she goes into the dining area with a smile plastered on her face, looking in the busser's direction, the way a normal person would when they pass by someone this closely. Briefly, his gaze flashes in her direction.

Don't look away, she tells herself. Zap! Darkness. Tunnel vision. He wants Rachel. No, he wants another woman ... or any woman? Something intense ... anger? Loneliness. An insatiable, grievous loneliness. A despairing loneliness.

They pass each other, and it's gone. The energy, his sensations are gone. *Fuck!* It wasn't enough. She needs a vision of Alicia, of her location. But she can't turn back and stare at the busser.

Rachel's vision is still tunneling and dark, but, somehow, her feet keep moving back towards her table. Wildly, her eyes search for her dad as her field of vision begins to widen.

There he is, her father. His eyes are on Rachel, were on her the whole time. He knows she had a premonition and looks like he could cry.

Sliding into her seat, Rachel lets out a big sigh. Her father's shoulders visibly relax. In between them are two plates of tiramisu and two steaming cups of coffee. Rachel could cry. Their tiramisu tradition has been ruined by this busser, by this situation. She hates her clairvoyance.

She reaches over and gives his hand a light squeeze. As soon as she touches his skin, a warm, solid, comforting sensation rolls straight up her arm and into her chest. Rachel isn't sure but thinks this is love; it isn't impending doom.

The thought pops into her mind that she needs to touch the busser, just a brush against his hand or arm. An accidental bump.

Nonchalantly, Rachel takes a sip of coffee and hopes her dad doesn't notice her hand trembling. "You going to eat yours or what?" she says, scooping up a bite of tiramisu.

He shakes his head and picks up his fork. "If I eat this, can we get the hell out of here?"

"Yep," she says, forcing another bite. As the creamy, rummy flavors melt in her mouth, her brain is scheming how to make a quick contact with the busser. Another sip of coffee. Another bite, for her father's sake. Her hand is still trembling.

What about a spill?

If she spills something when the busser is close by, she can ask him for a couple of napkins. Or just pop over and ask him for some more napkins. Better if she doesn't bring the busser over to their table; her father has had it with this clairvoyant escapade.

Quick, she thinks, before I lose my nerve. And Dad loses his tolerance. Don't even warn Dad. Just do it.

There her is, the busser, and their waitress is nowhere in sight. Her pulse is thrumming in her ears.

Do it. Go now.

She "accidentally" drops her napkin on the floor, then scoots out from behind the table. "Be right back," she mutters. Her dad freezes, his fork in mid-air, halfway to his mouth. That man is never going to eat tiramisu again.

"Excuse me," Rachel says to the busser, *the* busser. "Do you have another napkin? I dropped mine." Casually, she points in the direction of their table. Like what, he is going to scan the area under her table to make sure that she isn't lying?

Giving a slight, stiff nod, he reaches into his apron and pulls out a couple of thick paper napkins. His gaze lands on Rachel's eyes but he seems to look right through her. Rachel isn't seeing anything.

Damn it!

Her armpits grow damp with perspiration. He extends the napkins to Rachel, his movements stiff, robotic, as if he is uncomfortable this close to her. She isn't breathing. Reaching for the napkins, she barely brushes his hand.

Whoosh! The space between them goes dark. Darker. Now, almost black.

As if seeing through his eyes, images stream through

Rachel's mind. Deep in the forest. Huge trees. Thick moss. A shed or dilapidated cabin. Alicia is in there.

In a split second, the napkins are in Rachel's hand, and she turns away from the busser. Her blood is coursing through her brain, throbbing so loudly in her ears that every-thing—conversations of the people around her, the clattering of glasses and plates—sound far away.

Dropping back into her seat, her dad stares at her, his hands steepled in front of his lips. In his eyes, she can see that he is done.

He reaches over and rests a hand next to hers so their hands are touching, barely. Again, that warmth floods through her hand and arm, into her chest.

Rachel nods. "I'm okay—" her voice cracks "—I got it. I got one."

Looking down at her father's hand, she realizes that she is still holding the napkins. They are the high-quality, large, smooth rectangular type—dark burgundy red.

These were in the busser's apron, Rachel thinks. A perfect scent cue.

Lifting her hand off the napkins so she doesn't further contaminate them with her scent, she glances around for something to put them in. She has no baggie, her purse smells too much like her ...

"Can I get you two anything else?" their waitress asks.

"Just the check," her dad says.

"Uh ..." Rachel raises a finger. "I'd like a to-go container, please."

25

DAY EIGHT, 8:45 PM

AS SOON AS Rachel walks out of Bucatini, it feels like she can breathe again, as if something was constricting her chest and has, finally, snapped open. They're sitting in her car a few blocks from the restaurant processing what happened, when a Sheriff's cruiser drives past and parks up ahead.

When Chris climbs out of the cruiser and heads towards Rachel's car, she rolls down her window. A blast of cold air gushes in. "Want to jump in the back?" she asks Chris.

Rachel's father and Chris reach awkwardly through the seats to shake hands, then Chris says, "Well ... how'd things go?"

"It went great," Rachel says. Her dad gives her a sideways glare, which she ignores. "I got a premonition that might help us find Alicia."

Chris is silent for long enough that Rachel looks over her shoulder at him. He is frowning. "So, you could see or ... tell where she is?" Chris asks.

"Yeah. I saw the ... house that she's in."

"You mean, where she *might* be."

Scowling at Chris, Rachel says, "I saw the building where he has Alicia. Do you want to hear about it or not?"

Leaning back, Chris runs a hand over his head and sighs. "Yeah, but can we get in my cruiser so I can type this stuff into my laptop?"

Rachel's dad is noticeably uncomfortable with the tension between Chris and Rachel. Not as uncomfortable as he was in Bucatini, but, nonetheless, says, "I'm going to head on home." Looking over his shoulder, he says to Chris, "Can you make sure she gets back to her car okay? This whole thing makes me ..."

Chris gives her dad a quick thumbs up gesture.

"I'll be fine, Dad. And thanks for coming. Really ... I know it was ... I just really appreciate it."

In the cruiser, Rachel skips telling Chris about the sensation that the busser is full of longing for her ... or for some woman. Who isn't full of desire? She also doesn't mention that her carry-out container, which she nonchalantly set by her feet, is full of napkins with the busser's scent; Chris has made it clear that deputies need probable cause before they can do practically anything with a suspect.

Rachel focuses on the most important information: the cabin. Closing her eyes, she describes the cabin in as much detail as possible. "It's rundown and old, the roof partially caved in on the left, front side, slumping towards a rickety porch. The roof is covered with a thick layer of moss. Two windows in the front, not broken but very grimy, so it's hard to see through them. It's in a small opening in the woods, encircled by trees with a really tall one behind the cabin. It looked like it was up in the foothills because the trees surrounding the cabin were big, not old-growth but a heavy, natural forest."

Opening her eyes again, she pauses while Chris continues typing into the laptop. "Wonder if he has a cabin?" she mumbles.

Chris clicks something into the laptop and, after a minute, says, "Nope. Least not in this state."

"You know his name?" She is incredulous that he withheld this information.

"Yeah … we questioned all the staff, even if they didn't work the night Alicia went missing. Had she been seen there before, who saw her at the restaurant, what she ate, what she drank, if she left with someone—all that."

His nonchalance causes her anger to flare even worse. Here she is, telling this practical stranger about her ESP—something she has hid from just about everyone her entire life—and he already knows who the guy is, probably ran a background check and—

Oh, calm down, Sherlock. They probably ran background checks on all the staff. That would've been one of the first things they did.

Her gaze flits down to the carry out container, nestled discreetly at her feet. The one stuffed with napkins containing the scent of a predator whom she may try to track—without telling Chris.

How am I going to find that cabin?

As if reading her mind, Chris says, "There must be dozens of cabins like that up in the forest. Old hunting cabins. Old Forest Service cabins."

Well, there is that …

Chris starts typing again, and Rachel stares out the

window, waiting to see if he has any more questions. Up ahead, a figure is walking towards the parking garage. *The* parking garage, where Ruby found Alicia's earring. Squinting, Rachel watches as the person walks under a streetlight. It's the busser.

Nudging Chris with her elbow, she points and whispers, "That's him."

They both watch him enter the garage.

Less than a minute later, a car pulls out of the garage and turns right headed towards Third Avenue. Instinctively, Rachel slumps down in the seat. The busser saw her in the restaurant an hour ago; she doesn't want to be seen now, outside Bucatini, in a cop car.

The car is almost to the intersection up ahead, close enough that Rachel can tell it's an old Toyota, like a Corolla, a red sedan—with a trunk. She can't make out the license plate number. At the stop sign, the car's left turn signal starts blinking.

The Toyota turns in their direction. Rachel's entire body bristles with fear, but her eyes are glued to his front bumper trying to get that license plate number. The headlights blast into Chris' cruiser, causing pricks of pain as Rachel's pupils constrict. Momentarily blinded, she can't make out the plate number. Glancing up away from the direct beams, she sees the busser's face. He is looking directly at her.

Fuck! Her heart is thumping in her chest.

In another second, the bright lights glide away and the car passes them.

Quickly, Rachel cranes her neck to look out the back window, making a mental note of the license plate number: CAU-1863.

Turning back to face the front, she notices that Chris is watching her.

"You okay over there?" he asks.

"I'm good," she lies, hoping the busser didn't recognize her from the restaurant. "Should we ... follow him or ... something?"

Chris raises his eyebrows. "We?"

She nods.

He stares at her for a few beats, then blinks. "I know what you're doing ..."

As cheerfully as she can, given how fast her heart is still beating, she says, "Well ... I *am* a volunteer with the Sheriff."

Chris is not amused. His jaw muscles tighten. "Yeah—for *search and rescue* ops," he points out. "If this guy is who you ... sense or think he is, then you should steer clear of him." Pointing in the direction of Bucatini, he adds, "And stay out of there."

Rachel feels his anger—or concern, frustration, whatever—like a wave of heat rolling towards her. But all she can think about is that license plate number. Burned into her mind's eye is: CAU-1863.

As soon as Rachel gets home, she scribbles the license plate number on a scrap of paper then opens the to-go container and carefully, without touching them, shakes the napkins into a large plastic bag, zipping it shut. On today's date on the calendar, she writes: NAPKIN SCENT DAY #1. This is day one of the busser's scent. Counting back, it is day eight for Alicia Meyers' scent.

Staring at October twenty-seventh, the day Alicia went missing, Rachel gets a pang of regret that she and Ruby couldn't do more to find her, and now it's probably too late. She starts to berate herself for not telling Chris about her premonition sooner, then thinks that one through. That wouldn't have changed the outcomes. Or it could have—maybe Chris would have thought she was cuckoo and passed on using Ruby for searches. And Ruby *did* find Alicia's earring, and some very suspicious spray-painting activity.

Turning away from the calendar, she assumes the longer a person is missing, the lower the chances of finding them. There are probably stats on the internet about these chances, but Rachel doesn't want to read those stats.

What she needs to do is find that cabin or a way to track the busser.

Waiting for her computer to start up, Rachel gives Ruby a big belly rub. "I've got some more sniff-sniff work for you."

Ruby's tail eagerly thwops against the leg of Rachel's chair. It isn't Rachel's imagination; Ruby knows what "work" is, and she loves it. Rachel can relate; work is her great distractor.

Typing Bucatini's address into *Google Maps*, Rachel stares at the map on her computer screen. She locates the parking garage and the alley where Ruby tracked Alicia's scent. Zooming out, she looks at the surrounding area. The areas shaded green on the map, indicating forests, aren't that far away, maybe a ten- to fifteen-minute drive from the parking garage.

Cabins though? There could be lots of cabins in those forests, but those would be on private property. There is no way she is snooping around a hunter's cabin on someone else's property. That seems like a good way to get shot.

She clicks and drags the map further to the east, into the foothills, to the area where the National Forest land begins. These are some of her favorite areas to trail run and hike with Ruby. Until now, that is.

Mapping routes from the parking garage to points up one or two of the closest Forest Service roads, it would be a thirty-minute drive.

Rachel shudders at the thought of Alicia being locked in a trunk for half an hour, panicking, probably screaming. Unless she was gagged. Surely, she would have pounded and kicked on the trunk. The first several minutes he would have driven through town. At nine p.m. on a Monday. That part of town would be the least busy at that time, but someone would have heard her inside that trunk. Unless Alicia was unconscious or ... dead.

Rachel looks on the map at the route Ruby tracked Alicia —from Bucatini around the block through the alley and to the parking garage. That is only three city blocks. He could have pushed her into the trunk, then shot her ... or bludgeoned her.

Rachel shakes her head, trying to push those thoughts away. Don't go there, she tells herself, inhaling, holding, and slowly releasing a few deep breaths.

This breathing technique of Glen's doesn't work for shit.

Rachel stares at the computer screen. From where Alicia's car was parked on Marsh Street, it is only one block to the parking garage. Through the alley. The lens of the single camera in the alley was spray painted over. One city block in an unlit alley with no camera at nine o'clock at night.

She could have been at gun point and threatened to walk

quickly and not say a word. But would a woman willingly climb into a man's trunk rather than risk being shot? In a public parking garage with businesses nearby? I wouldn't, Rachel thinks. I would've bolted. And maybe dodged back and forth hoping not to get shot in the back.

Or, the guy could have had his hand over Alicia's mouth, dragged her down the alley, then forced her into the trunk. But the busser didn't look *that* strong. Tall but lanky, not strong.

Maybe, by the time Alicia was pushed into the trunk, she was unconscious.

Rachel recalls the busser refilling their water glasses. He could have easily drugged Alicia's drink. Or her food, if he brought her plate out. Chris said they questioned Bucatini staff about what Alicia ate and drank that night, but all those dishes would have been run through the dishwasher long before anyone knew she was missing.

Quickly, Rachel scans the internet for information on date rape drugs. The effects can occur five to thirty minutes after ingestion, depending on the amount consumed and the drug used—turns out, there are a few of them. See if I ever drink from a glass or opened container again, Rachel thinks. In addition to amnesia, the drugs can reduce muscle reflexes and physical responses; some can result in the victim slipping into a coma-like state.

Holy shit! If she was getting drowsy from drugs, he could have guided her and half-carried her through the alley. Maybe he didn't put her in the trunk but just laid her in the backseat. Trunk or backseat, either way, if she was uncon-scious, there wouldn't have been a peep from her as he drove out of town.

Alicia could still be very much alive.

Wildly, she turns back to the *Google* map and begins searching the Forest Service lands for anything that looks like the roof of a cabin near a road. When she hovers over and clicks on the first obvious building, a label pops up that says it is the ranger station. Okay, so she is looking for a building much smaller than that.

This will be impossible. Several areas that look like small cabins are, upon zooming in closer, only boulders or rock outcroppings or trailheads. Rachel's eyes follow several trails on the internet map, along which she finds nothing that looks like a small cabin.

She searches until she is bleary-eyed but finds nothing.

Rachel is chasing ghosts. That busser could be a nice man who is just super lonely. Everyone wants people, lusts after them in the privacy of their own heads. We're all just animals, biological creatures. And maybe he dreams of owning a cabin in the woods, so that was on his mind when she brushed his hand.

Who dreams of owning a collapsing, moss-covered cabin?

26

DAY NINE

ONE OF THE requirements of the sex offender program is the men must agree not to enter into a physical relationship with a woman while they're enrolled. Friendships with women are okay. What a joke, Patrick thinks. None of us guys have a clue how to be friends with a woman. Besides, how many women wanna be friends with a sex offender just outta prison? Zero. Less than zero.

Still, Patrick has been trying to fantasize about being friends with women, instead of having deviant sex—or devious? He will get that straight one of these days. His "friendly" scenario involves the woman he saw at work a couple of weeks ago, the edgy one who never looks at anyone. In these friendly, nondeviant fantasies, he imagines asking her to dinner, watches her blush—no, she isn't the blushing type—watches her nod, somewhat aloof, but he can see the eagerness in her eyes, those stunning eyes of jade. He pictures them dining at a restaurant, a fancy one with white tablecloths. They lean in close, talking to each other all quiet.

This scenario fizzles when she asks what he does for a

living. In his fantasy, he tells her that he works with horses, which isn't a lie. But in his daydream, he tells her that he is an equine veterinarian instead of a volunteer who scoops up manure. After helping the vet with an injured horse last month, he would love to be a vet. He didn't mind the horse being sedated, the wound being drained, the stitches ... But becoming a vet is a pipedream.

Besides, he likes cleaning horse stalls because he loves being around those animals. But Patrick is no idiot; no woman is going to date a man who mucks horse stalls or has a minimum wage job because he didn't graduate from high school.

Except Alicia; she would never judge him. Patrick talks to her most every night in their secret place. They're getting to know each other, talking, like friends. Well, he talks; she listens. He hasn't touched her. Not once. He can't—no physical relationships allowed. Dr. Levitsky would approve.

Sometimes, Patrick imagines stroking Alicia's hair. She would like that. He wonders if she is one of those women who like their hair grabbed, who wanna be pinned down by their hair, their ass up in the—

One is a gun, you're gettin' triggered! Two: it ain't true that women wanna be pinned down. Three: re-see. Focus on the horses.

Patrick doesn't want to do anything that will jeopardize working at the ranch with those magnificent, powerful animals. Not even having deviant fantasies.

27

DAY TEN, 1:45 PM

RACHEL SPENDS the morning at work in a fugue state, going through the motions of work but completely uninspired by the project permits, the calls with clients, even the large invoices she submits for payment. But at least her brain isn't churning about cabins in the woods. Until she takes a break to eat a late lunch.

The image of that cabin is burned into her mind, yet there is no way to find it. A cabin in a forest. A woman in a cabin. A needle in a haystack.

Or maybe this is all just in her imagination. A paranoid mind.

No. This is gut instinct. Trust your instinct—that is the message she keeps hearing in her head.

"That's it," she mutters, chucking the rest of her sandwich in the trash. She is sick and tired of her mental waffling, constantly second guessing herself. I have to track that busser, she thinks. I'm not a police officer with a bunch of legal sideboards. I can follow whoever the hell I want.

It's almost two o'clock. She wonders if the busser is at

work or at home. Maybe he is up in the woods. If he is at work, he won't be getting off until much later. There is no harm in cruising the area around Bucatini, including the parking garage, looking for a red Toyota with plates CAU-1863.

Ten minutes later and two blocks from the restaurant, she hasn't seen his car and realizes, even if she does find it, she can't park nearby and watch his car for hours. It's broad daylight. People will get suspicious. She decides to scout the area for his car and, if she finds it, locate a good, out-of-the-way place to wait this evening. Basically, she will plan a stakeout.

This is starting to sound crazy, she thinks, partly hoping she doesn't find his damned car.

At a regular speed, not too slow, not too fast, Rachel looks straight ahead and drives past the restaurant, as if she is headed somewhere. *Oh, I'm headed somewhere alright: to a looney bin.* All the while, she checks for his car out of the corners of her eyes.

Nothing.

Turning right onto Marsh Street, there is still no older, red Corolla. She circles the block and finds no sign of his car. Next, she turns into the parking garage.

As soon as Rachel enters the garage, she sees a Sheriff's car pulled to the side, near the elevator.

Maybe they found more evidence. Or caught the busser!

She has no choice but to drive past the cruiser. Squinting in the dimly lit garage, it doesn't look like anyone is detained in the back of the cruiser. There is only one person in the driver's seat.

If that's Chris, I'm in trouble.

As she gets closer, she can't tell. Maybe that is him.

Next to the cruiser, and ... yes, it *is* Chris.

Though she has her straight on, I'm-headed-somewhere look, she can't help but glance to see if he catches a glimpse of her—the crazy lady. His mouth falls open as Rachel's car creeps past.

Rachel continues circling level one, no longer looking for CAU-1863 plates, just heading for the exit, telling herself that this a free world, that she is allowed to use the freaking parking garage.

Two more turns and she will be out of there.

Her phone rings.

Hey, can't answer the phone; I'm driving.

One more turn, and she will be at the exit. Her phone keeps ringing.

As she slowly takes the last corner, there is Chris, walking towards the exit, phone to his ear

Seeing her car, he takes the phone away from his ear and holds his hands in the air, questioningly. He is glaring at her, his dark, straight eyebrows now bunched up. Those brows are the only part of Chris that Rachel can read. They are saying, What the hell are you doing here, and why the hell are you driving away from me?

Rachel pulls into a parking spot, why, she isn't sure. To pretend like she is simply out running errands? So he can come over and chastise her?

In her rearview mirror, she watches him stride over to her car with that swagger of a tall, athletic man. Against her better judgement, she finds herself thinking that he is really sexy. Rachel's very next thought is, Don't even think about it.

He's a cop—there would be a stream of impending doom radiating off this sexy man.

He doesn't wait for her window to slide all the way down before starting in. "What are you doing over here?" he says, serious and stern.

She gives him a sheepish smile. "Volunteering?"

Naturally, he doesn't smile. "I told you—" He scans the garage around them and says in a lowered voice. "You *need* to stay away from this guy."

"How? How can I do that?"

"You just don't come over here. Period." Daggers shoot from his eyes at her. "Don't park in this garage. Don't go to his workplace. None of it."

"All I can think about is this man and that damned cabin. I spent hours last night searching the internet for cabins in the woods. It's impossible. The only way to find out where that cabin is—" she swallows "—is to follow him."

He releases a big exhale, an exasperated gush of air. Leaning over, his arms on the roof of her car, his face close to her, he says, "I got this, okay? You have to trust us to do our job. And don't get on this guy's radar. You know what I mean?"

She blinks. "You mean so I don't become one of his victims?"

"Exactly. For all you know, *he* could be watching *you*."

That gives her pause. That is a risk she hasn't seriously considered. Until a few weeks ago, she wasn't aware that the busser even existed, but was he aware of her? She estimates how many times she ate at Bucatini with her father or Lorena over the past several months: eight or nine times. Except for the night she was there with her dad and Margaret, she honestly can't recall if he ever bussed their table.

She does know that every time she ate there, she always drank from her water glass—that was, no doubt, filled by a busser. That gives her a chill.

"So, you're watching the busser?" she asks.

He straightens up, stretches his neck to the left and right, then says emphatically, "Again, you just have to trust me."

"Please stop saying that. If it hadn't been for my premonitions, this guy might not even be on your radar ... If he is."

He doesn't say anything for a few seconds. "Listen, we have watch lists and suspects for lots of cases. I can't tell you about suspects we're investigating. But I can tell you this case is high priority. I'm working on it twelve, fourteen hours a day."

Yeah, the busser is on Chris' radar. Probably anyone who worked at Bucatini that night is. He just can't tell me.

Rachel has hit another dead end. The thought of giving up, of acquiescing and trusting the Sheriff's department—no, trusting Chris—to handle this, fills her with dread. She is terrified they won't find Alicia in time. But she is powerless; there is nothing more she can do. Plus, she is mentally and physically stressed out from lack of sleep and her evolving premonitions and doing searches while withholding information about the busser and then telling Chris the entire truth.

With all this boiling inside and spilling over, she feels as if she could explode. She could step out of this car and rage and stomp and scream until her voice gives way. Scream until she collapses onto the ground, a puddle right there at Chris' feet. She imagines he would let her finish then scrape her off the concrete, put her back in the car and send her on her way.

Maybe he'd give me a hug, too, she thinks. Where the hell did that come from? And what a perfectly good way to get sideswiped by a premonition—hug a cop.

"I'm really not trying to be stubborn," she says defensively. "I don't ask for these premonitions, and I almost never say a word about them. To anyone. And I never act on them. *Never*. But this one was unlike any premonition I've ever had. I feel ... obligated to do something about this one. You can't imagine what it's like."

"You're right, I can't. Not exactly. But I get all kinds of information about crimes and suspects and, sometimes, I can't do jack shit with that information. And I'm not just talking about your—ESP, or whatever—I'm talking about hard, cold facts when I have no probable cause. I'm talking about evidence that I can't seize because I don't have a warrant. I've got a job to do but only one way to do it."

She puffs out her cheeks with a huge, drawn-out exhale. She and Chris stay where they are, unmoving and not talking, for a minute. They're at an impasse. Yet another dead end for Rachel.

"Can you do one thing for me?" Rachel says. "Please?"

"Depends ..."

"If he—if your investigation leads you near a Forest Service road or trailhead or someplace a cabin might be, can you let Ruby track Alicia there?" Unfortunately, it's probably too late for Alicia. Scent-wise.

"That, I can do," he says, nodding. Then wearily adds, "In the meantime ... please stay away from this guy."

28

DAY ELEVEN, 3:00 PM

CHEERFULLY, Wayne packs a box with supplies: baby wipes, a gallon of water, four bottled protein shakes—the chocolate and strawberry ones his mother likes—and a surgical mask and gloves so he won't expose her to any germs. The doctor said it was very important that she avoid germs and sick people during and after chemo.

Starting at the box to see if he forgot anything, he smiles because it looks like a picnic basket. She'll be so happy, he thinks. Over the top of the box, Wayne lays a soft, warm blanket, in case the other ones haven't been keeping her warm. Gently, he tucks the blanket around the supplies so nothing falls out.

Reviewing the list of her medications, he makes a check mark next to each one that he added to the protein shakes: ketamine in the strawberry shake and oxycodone and nabilone in the three chocolate shakes. Checking off nabilone, he snickers because the doctor explained this is a form of cannabis. *Marijuana! Mama is taking marijuana.* It's supposed to help with the chemo sickness. Secretly, he tried one of the nabilone pills the other night because sometimes he worries so much about Mama that he can't sleep. But the pill just made his mouth and head feel like they were full of cotton.

On the drive up to his mother's cabin, Wayne stops by work to get some carry-out food. Parking in the alley with his flashers on, he hurries through the back door.

"Wayne, my man," the chef, Marco, calls out to him. "Thought you was off today?"

"Yeah, I wanted to get some dinner. To go. I can pay—"

"Ah, don't worry about it." Marco dings the bell to let the waitstaff know an order is ready.

Ximena hustles back for the plates of food and smiles at Wayne. "Uh-oh," she teases him, "here comes trouble."

Wayne's cheeks grow hot. Ximena is his favorite waitress because she doesn't treat him like he is stupid and slow—like some of the other waitstaff do. Plus, she never gets mad when he says her name wrong; she just reminds him to say the letter "X" like an "H."

"Okay, what's it gonna be?" Marco says to Wayne.

"You got lasagna?"

"Always."

Wayne's mouth waters as he watches Marco slide a slab of lasagna into a clamshell container.

"I made a new cheesecake recipe," Marco says enticingly. "White chocolate raspberry. Guy that delivered the wine earlier said it was my best ever."

Maybe today, Wayne thinks, Mama can handle a few bites of cheesecake. It will be such a nice treat for her after months of chemo sickness. And a little celebration—he still can't believe she got out of the hospital.

Ximena comes back with another order for Marco, just as Wayne says, "I'll take a piece of cheesecake, too? If—" he glances, sheepishly, at Ximena then back to Marco "—if that's okay." He gets a free meal on days that he works, but the few times Wayne has come in on a day off, they never charged him.

Ximena waves away Wayne's concern and slices him a piece of cheesecake while Marco sautés garlic and onions for the next order.

"Thanks," Wayne says. "See you tomorrow." Slipping out the back door, he mutters, "Mama is going to be *so* happy."

"Did he say that food was for his mom?" Ximena asks Marco.

Sliding grilled shrimp over a bed of pasta, Marco shrugs. "Couldn't hear him back here in the kitchen."

"Hmm. I must've heard him wrong ..." Ximena gets a deep crease between her brows, her face frowning with concern. "His mom died like ... three or four weeks ago."

29

DAY TWELVE, 10:00 AM

RACHEL IS RUMINATING over her last conversation with Chris. She has spent most of her life minding her own business where her premonitions are concerned, and now, with the one premonition she can't ignore, she has been told to mind her own business. It isn't the irony of the situation which is troubling, it is her helplessness. It is almost unbearable for her to stand by and do nothing. She can't stop dwelling over ways she could take some kind of action to find Alicia.

To get a break from her brain, Rachel takes Ruby for a run. But not in the woods.

While running, instead of trying to figure out what to do next, for her sanity or for Alicia Meyers' life, she puts in her earbuds and cranks up her playlist. Her brain needs a break. The last thing she wants right now is more information entering her brain. No more random, outside information. No more thinking, scheming, analyzing. Brain closed for repairs. And for some Rolling Stones music.

She runs for a long time, losing herself in "Sympathy for

the Devil," pushing herself harder and faster, hitting, finally, a runner's high. As she loops back closer to home, she slows her pace and her high dissipates. The world returns. So does her brain.

For once, though, her brain comes up with an idea that isn't half bad. In addition to eye-contact avoidance, maybe listening to music around people will decrease the chance of receiving a premonition. Like a brain buffer, calming her synapses—or what does Glen call them?—her receptors. Music though earbuds, with no space between the music and her brain, or between people and her brain, might occupy those receptors. It would be like a mental Do Not Disturb sign.

Jeezus! See no evil, speak no evil. Now, hear no evil. Don't go to Bucatini. Stay away from the predator. Don't go into the woods. Don't drink anything that's already opened. And I thought my world couldn't get any smaller.

Trying out her newly discovered mental and auditory Do not disturb sign, Rachel takes Ruby for her annual checkup that afternoon. Not wanting to be obnoxious, she removes her earbuds while talking to the vet and paying the bill. That was her first mistake.

Ruby is hamming it up with the front desk staff, soaking up the love and attention and, literally, inhaling the treats, when someone comes through the door with a German shepherd. The two dogs engage in the usual nose and butt sniffs.

After paying the bill, Rachel gives Ruby's leash a gentle pull to signal it's time to leave, then glances down at Ruby and the shepherd. That was her second mistake.

The German shepherd looks at Rachel. Instantly, the

room darkens, Rachel's vision tunnels and she senses, no she *sees*, that the German shepherd is not long for this world.

Oh, no, no, no, no.

Scrambling in her purse for her earbuds, Rachel tries to push the image away, but she can't unsee it. Unleashed, the dog will run into the street. A car will not have time to stop.

Quickly, she heads for the door, sidestepping the shepherd's owner, a young man of maybe twenty-five. Another vision: a woman, about fifty, in the car that will hit the German shepherd. The woman is crying, wild with grief, covering her eyes, also trying not to see the dog on the asphalt.

Grief wells up inside of Rachel. It's just a dog, she tells herself, shoving in her earbuds. Just a dog. Get out of here. Mind your own business.

She turns up the volume. Pearl Jam's "Just Breathe" is not working. Another image streaks through her mind's eye: the dog motionless in the road, tongue hanging out of its mouth, eyes like glass.

Desperate not to see any more, Rachel clenches shut her eyes for a second. Opening them, she reaches for the door knob and sees the sign on the door asking clients to have their dogs leashed in the office. That German shepherd isn't on a leash.

Anger wells up inside of Rachel at the man's irresponsibility. Not for having his dog off-leash here, in the vets, but for the accident that he could prevent. What the hell is wrong with this damned idiot? She is outraged.

Time slows for Rachel. The front desk staff mutters to the man that he needs to have his dog on a leash. Rachel wants to scream, You can prevent a senseless, heart-breaking accident. You can stop your dog from dying!

Then like the cogs of a gear slipping into place, *clck, clck, clck*, Rachel hears what she is thinking: You. Can. Stop. A. Dog. From. Dying.

Sometimes I can.

Rachel slowly turns to face the young man. He is grumbling about his dog being well-behaved while hooking a leash onto his dog—the staff keep a few leashes on hand for obnoxious people like this who think the rules don't apply to them.

Sometimes, you can stop a dog from dying.

Pulling out her earbuds, Rachel clears her throat. "You know, leashes can save a dog's life." She waits for the negligent dog owner to look at her before continuing. The front desk staff also pause what they're doing and watch the stare down.

Boldly, Rachel holds the dog owner's gaze for several long moments then says, "I know this for a fact."

She hopes that he sees the truth in her eyes.

30

DAY TWELVE, 2:00 PM

BACK AT HOME, Rachel is unhinged by the encounter at the veterinarian's office. Intervening with that dog owner completely contradicted her entire approach to a functional life. Minding her own damned business has been her fail-safe, serving her very well for over a decade. Yet, today, for some unknown reason, she chose to intervene in someone else's life. Over a dog. Rachel is unmoored, as if she lost her compass. What happened to the better-safe-than-sorry rule? There was nothing safe about getting in that man's face and staring him down. Nothing safe for Rachel, that is; hopefully, safe for the dog.

She can't stop wondering if she did, in fact, just stop a dog from dying.

Trying not to analyze the hell out of her every move, Rachel spends the next hour squinting at *Google Maps*, zooming out enough to see the forested lands as well as Bucatini and the parking garage. Leaning back to take in the bigger picture, she clicks off the satellite imagery on the map to make the roads more visible. There is an almost straight shot, as the crow flies, from the parking garage to Forest Service Road 2068 to the northeast. It's a road Rachel hasn't yet scoured for cabins.

Scrolling northeast to follow the road on the screen, several miles up that road, heading into the mountains, are a scattering of small square building symbols. A label reads: ADA CREEK CAMPGROUND. She clicks the satellite imagery on again, but the trees conceal the cluster of small buildings. She tries to use the street view feature, but it isn't available because the area is too rural.

A remote campground with buildings. There could be an old, dilapidated cabin among those buildings, and the campground would be closed for the season. No campers. No Forest Service staff.

Reading about Ada Creek Campground on the Forest Service website, it's a small campground with potable water, outhouses, twelve campsites for tents and two sites with electrical hookups for recreational vehicles. There is a horse camp nearby, accessed from a different Forest Service road, and a network of horse trails, including one that runs fairly close to the campground. There is no mention of cabins and no photos of the campground. It sits at an elevation of just over two thousand feet, low enough that there wouldn't be any snow yet.

Rachel's first instinct is to drive up there and search with Ruby, but she doesn't have Alicia's bra, the scent cue. On what basis would Chris be willing to search again for Alicia, this time near random cabins that Rachel found on an internet map? Especially after he just told her to let the Sheriff's department handle this case. None. There is no basis for Chris to agree to another dog search.

Even if she could, somehow, finagle that bra back from Chris, Alicia has been missing for twelve days. Rachel figures those are dirt or gravel roads, on which Alicia's scent could still linger, but asking Ruby to search for a scent *that* stale isn't fair. Plus, who is she kidding? Chris isn't going to give her Alicia's bra. He was crystal clear that she is to let the Sheriff's Office handle this case.

Rachel's mind just took her in a complete circle. A wide, murky, complete circle.

Looking over her shoulder, Rachel stares at the bag of napkins from Bucatini. That is a fresh scent. Using those napkins as a cue, Ruby could search the campground for the busser's scent.

This is crazy, she thinks. I can't go search for a predator in an abandoned cabin. By myself. She remembers Chris' warning about the possibility of her being watched by the busser.

Nah, that's paranoid.

Between her ESP, her hypervigilance and Chris' warning, things are getting murky for Rachel. Still, she goes to the front door to see if she locked it. As she turns the deadbolt, the memory of the busser's haunting eyes flash in her mind. Nothing murky about that image.

Back at the computer, Rachel stares again at the almost straight line between the parking garage and Ada Creek Campground. Her brain likes straight lines. Clean. Simple. Obvious. She clicks the campground then taps on GET DIRECTIONS, entering the parking garage address as the FROM location. It's about a forty-minute drive. Forty minutes in a trunk.

Sometimes, you can stop a person from dying.

This area looks like a perfect place for a trail run—except for the possibility of stumbling onto an abducted woman and a predator. Her dad won't go up there with her; he is too protective. Even if she could talk him into it, she has caused him enough heartburn. Rachel wants her dad to enjoy some peace with Margaret. Even on her mother's couch.

Lorena is not an option. Rachel is done considering her as a partner in hunting down a predator. Lorena *and* Fletcher might be a possibility to check out the campground with her, but she would have to be honest about what she is doing.

Rachel plays out that conversation in her head. First, she would need to tell Fletcher about her ESP—about which he would probably scoff—then fill them in on all the convoluted details: her cabin premonition; her needle-in-the-haystack internet searches for similar cabins; why she thinks Ada Creek Campground could be the place; how she acquired napkins with the busser's scent; why the Sheriff can't be there with them. Fletcher would then say, You want me and my wife to help you search for a cabin in a remote area where a missing woman might be held captive, and where her abductor might also be present? Without involving the cops? Based on your "premonition" (and he would definitely air quote those words)? Yes, Rachel would say. Do you two want to come along? It will be fun. Uh, no thanks, they would say.

Another dead end.

"Ruby, looks like it's just you and me tomorrow."

Ruby perks up and gives a little tail wag.

———

Preparation for tomorrow's "hike" involves a quick trip to the sporting goods store for some kind of self-protection.

Perusing the handguns, Rachel tries to fend off a very eager salesman by explaining that she has no experience with guns and is just looking.

Undeterred, he says he has just the gun for her. "This thing is *super* easy to shoot," he says excitedly. "No experience required. Double action. No hammer. Just point"—he reaches under the glass counter—"and shoot."

Beaming, he slides across the counter a small revolver. The gun is pink.

Rachel stares at the gun for a few beats.

"Called the Pink Lady," he says proudly. "Only weighs twelve ounces. Tuck it right in your purse."

She looks at him and arches an eyebrow.

"I mean ... if you have a concealed carry. If you don't, you can apply for one at the Sheriff's Office." He is losing momentum. "Or just holster it on your waist ..."

Rachel passes on the gun because she doesn't have time to get a concealed carry permit and has no clue how to shoot a gun. Even a pink one. Maybe someday Chris can give her lessons.

In the end, she buys a powerful, handheld taser. She considered the taser gun like the police use, the ones that don't require contact with an assailant, but it was bulkier than the Pink Lady. And it was bright yellow. She couldn't imagine walking around with that big, yellow beast strapped onto her waist tomorrow.

On the way to her car, Rachel has an uncanny feeling that she is being watched, making the hair on her neck bristle. Scanning the cars around her, there are no red Corollas.

In her car, she plugs the USB cable into the taser to charge while reading the instructions. Pretty simple. It has a holster—of sorts—to clip onto a belt or purse strap, within easy reach. To use it, make contact between taser and your assailant and press the trigger button.

Casting an eye over the parking lot again, Rachel sees nothing suspicious. Not a single assailant in sight.

All this weapon stuff has me on edge, she thinks. Little Pink Lady guns and giant yellow tasers ... and tomorrow's hike is more than a little nerve-racking.

That evening, she calls her father just to say hi. She reassures him that, yes, she is taking care of herself. She tells him that Ruby had a good check-up with the vet. During the brief call, she casually mentions that she and Ruby are going for a hike tomorrow morning at a pretty area around Ada Creek Campground.

At least someone will know where I'm headed if ... well, always better safe than sorry.

31

DAY THIRTEEN, 10:00 AM

BEFORE HEADING up to Ada Creek Campground, Rachel makes a quick drive by Bucatini, scouting for the busser's car (and keeping an eye out for a Sheriff's patrol car). The busser's car isn't anywhere in a five-block radius of the restaurant.

Next, Rachel drives into the parking garage, her palms growing sweaty on the steering wheel. Only half the spaces are occupied. She cruises through all three levels of the garage. Not one Toyota with matching plates.

With her car idling near the garage exit, she checks the time. Bucatini doesn't open until eleven a.m., another forty-five minutes. The busser could be on his way to work right this minute. Or, for all she knows, he could be out grocery shopping or visiting his grandma.

Or out stalking another woman.

That does it. She is going to search for that cabin. If she sees his car up in the woods, she will just turn around.

Typing the campground into her phone's mapping app,

she punches Start and exits the parking garage. There is still no busser in sight.

Driving out of town, she checks every cross street for a Corolla. Constantly, her eyes flit to her rearview mirror watching for a red sedan with the busser's menacing face staring back at her.

Ruby gets excited when they turn onto the gravel Forest Service Road 2068, or maybe it's the smells of the forest. In the woods, Ruby lives her best life—digging after moles, chasing squirrels, jumping after birds. Or maybe Ruby loves the forest because it is where her owner is happiest. Or where her owner used to be the happiest. Since Rachel brushed against the busser's hand and saw that cabin, she hasn't stepped one foot in the forest.

Rachel loses cell reception right away. That gives her a lump in her throat. She wishes she *had* bought the Pink Lady yesterday. I've got the taser, she tells herself. Still, she pops open the glove box to see if her pepper spray is in there.

Without cell reception, the phone's directions to the campground are no longer active, but her location still shows on the mapping app, which is reassuring. At least she knows exactly where she is. So far, no other cars pass Rachel coming down from the mountains, no cars are behind her. Not a Corolla in sight.

Up ahead, she glimpses a sign that appears to be in the middle of the road. Glancing at the map, she isn't yet to the campground. Maybe the satellite feed has her location off a bit.

She rolls her car to a stop in front of a Forest Service gate and a sign that reads: Campground Closed for Season. From her vantage point, Rachel sees no buildings, cabins or campsites. Zooming into the offline map image, which makes it pixelated, Rachel estimates the campground structures are, indeed, at least a half-mile up the road. Ruby is panting excitedly, pacing across the backseat from window to window, taking in the scenery—or the smellery—ready for action.

She lets Ruby out of the car to pee and race around, releasing some of her pent-up energy from the forty-minute car ride. Rachel zips up her jacket, pulls on her knitted cap, clips the taser onto her belt loop and throws the pepper spray into her backpack. Sliding on medical gloves to avoid scent contamination, she picks up the bag of napkins from the busser. Her stomach pinches with tension. She wishes Bucatini didn't use dark red napkins.

What if we do find a cabin and the busser is in there?

That scenario paralyzes her for a moment, and she stares at the napkins. Ruby spots the plastic bag, races over and sits at Rachel's heel.

Rachel tells herself that she can turn back at any time.

With an exuberant, sing-song tone, wishing she felt the way she sounds, Rachel says, "Ruby, you ready to do some sniff-sniff?" Opening the plastic bag, Rachel lowers it to Ruby's snout. "Find it," she commands.

Ruby starts off with her nose in the air, trying to find the scent. Running up and down the road, along both sides, nudging into the thick layer of fallen leaves under the bare bushes, she can't find the smell. Could be the scent on the napkins has gone stale; it is five days old. Or the busser never came up this road. Or that wasn't even a premonition she had with the busser; it may have simply been her brain in overdrive or triggered, as Glen suggested. Maybe she simply can't turn off her danger receptors.

Ruby's nose is to the ground now, back and forth, up and down, until she smells her way to the gate. Placing her front paws on the gate, she snorts at the gate latch, then sits in alert position.

"Good girl," Rachel says, checking the forest all around her. It appears she could open the gate and drive through, but if someone came along and put a lock on this gate, she wouldn't be able to drive out of here.

Scooting around the gate, Rachel starts up the road at a jog, while Ruby bounds ahead. Rachel breaks into a run to keep Ruby in sight.

After several minutes, Rachel slows her pace some to unzip her jacket and stuff her knitted cap in her pack. She is starting to wonder if she psyched herself up for nothing, if there will be no cabin, no Alicia, no busser. Maybe she should just turn around and get the hell out of there. Except ... Ruby did alert at the gate latch.

Trust your instincts, Rachel reminds herself. A woman's life is at stake.

When Rachel and Ruby reach the campground, there are several openings in the forest: campsites with metal campfire rings and water spigots. Nearby, are two covered areas with picnic tables. Beyond those are two concrete outhouse buildings, locked up for the season. There are no cabins.

Past the outhouse buildings, the road peters out into more of an off-road vehicle type of road: mostly dirt, no recent grading or new gravel, big potholes. It is right there that Ruby practically skids to a stop. Sniffing diligently around the narrowing road, she noses her way fifteen yards up the road, looks back at Rachel and alerts.

Rachel stares at Ruby. Ruby stares back. When Rachel walks towards her, Ruby darts further up the road.

The road narrows, the forest closing in around them and becoming colder. The forest smells strongly of decaying leaves and musty, damp earth. Rachel zips her jacket back up and pulls on her cap.

Now the old road bed becomes more of a wide path. With little sunlight reaching the forest floor through the dense trees, it becomes darker, as does Rachel's mood. Her mind niggles over the fact that she is alone and has no cell reception. Continually checking the woods in every direction as far as she can see, which isn't far, there is no cabin.

After a few more minutes, Rachel contemplates her options. Her head screams for her to get the hell out.

Then that still, quiet internal voice whispers, Sometimes, you can stop a person from dying.

Rachel clicks her tongue, and Ruby circles back to her side. Opening the bag of napkins, she puts it in front of Ruby's face, again, to be certain she is still following the busser's scent.

Ruby stuffs her nose in the bag for a split second, then pulls Rachel further along the old road bed.

Up ahead, Rachel spots a short, perfectly straight, horizontal surface that is mottled brown and green. *What the hell is that? A fallen tree?*

Slowing her pace, Rachel tries to figure out this horizontal anomaly. It's too far off the ground to be a fallen tree. Calling Ruby back to her side, Rachel clicks the leash onto her collar.

As they draw closer, Rachel squints and makes out a

cedar-shingled rooftop covered with a thick layer of lime-green moss.

She becomes aware of her heartbeat, like a small drum in her ears—*boomp-boom, boomp-boom.*

Closer now, she sees a break in the horizontal line where the roof slumps. The corner of the roof is partially collapsed over a wobbly looking front stoop.

Rachel breaks out in a cold sweat. Literally. A film of perspiration forms on her temples and neck and under her arms, yet she is icy cold. Something inside her—fear or instincts—won't allow her feet to take one more step.

The cabin has two windows on either side of a wooden door. It is identical to her premonition. It sits in a small opening in the trees with one giant cedar growing behind it. Exactly as it appeared in her premonition.

32

DAY THIRTEEN, 10:45 AM

MOST PEOPLE LOVE HAVING a day off. Not Patrick. No work means no distractions, and that means battling demons. The day starts off shitty because he dreamt about Alicia. A sexual dream. Deviant, to say the least. He wakes up hard as a rock. None of the counselors at the sex offender program have talked about how to handle morning wood, especially after a dream like that.

Lying in bed still, he doesn't want the dream to end. With his eyes closed, he can still see Alicia's face, can imagine running his fingers through her hair, yanks on her hair. She lets out a gasp, part pain and part excitement.

Patrick growls, "Fuuuck!" *Now this bitch is triggerin' me in my goddam sleep.*

His mantra starts rolling through his brain. One is gun. Two: is it true? Three: re-see. One is a gun.

It isn't working—he can still imagine her unsuspecting face. He needs to see her face in person, run his hands through her hair. He needs release.

Groping the mattress, his hand brushes against her,

stretched out next to him, waiting, always ready for him. Shifting onto his elbow, he stares into Alicia's face. She always gives him that same inviting smile. He has been resisting her but wants so badly to feel her hair, needs to feel her hair.

Reaching over, his pulse quickens. Gently, he runs his hand over and down her hair. Guilt washes over him. Under the weight of his hand, her hair crinkles. The sound sends a jolt of fury and embarrassment through him. He is stroking a poster—Alicia's poster.

Last week, when no one was looking, he snatched the MISSING WOMAN poster off a billboard and quickly tossed it in his car.

Back at home, he carefully unrolled the poster and tucked her safely inside his pillowcase. Each night, he takes her out and presses her flat on the bed next to him. He likes waking up next to her.

His erection is throbbing. It has been weeks since he had a decent fantasy about her. What's the big fuckin' deal, he thinks. It's nothin' but pretend now. What's a few minutes of pretending?

Grabbing her by the hair, he pulls Alicia's face down, moaning, as he presses the poster against his erection. Under his breathe, he mutters, "There you go, you little whore. That's what you want, ain't it? Wanna be choked like that? You like to gag on me, don't you?"

As soon as he climaxes and the contractions stop and the wave of release passes, here comes the shame and the rage. The poster is destroyed from being rubbed up against him, Alicia's smiling face is crumpled and distorted, damp with his cum. He smears it into her mouth, his thumb punching a hole between her lips.

I wiped that smile right off your face, bitch. You got what you deserve.

Patrick starts shredding the remnants of Alicia's face, then stomps around the room, angrily shoving pieces of the poster in his mouth. "I will turn you into the piece of shit you are," he says, laughing like a maniac, bits of chewed up poster spraying from his mouth.

His craving, his need, to see Alicia wince in painful ecstasy is physical. His body is screaming to hear Alicia plead. Desperately, he needs a woman.

No. No women. Find somethin' else to focus on. That is part of the mantra, which, at this point, he can barely recall. Patrick runs his palm over his mustache and goatee, glancing around his apartment. There isn't a distraction good enough to take his mind off Alicia, the real Alicia, a flesh and blood woman.

There is no booze in his apartment, but there is a store down the street. He peeks out the window, checking for what, he doesn't know. A bottle of cheap whisky? A woman? His parole officer? The cops?

No booze. No parole violations. What he has done here, so far, no one will ever know about. But drinking could land him back in prison.

Go find a woman. No.

Just go outside. Run. Yes. Go run.

Or he could go for a drive.

33

DAY THIRTEEN, 11:15 AM

RUBY STRAINS AGAINST THE LEASH, and Rachel gives it a tug. When Ruby looks back at her, Rachel, without uttering a word, gives her the hand signal to sit. Scanning the cabin's surroundings, Rachel sees no indication of recent activity. She listens intently for any signs of life from the cabin. The entire place looks untouched, as if no one has been there for years. She isn't sure why, but it looks meticulously untouched. Intentionally untouched.

They stand motionless for long enough that the birds around them resume their sing-song. She wants to slink up closer and peer into a window to see if Alicia is inside, but Rachel's body is screaming at her to get the hell out of there!

The stillness around them is broken by a soft grunt from Ruby who is staring at Rachel, probably getting bored because she never has to stand still in the woods for this long, especially when she is working. Rachel looks at Ruby for a moment, trying to decide what to do.

I could tell Ruby to stay here while I scout around the cabin, she thinks. That way, if anyone else walks up this trail,

Ruby would bark. Or, do I want Ruby's nose sniffing the cabin before I go up there? Yes, that is best. Besides, Ruby can outrun any human. Unless the busser has a gun.

Rachel unhooks Ruby's leash, then, as silently as possible, slides the plastic bag out of her pocket again and lets Ruby sniff the napkins—her cue to get back to work. Ruby immediately resumes following the scent trail.

Staying put on the trail, Rachel watches Ruby sniff the base of two trees in front of the cabin. There are rays of late morning sunshine refracting through the tree tops into the small clearing in front of the cabin. Next, Ruby noses her way straight to the door of the cabin.

Fuck.

Ruby sits in her alert position and stares back at Rachel.

Fuck, fuck.

A taser and pepper spray, Rachel thinks. Really? Trying to calm her nerves, Rachel reasons that if the busser *was* in there, Ruby would be barking or growling or acting cautious. Taking a huge inhale, Rachel holds it for several seconds, then exhales. Her pulse, immediately, accelerates again.

Ruby, still sitting at the cabin door, tips her head with curiosity at Rachel.

Digging the pepper spray out of her pack, Rachel removes the taser from her belt loop and clips the pepper spray there instead. Then, taser in hand, she heads towards the cabin.

Tiptoeing isn't necessary; the forest floor is a soft duff of earth and decaying pine needles. Walking decisively towards the cabin, Rachel identifies a long crack in the wood to the left of the door. That crack becomes her target, hoping she can see through the crack into the cabin. If not, she will try a window.

Putting her face up to the crack in the wood, Rachel moves her head left and right until her eye can focus on something inside. The wooden leg of a table—no, a chair, because there is a corner of dirty, worn upholstery. Moving her head to get a different view, the dry, splintery wood of the cabin scratches her forehead. Her view through the narrow crack is too restricted to see much.

She needs to look through a window but is afraid of what she might see. Someone staring back at her. Or worse, Alicia tied to the chair, her throat slashed.

No! Stop it.

Moving over to a window, Rachel inches her head up until she can see through the corner. There are no signs of anyone inside. There is the chair, mercifully, empty. Next to the chair is an upside-down wooden crate. Beyond the chair is a closed door to another room.

Looking at the front door, there is a heavy metal clasp bolted to the door and the door jamb and secured with a heavy padlock. Both the clasp and lock look shiny and new. Absurdly, she tries the doorknob. It turns but the door won't budge with that padlock. When she releases the doorknob, a faint metal-on-metal sound clunks from it.

From inside the cabin comes a faint, muffled sound. Rachel's skin tingles with fear. Ruby cocks her ear up, listening intently.

There it is again. It sounds like a moan. Pressing her ear against the cabin door, Rachel hears a woman whimpering from somewhere inside the cabin. It has to be Alicia.

Adrenaline zings through Rachel's entire body.

Fuck, fuck, fuck.

Rachel can't think straight. If the busser is in there, then he heard them already. He would've come out by now, looking for them, chasing them away. No, the door is locked from the outside; he can't be in there. Unless this is some kind of trap.

Slinking around the cabin with Ruby close on her heels, Rachel finds no other doors or windows. Alicia's pleading is louder at the back of the cabin. Alicia must be in a back room. Ruby sniffs wildly then begins a mad dig at the base of the cabin, dirt flying up in all directions. Clearly, the busser's scent is also strong in that back room.

As Rachel starts around front again, Ruby lets out a short, demanding bark. Startled, Rachel jumps.

"No bark," she whispers. *Well, if the busser is in there, he knows we're out here now.*

In response, Ruby catches Rachel's eyes, sits down in a firm alert stance, stares at the back of the cabin and then back at Rachel.

For several seconds, Rachel listens through the back wall but hears nothing but plaintive mumbling from Alicia. No man's voice.

Determined to get in the cabin, Rachel races to the front and tries to open the windows, to no avail. She jams her shoulder against the door, then again, harder. The last one sends pain shooting down her arm. Kicking at the door does nothing. That clasp is attached with heavy screws; the door won't budge.

Scanning the area, Rachel finds a big rock.

Standing several feet back from the cabin, she commands Ruby to sit next to her. Then she hurls the rock through the window, shattering it, glass flying in all directions. Using a dead tree limb, she knocks the splintered window panes and pieces of glass out from the window frame.

Alicia is screaming. "Help me! Please! Help! I'm in here."

"I'm getting you out of here," Rachel calls back. "Hold on. Just hold on."

Rachel is wild with fear and panic and determination. Her body is on autopilot, focused only on getting Alicia out of this horror.

Louder now, big, gasping, muffled sobs, desperate sobs are coming from the back room.

Rachel hollers back to Ruby. "Stay. Stay, Ruby." Firmly, she pumps her palm towards Ruby.

Adrenaline surges again through every fiber of Rachel's body as she hoists herself into the window opening, scrambling to get her legs through next. Teetering on the window frame, trying to get her feet down first so only her shoes land in the shards of glass inside, Rachel half swings, half flops into the cabin. A sliver of glass still in the window frame punctures her hand.

"Shit," she yells, which gets Ruby to barking.

Sticking her head out the window, Rachel says firmly, "I'm okay, Ruby. You stay. Stay." Palm out, her non-bleeding one, she gives Ruby the stay hand signal again. The last thing she needs is Ruby running into all that glass.

Blood drips from her hand, but the glass sliver is large enough that it is visibly sticking out of her palm. As she moves towards the room where Alicia is, Rachel grimaces and plucks the glass out. A thin stream of blood now flows from the cut.

With nothing else to staunch the blood, Rachel takes a napkin from the plastic bag and stares at it for a second. Just thinking of the busser's scent makes her shudder. Then, quickly, she presses the napkin against her bleeding hand and slides a medical glove over the mess as best she can.

Grabbing the doorknob to the back room, Rachel takes a deep breath, hoping beyond hope that this door isn't locked.

34

DAY THIRTEEN, 11:20 AM

PATRICK DRESSES HURRIEDLY, anxious to get out of his apartment. His heart pounds with anticipation. He is desperate to find an escape. And petrified that he *will* find one.

Shoving his foot in his tennis shoe, it is wet. Again. This time from hosing down the horse stalls last night. He never found boots in his size at the thrift store and couldn't afford new ones after buying car tires. It infuriates him that he can't afford tires *and* a couple pairs of new boots.

Why can't I have both? Is that askin' too much?

As hard as he can, he chucks the other shoe across the room and watches it bounce off the wall and flop across the floor.

Staring at that shoe, he is transported back to when he was a boy with only one pair of shoes. *Thirty years later, and I still got one pair of fuckin' shoes to my name. I'm goin' nowhere.*

He drops onto the floor and shoves his foot into the other shoe, his sock instantly becoming damp. The soggy shoe sickens him, makes his body grow cold. His mouth starts to water, like he is about to vomit.

Leaning his hands into the mattress to push himself up off the floor, instead he drops his head and chest onto the bed. Clutching handfuls of the blanket, he squeezes them so hard his fists hurt.

"No! I'm not goin' back there. Not again."

Deep in the recesses of his mind, from long, long ago, he hears a pathetic, whimpering voice. *Stop it! Mommy, don't! Please. Stop.*

C'mon, his mom coaxed, *be a good boy. Just one kiss. Right there between Mommy's legs.* Grabbing his hair, his mom pulled his face between her crotch. *There you go,* she said all sugary sweet. *Right there, baby. That's it.*

He gagged as his mom pushed herself against his mouth and nose, holding onto his hair so he couldn't back away. Unable to catch his breath, he gasped and choked. Once he even threw up. She laughed at him that time and called him a little wuss.

The flashback makes him want to wretch. He loathes that pathetic little boy, begging like he was helpless.

Willing away the memory, Patrick's eyes fly open, and he bolts upright, kneeling now at the foot of his bed. He starts twisting the blanket, rage for his mother boiling inside of him. Tighter and tighter, he twists the blanket until it becomes a thick rope. More twists and the blanket coils onto itself, like a noose. He imagines strangling his mother with it.

"Be a fuckin' man," he shouts and storms out the door.

When Patrick breathes in the cold air outside, his rage drops a few degrees. Way too cold to run in soggy-ass shoes, he thinks, and climbs into his car.

For no reason except it is where Patrick usually drives, he heads in the direction of work. He passes the liquor store then the pot shop.

Just keep drivin', man.

Up ahead, he sees the trees of Derby Park and is drawn in that direction.

In the parking lot, Patrick shuts off the engine and stares at all the people roaming around Derby Park. His thoughts are dark, very dark. He feels like he has been filleted, his guts stripped open, and he can't push his nasty mother back out of sight, back out of his memory. The image of being forced to go down on her is seared into is brain, fresh and raw, like it happened yesterday. He wants to hurt her. Burning in his chest is a screaming, boiling urge to choke his mother.

Or that woman there, who just ran past.

There are tons of women there today. They are jogging with baby strollers, pushing kids on swings, the children all bundled up in dry, warm coats. There are soccer balls rolling by. This isn't what his childhood looked like. All these normal families fill Patrick with—what is that? Disgust, he thinks. Depression, maybe. Whatever it is, it is calming his anger.

Jumping out of the car, he runs through the park trails, past the happy families, past the women, past the fathers. He runs until he can hardly breathe, runs until a stitch in his side pinches until the only thing he is aware of is that pain.

Leaning forward, hands on knees, he gulps air. Then he stands and stretches out the cramp, walks around, waiting for the pain to pass.

Pain. That is what he has been trying to inflict on his mother for years. But that woman don't feel pain, he thinks, cuz she don't care about no one but herself. *Ain't nothin' I can do to make that whore sorry for what she did.*

What the hell am I s'pose to do with all this fuckin' pain?

Something in the back of his mind tells him to call the hotline.

He forgot all about the hotline. The sex offender program has a twenty-four-hour hotline to call when you—well, he guesses you call when you get deviant thoughts. Rifling through his wallet, he finds Dr. Levitsky's business card. There, in bold, is the hotline number.

It would be so easy to get back in his car and chase down another escape—not Alicia, a different woman. That would take away his anger and pain, at least, for a while. For a little while, it would feel so good.

Agitated, Patrick flaps the sex offender hotline card against his palm. Dr. Levitsky is always telling him that he has choices, that it all comes down to choices. This doesn't seem like much of a choice. Patrick looks down again at the hotline number on the card, then squints over at his piece-of-shit Subaru, the dark gray body bruised with pockets of crumbling rust. That car will lead him to relief. And trouble. That car will lead him to a woman. And prison.

But if he calls the hotline ...

35

———————————

DAY THIRTEEN, 11:30 AM

RACHEL IMMEDIATELY RECOGNIZES Alicia from the news. Her face is streaked with dirt and tears, and her coat and jeans are filthy. Rachel sees no blood anywhere. One of Alicia's shoes is missing, and the sock on that foot is covered with dirt. Tangles of strawberry blond hair jut out in all directions from underneath an absurdly fluffy, white—now, dirty white—knitted cap. On top of the cap is a big, pink pom-pom.

The small room reeks like an outhouse, like old, festering urine and feces. Alicia cowers in the corner on a pile of blankets. A long, handicap rail is mounted to the wall. Handcuffed to that rail is Alicia's right hand.

Oh, fuck me, Rachel thinks. Handcuffs! How am I getting those off?

"It's going to be okay," Rachel says pumping her hands a little. "I'm getting you out of here." *I'm going to race back to my car, drive down until I get cell reception, call nine-one-one ...*

Alicia's eyes dart around the room—to the bathroom door, to Rachel, back to the door. Afraid Alicia is warning her that the busser is coming up behind her, Rachel peers over her shoulder.

Nothing.

Rachel can't run out and leave Alicia. If he comes back, he will know someone else was here, and who knows what he will do then.

Walking slowly over to Alicia, Rachel notices a five-gallon bucket with a roll of toilet paper beside it and a bedpan perched on top—the obvious source of the stench. There are numerous water jugs, some empty, some partially full, and dozens of plastic bottles of high-protein nutritional drinks.

What the fuck is this place? It's like a third-world, prison hospital.

Alicia doesn't look weak or emaciated, but Rachel kneels and asks her if she can walk.

Alicia nods.

Scanning the room, Rachel berates herself for being so unprepared. Stupid, stupid idiot. You came out here looking for a kidnapped woman! You should have tools—

Shut up. I'm a goddamn attorney not a cop. I don't even own bolt cutters.

Looking at the handicap rail, it has scratches all over and the drywall around each end has been gouged and scraped, no doubt by Alicia trying to get free. On the floor is a hefty black, metal flashlight. Rachel picks it up and gives it a bounce to assess if it is heavy enough to do anything to the handrail.

Shaking her head, Alicia says, "Tried. Too short to pry bar off."

What Rachel needs is a crowbar or a hammer to bust at

least one end of the rail off the wall to slide off the one end of the cuff. Alicia would still have the other cuff on her wrist, but that won't stop her from walking, or running, out of this hellhole.

"I'm going to look around the cab—"

"Don't," Alicia says, her eyes flying open wide with terror. "You can't leave me her. Please don't leave. Please! I can't—"

"I'll stay where you can hear me the whole time. I just need to find something to get this rail off the wall. Okay? Then we can get out here."

Alicia lets out a pained grunt of defeat, her body crumpling some, her eyes still wide with terror.

"I'm not leaving here without you. Promise." Slowly backing out of the bathroom, Rachel keeps her eyes locked on Alicia, repeating, "I'm right here. I'm right here. I'm right here."

In the front room, Rachel grabs the chair, but it's too light, the wooden legs would snap in half. She lifts the wooden crate, which is also too flimsy.

A rusty woodstove sits in the corner at the other end of the cabin. With two strides Rachel is there but finds no metal poker rod, not even a piece of firewood.

Continually reassuring Alicia that she is still here, tears of frustration and anxiety and powerlessness and fear start streaming down Rachel's face.

Near the woodstove is a small table with a drawer, an ashtray on top. Inside the drawer there is only a lighter and a tiny, useless pocketknife.

A pocketknife! With a jolt of excitement, Rachel remembers the very sturdy, multi-tooled pocketknife Aaron gave her on one of their hikes. That handrail must be screwed onto the wall. Her knife has screwdriver heads. Small ones, but they should work.

Swinging her backpack off, she shoves her hands into the pack, digging, hoping. "I'm right here, Alicia." *Please let it be —there! The pocketknife.*

Swiping away her tears and putting on what she hopes is a calm face, Rachel goes back to the bathroom and examines the handrail. There are four screws at each end where it is mounted to the wall.

"I've got a screwdriver," Rachel says, starting on the first screw.

Clenching her eyes shut, Alicia nods vehemently.

It takes more time and hand strength than Rachel expected to remove the screws with a pocketknife screwdriver. The whole time, Rachel keeps the doorway in her sights, dreading the thought of the busser's silhouette appearing.

By the time she removes the last screw, the pressure on her palm has Rachel's hand bleeding again and has shredded the medical glove.

With one end of the rail loose, Rachel puts her foot on the wall for leverage and pulls the rail far enough away from the wall that Alicia maneuvers the handcuff off the rail. It comes free with a *thunk*, and Alicia falls back onto the blankets. The cuff dangles from Alicia's wrist, the sleeve of her coat bunched up above it. The skin on her wrist is red and raw.

Before Rachel can try to help Alicia up, Alicia scrambles to her feet—looking shaky but determined—and heads to the front of the cabin.

"Front door's bolted shut, so we go out this way," Rachel says, kicking the bigger glass shards out from underneath the window. She drags the chair to the window and, pointing at Alicia's shoeless foot, warns her to be careful.

Alicia doesn't hesitate. In seconds, she is up on the chair and out the window.

36

DAY THIRTEEN, 11:50 AM

AS THEY START off down the trail, Alicia looks wobbly, so Rachel wedges her hand under Alicia's upper arm for added support. Alicia breaks into a jog for a few minutes but quickly slows back to a fast, stumbling walk. After Alicia catches her breath and gains momentum again, she breaks into another jog. If she is stepping on sharp or hard rocks with her stocking foot, she isn't showing any signs of it. Or doesn't care about the pain.

Ruby, meanwhile, appears to be having a blast, racing through the woods, her ears flapping like wings. If somebody else was out there, she wouldn't be so oblivious, she would be on Rachel's heel. This should comfort Rachel. It doesn't.

Rachel wants to ask Alicia when the busser was last at the cabin, how often he comes, at what time, but she doesn't want to cause any more trauma. And she certainly doesn't want to do anything to slow Alicia down. So, Rachel keeps looking over her shoulder, scanning the woods around them, certain that he will, any moment, crash through the forest.

When Rachel finally catches a glimpse of her car, she is

flooded with relief. So giddy with relief, she could break into laughter. Instead, she breaks into tears. She is feeling slightly hysterical. Not hysterical as in funny; hysterical as in she is about to lose it.

Pointing at the car, Rachel says, "We made it. There's my car."

Alicia's gaze follows Rachel's finger, and she sees the car through the trees. She starts stumbling, probably from exhaustion and euphoria and blinded by the tears also streaming down her face.

To steady her, Rachel slides her hand under Alicia's arm again. Alicia leans hard into Rachel, who half carries, half pulls Alicia the last hundred feet.

As gently as she can, Rachel hurries Alicia into the car, constantly sweeping her gaze around the woods, up and down the road. She doesn't bother snapping a seatbelt on Alicia because Alicia is rocking back and forth, muttering, over and over, "Thank you. Oh, god, thank you. Thank you."

Scrambling into the driver's seat, Rachel locks the doors, first thing. They are both breathing heavily. Even Ruby is panting loudly from the backseat.

Rachel does a three-pointer to get the car turned around on the road, constantly checking all around them and murmuring, "You're safe. You're safe now. It's okay."

Once they are headed down the Forest Service road, Rachel's pulse slows but her heart feels like it is lodged in her throat. To make matters worse, Alicia starts shivering.

Assuming her shivers are from sweaty, damp clothes chilling her now that she is no longer on the move, Rachel cranks up the heat. Alternating hands on the steering wheel, Rachel shimmies out of her jacket and clumsily, while driving, drapes it over top of Alicia's coat. Somewhere on the trail back there, Alicia lost the pink pom-pom cap, but Rachel isn't stopping to put her ski cap on Alicia.

The shivering becomes more pronounced, almost violent. *Fuck! Is she having a seizure?*

Driving as fast as she can on the gravel road, watching Alicia in her peripheral vision, Rachel figures the quicker she gets her to a hospital the better.

Gradually, the shivering slows to periodic trembles, then Alicia leans her head against the passenger window. Rachel flits her gaze off the road long enough to ensure Alicia is still breathing.

She is going into shock, Rachel thinks.

As soon as they reach the paved road, Rachel's phone starts dinging with notifications. Cell reception. Alicia hears it, too, and rolls her head in Rachel's direction. In Alicia's eyes there is a glimmer of hope.

Gently, Rachel says, "I think it's safe to pull over, real quick, so I can text the police."

Alicia nods.

Pulling to the side of the road, the engine still running, Rachel holds her water bottle in front of Alicia, who grabs it greedily and starts drinking. Her head back, eyes closed, she looks as if she is in ecstasy. Water spills from around her lips and darkens the front of her filthy shirt as she swallows, loudly, glurg after glurg, until the bottle is drained.

Dropping the bottle to the floor, Alicia lowers her forehead to the dashboard. Rachel can see her eyes are wide open, glassy, staring vacantly at the floor.

Keeping an eye on the rearview mirror and the road ahead and the bare, woody bushes next to the car, Rachel quickly texts Chris: Have Alicia Meyers. Taking her to St. Michael's ER. Should be there in 10 mins.

She doesn't wait for his reply before pulling back onto the road.

Driving now on blacktop, close to the highway, the road is straight and flat, so Rachel accelerates to fifty-five miles per hour. Silently, she lets out a long, slow exhale.

Then she spots it. A quarter of a mile ahead is a red car driving towards them.

Her heart plummets.

Glancing at Alicia, Rachel figures she won't be visible to the busser since she is all crumpled forward. Besides, she isn't about to ask Alicia to duck down and hide.

Flicking the sun visor to her left, Rachel fumbles to put on her sunglasses then pretends to rub her nose, hand over her mouth. It's the best disguise she can come up with in the ten seconds it takes for the cars to be almost side-by-side.

Shit, shit, shit. That is him.

As she passes the red car, Rachel stares straight ahead. She doesn't breathe. Her only movement is the feigned nose rubbing.

In her rearview mirror, plain as day, Rachel sees the license plate: CAU-1863

37

DAY THIRTEEN, 12:00 NOON

ON TODAY'S drive to his mother's cabin, Wayne listens to the live broadcast his father told him about. When he loses cell reception, he takes off the headset. They weren't talking about much of anything today anyway.

When he pulls up to the gate, he hops out of the car, whistling as he lifts the latch and starts to swing the gate open. In a muddy section of the gravel road that is still damp from last night's rain, he spots tire tracks. He freezes.

Tire tracks? From who? This is Mama's place.

Whipping his head around, he scans the area in front of the gate, the edges of the road. A car was here, then backed in and out to turn around. There are a few pawprints that look like they were left by a small dog.

Frantically, Wayne pushes the gate all the way open, drives through and doesn't bother getting out and shutting the gate. He pushes play on the broadcast then remembers there is no cell reception. Gunning the engine, he races up the road, slowing at the big U-turn.

He drives through the campground and straight past his

usual parking spot. His fingers are white knuckled around the steering wheel as the car is jostled left and right, up and down, on the overgrown road, branches thwacking against his windows and screeching against the side of the car.

When he can drive no further on the overgrown road, he flies out of the car and runs to the cabin.

One of the windows is shattered, the glass knocked out of the frame.

Fumbling to unlock the padlock, he finally opens it and skids into the back room.

Slapping his hands over his mouth, his words come out muffled. "No, no, no, no, no."

Sobbing and muttering that he has to find his mother, Wayne stumbles back to the car.

From the backseat comes Papa's harsh voice. *You blew it. I knew you couldn't handle this.*

Wayne doesn't even look over his shoulder. His mother taught him years ago to pay no mind to his father. Just put on your headset or turn on a TV show, she always told him.

The road is too narrow and overgrown to turn around here, so Wayne jams the car in reverse and backs up as fast as he can without smashing into trees.

You were supposed to take care of her here, Papa hisses.

"I did *everything* you said," Wayne snaps. "Gave her the meds. Put a lock on the door."

At the campground, Wayne turns the car around. "Just leave me alone, Papa. *Please.* I have to think."

That is when he spots it. Near the edge of the campground, stuck on the low branch of a tree, is his mother's favorite ski cap.

Slamming on the brakes, Wayne stares at the cap for a

few seconds, his jaw hanging open. He doesn't want to leave it there but can't bear the thought of touching it. That cap, dangling from its pink pom-pom, is proof that someone took his mother because she would never leave it behind. And wherever she is, she will be so cold without it. It kept her warm through all her chemo, all her hospital stays, while she was at the cabin ... she needs her ski cap.

Hurrying out of the car, he snatches the cap off the branch.

Back in the car, Wayne drives like a maniac, taking the big U-turn so fast that the back wheels skid off the gravel and churn into the soft soil at the edge of the road.

"Aaahh!" He jerks the steering wheel the other way to get all four tires righted onto the gravel road again.

When he sees the open gate ahead, he flies through it. There is no point in stopping to close the gate, he thinks, his lips pinched tight in anger. Mama is gone.

38

DAY THIRTEEN, 1:05 PM

THERE ARE two Sheriff's cars at the curb in front of the emergency room and one at each of the three hospital parking lot entrances. Chris is standing in front of the emergency room door with four other deputies. As soon as Chris sees Rachel's car, he points and three medical staff push a gurney towards the car. All five deputies follow them to the car.

"We're at the hospital now," Rachel says softly. "Some nurses are coming over. They will take care of you."

"Will someone get my—" a sob jerks out of Alicia "—get my daughter? Is she okay?"

"Uhh ... the police are here. I'm sure they're going to call ..." She isn't sure who they will call, so she doesn't say anything more.

As soon as her car stops, a female nurse opens the passenger door, kneels and starts talking, soothingly, to Alicia, while the other two medical staff stand at either end of the gurney. Three deputies flank them, at a slight distance, and continually scan the parking lot.

Chris and the other deputy come to the driver's side as Rachel steps out of the car.

"You hurt?" Chris asks.

Numbly, she stands there, fingers still on the door handle staring blankly, eyes unfocused. "Uh ..." She shakes her head, trying to snap back to reality.

"Let's have someone look at that." Chris points at her bloody hand.

"Huh?" Rachel looks at Chris then at her hand. "No, it's not ... I don't need a doctor. It was just glass ... a little sliver."

She hears the gentle murmur of the nurse talking to Alicia. From the backseat, Ruby lets out a, *Boof!*

Rachel opens the back door, and Ruby jumps out and gives a quick lick to Rachel's wounded hand.

Alicia is on the gurney now, curled up on her side. The deputies maintain their perimeter as Alicia is wheeled into the emergency room. The female nurse walks alongside the gurney, and Alicia clutches the nurse's hand with both of hers, as if she will never let go. The handcuff still dangles from her wrist.

"I can't believe I found her. I can't believe she's—" alive, is what Rachel thinks "—that she's okay."

"Tell me exactly where you found her," Chris says. "And what happened. If anyone else was there."

Turning to Chris and Deputy Williams, reality swoops down onto Rachel in full force. Everything rushes back to her like a horror movie spooling out before her eyes. They need to get back to the cabin.

Her words tumble out. "He passed us on the way out. The busser. Drove right by me..." She leans into her car and grabs her phone, taps open a map and points at the screen.

"He passed us right here on Mountain View Road. About a mile from the highway. The red Corolla. It was him."

"And where'd you find Alicia?" Deputy Williams says, finding Mountain View Road on his phone.

"In a cabin right here off a road. Let's see ... okay, well, the road doesn't show on the map. It's really more of a wide trail, overgrown, that heads into the woods past the outhouse building. You can't see the cabin from there. You have to go up that road about ... a few hundred yards."

"Anyone else up there? In the cabin?"

She shakes her head. "No one."

"At the campground?" Chris asks.

"No. No people. No cars. There's a gate across the road. It's not locked, so—"

"I'll call for back up," Chris says to Deputy Williams. "You get up to the cabin."

Deputy Williams speeds out of the parking lot, the red and blue lights atop his cruiser swirling, while Chris climbs into his car, leaving the door swung open, and talks to dispatch at length.

A loud ringing begins in Rachel's ears, so she only picks up some of Chris' words. "... Ada Creek Campground ... suspect could be in vicinity ... red Corolla ... road blocks ..."

Rachel becomes chilled and light-headed so sits down on the curb, which is painted red there in front of the emergency room entrance. The concrete is cold, sucking any last warmth from her. Crossing her arms against her chest, her eyes focus on the asphalt under her feet and at the red line on which she is sitting. Ruby sidles up next to her.

The ringing in Rachel's ears has become a deafening

buzz. A car drives by, but she can't hear it. She can see Chris' mouth moving, but all she hears is a persistent, whirring *bzzzz*.

Then, without knowing how much time has passed, Chris is suddenly next to her. "Let me get—"

Startled, Rachel recoils.

"Whoa," he says, "didn't mean to—" He notices she is trembling. "Come on. Let's get in my car, get some heat going."

Chris hooks Rachel's elbow and helps her up from the curb. As they walk towards the cruiser, Ruby hops in the open door like she owns the place, settling in the passenger seat. Sliding in next to Ruby, Rachel appreciates the dog's warmth against her leg.

As the car warms up, the ringing in Rachel's ears lessens into a faint humming. A car drives past, which she hears this time. Next to them, the emergency room doors slide open with a soft *whoosh*.

No longer numb, Rachel feels overwhelmed. As if she was holding it all together in front of Alicia, the world now seems to crash down around her—all the fear and adrenaline, the scene in the cabin, Alicia's condition, the handcuffs, the nauseating smells. Rachel is sickened and enraged and devastated. Somewhere, too, deep in her gut, she is euphoric. Alicia is alive. Alicia's daughter still has a mother. A mother is still alive!

With that, Rachel begins to cry. Ruby immediately licks Rachel's chin, and Rachel pulls back out of reach of the dog's tongue. Rachel loves Ruby almost more than anything, but that scavenger will *eat* just about anything. When Chris hands her some tissues, Rachel continues to cry. After a minute, she takes a shuddering inhale and is, finally, done. Drained. Empty.

Wiping her eyes and cheeks, she notices Chris is staring out the windshield, his jaw set with—what? Anger? Pity because he can't stand people crying? She can relate. No, he looks disappointed, Rachel thinks. He probably wants to get my statement and get up to that cabin. Instead, he's stuck here waiting for me to stop blubbering.

Wanting him to find every shred of evidence to arrest the busser, Rachel forces herself to focus. "Uh ... let's see ..." The shrill ringing in her ears is gone, and she no longer feels icy, but she can't think straight.

"You okay to do this now?"

Probably not. Rachel nods.

"Tell me about the cabin," Chris says.

"Uh, the broken window, that was from me." Her voice is quavering. "That's how I got in and when I cut my hand." It's all coming back to her. "She was in a back room. There's a handrail on the wall. She was cuffed to it. Uhh ... what else? Something else. Something, something. I can't remember. There's all kinds of evidence in the cabin: water jugs, protein shakes. Lots of stuff. We have to get back up there."

Chris lets out a snort. *"You're* not going."

Her eyes grow wide, but before she says a word, Chris puts his hand up to shut down her protest. "I'm going to call the rest of this in." He points at the radio mic. "That cabin is a crime scene. Very soon, deputies will be swarming all over that area. You're *not* going back up there."

Listening to the back and forth between Chris and a

dispatch operator, his words sink in to Rachel's rattled brain: *You're not going back up there.*

Of course, she thinks. I'm not going back to that cabin. Never.

39

DAY THIRTEEN, 1:15 PM

WAYNE JUMPS when a sound crackles from his phone. He is back within cell reception. The broadcast is back on. His father told him to start listening to the live Sheriff's dispatch scanner after his mother was brought to the cabin.

Speeding out of the forest, gravel spitting up from his tires, he can't make out the dispatcher's words. Groping in the passenger seat for his headset, he slides it over his head and cranks up the volume.

"... units report to Ada Creek Campground on a ten-fifty-seven."

A ten-fifty-seven? What is a ten-fifty-seven?

No longer on the gravel road, he steps harder on the gas pedal, driving way too fast for this winding, two-lane road. If his mother was here, she would say, Now, Wayne, you slow this car down before you wreck. You hear me?

"Sorry," he whispers. "I'll be careful." Quickly, he swipes the back of his hand across his nose and mouth, wiping away the tears and snot tickling his skin there. He wipes the mess onto his pant leg.

More staticky, garbled talking comes from the phone. "...Forest Service Road two zero six eight. Repeat: Road two zero six eight."

That's the road I was just on, Wayne thinks.

Faster, Papa commands. *Get to the highway before the cops get here.*

There is no time to waste, no time to be stopped or questioned by a policeman. Wayne needs to find his mother.

He stomps the gas pedal all the way to the floor.

As he nears the interchange with the highway, Wayne slows his car enough to turn onto the highway heading west. This is exactly when he sees not one or two but four Sheriff's vehicles exiting the eastbound highway. One by one, the cruisers drive through the underpass, right underneath Wayne's car, and head in the direction of Forest Service Road 2068.

"Unknown if suspect is in the vicinity," the dispatcher says. "Unknown if suspect is armed."

The suspect? The person who took Mama? Maybe the police will find Mama, Wayne thinks, feeling confused and foggy. That might be good but, for some reason, this thought makes his body tense and his armpits sting with perspiration. Fully expecting to hear something from the backseat, he peeks in the rearview mirror. Nothing. Silence.

Blowing out a big gush of air and tension, he drives at the exact speed limit. He drops his phone in the passenger seat. *Mama would scold me if I so much as touched my phone while driving.* That makes him smile, remembering the last time she scolded him about that, and he told her to get him a car with Bluetooth then.

Thinking of her reminds Wayne that Mama is going to need her pain medication soon.

More chatter and squawks come from the phone. Now that he is driving on a smoother, quieter road, Wayne can hear the dispatch broadcast loud and clear.

"Ten-fifty-seven victim no longer on site," the dispatcher says.

Wayne's eyes go wide. *The victim? Is that Mama?*

As if the dispatcher read his mind, there is a clicking sound, static, then, "Repeat, victim not on site. Victim has been taken to hospital."

Wayne's vision blurs. Exiting the highway, he pulls to the side of the road.

"Not the hospital," Wayne whispers. "Don't take her back there."

His papa starts in on him again. *She's probably there for good this time cuz you couldn't keep her at the cabin.*

Clenching the steering wheel, Wayne begins rocking back and forth, more and more forcefully. "I tried to keep her there," he screams. "Kept the hospital ... safety ... thingy on her wrist, but ..." Repeatedly, he smacks his chest into the steering wheel then slams his back against the seat. "But she kept ... trying to get the handcu—"

Safety restraint, Papa corrects.

"She wanted the—" Wayne starts sobbing. "She wanted—that safety—restraint—off." He lets out a wail. "And begging—she kept begging—to leave."

PART 3

A WITNESS

40

DAY THIRTEEN, 1:30 PM

WHILE CHRIS' police radio explodes with communications about the cabin, he drills Rachel about any more information.

Her brain is on overload.

What else? Think. Think. Closing her eyes, she pictures the scene. The cabin location, check, she told him. The handcuffs, check. Handrail, check. The broken window, check. Oh, right, the bloody glove.

"I'm not sure how important it is—"

"Just tell me. I'll decide," he says, opening his laptop.

Rachel charges on. "There's a torn up medical glove, might still have a bloody napkin stuffed in it. I think I just dropped it on the floor of my car. That's not her blood, it's mine. From the cut"—she points at her hand—"when I climbed through the window. It was a dark red napkin to begin with, so ... it wasn't that much blood."

She is forgetting something and berates herself for not taking pictures.

Oh, like I was going to take pictures of a poor woman,

scared for her life, while I was having a panic attack. For once, Rachel's brain is on her side.

Remembering the terror in Alicia's eyes reminds Rachel how she rummaged through the cabin looking for tools.

"I couldn't find a ... anything to pry the handrail off the wall, but I looked through the cabin, touched a few things. The chair, wooden box, a drawer. There was a lighter and a little pocketknife in the drawer. I had on a medical glove, so my prints shouldn't be on them, but ... I don't know, maybe."

The car grows quiet except for the sound of Chris clicking away on the laptop keyboard.

When he stops typing, he looks over at her. "So, how'd you find that cabin?"

Her mouth is, suddenly, quite dry. Parched. Licking her lips, Rachel begins. "Umm ... Ruby—" she glances down at her "—she found the cabin."

Chris rolls his finger in a circle, indicating for her to keep talking.

Clearing her throat, she says, "When Dad and I were at Bucatini the other day, I asked the busser for some napkins. That's how I got close enough to get a premonition about the cabin. When I realized the napkins would have his scent on them ..." She cringes guiltily.

"Ruby found the cabin using the scent on those napkins?"

She nods. "It isn't visible from the campground. I would've never walked into the woods that far because the road is all overgrown."

"Why'd you think Alicia was up at that campground in the first place?"

"I'd been scouring internet maps for days—"

"Me too," he says.

Surprised to hear that because she really thought he was dismissing her premonition, she stares at him for a few seconds before continuing. "On a map, that campground is, pretty much, a straight shot from the restaurant. And it had these clusters of buildings ... I thought one of them could be a cabin. Once Ruby started tracking his scent at the gate, I had to keep going. She practically dragged me to that cabin. Then I heard Alicia—" Rachel's eyes sting with tears remembering her frantic, pleading whimper.

Chris stares at her profile for a few beats then shakes his head. "That was brave ... and really dangerous. You're lucky the perp wasn't there."

"I know. Believe me, I was scared shitless. But once I heard her in there ... I couldn't walk away."

Sometimes you can *stop a person from dying.*

Glancing in his rearview mirror, Chris says, "Listen, I hate to tell you this, but ... we need to impound your—"

"Wait, am I"—she whips her head around to see a tow truck turning into the parking lot—"a suspect?"

"Of course not." He gives her a look like she is being ridiculous. "But your car's got evidence, victim's DNA, probably the perp's DNA. We can't risk losing anything. We've gotta scrub it for evidence. Your car's ... basically part of the crime scene."

"Chris, I didn't have a choice up there. I had no cell reception and couldn't call for—"

"I'm not saying you did anything wrong. You probably saved her life. This is all just procedure. The victim was in your car and ... you're a key witness."

It takes several seconds for her to grasp the gravity of what he is saying. She is a witness and might have to testify. Under oath. She can't say that she was out for a hike and stumbled onto Alicia in the cabin. That would be perjury. And her premonition, getting the busser's scent from the napkins, she can't withhold that information if she gets put on a witness stand.

Fuck! I'm an attorney. I know all this.

Rachel is too spent, physically and mentally, to analyze all the ramifications of what she has done. And something inside of her wants to give up the battle. Let everyone hear about her damned premonitions. What is the worst thing that can happen? This isn't the Salem witch trials. Are they going to burn her alive for saving Alicia's life?

"And you should know," Chris says, "the media listens to our dispatch scanner twenty-four-seven. I'm sure they started calling the Sheriff's office soon as they heard the chatter about a missing person being found. They're probably headed up to the cabin right now to try and get video footage. And witness statements *are* part of the public record."

"Please do not release my name until the busser is arrested."

"Until a *suspect* is arrested," Chris interjects.

Rachel glares at him.

"I'm trying," he says, "but ... names have a way of getting out there."

"A way of getting out there?" Her voice grows louder.

"Whoa," he says, his hands up defensively, "I'm on your side here, trying to protect your ident—"

"Can I get some kind of witness protection?" From the

apologetic look on his face, she can tell *that* isn't going to happen.

"I'll get a detail put on your house. Have a deputy cruise by regularly. At night, too."

Terrific. Well, this isn't the mafia I'm dealing with. It's a busser.

DAY THIRTEEN, 3:00 PM

BACK AT HIS HOUSE, Wayne races to the bathroom, his stomach in spasms, and kneels in front of the toilet and retches. Clinging to the toilet, he heaves until there is nothing more to vomit.

After rinsing his mouth, he dares a few sips of water, recalling that this is what his mother did when she had the chemo sickness—little sips. The thought of her makes him sad and worried and lost.

Wayne splashes his face with cool water. "What do I do?" he mumbles, looking in the mirror. His mind is reeling and muddled with information, so much information that his brain hurts. "Report her missing to the police?"

Nooo, comes Papa's voice, angry, as usual. *Absolutely no police. Can't trust the bastards.*

Wayne cowers, hating it when his papa cusses.

Baffled, his thoughts begin drifting, imagining the picnic he and his mother should be having. An indoor picnic, of course, because she was supposed to stay inside the cabin where it was warm and safe. Remembering how much his mother wanted to leave the cabin fills Wayne with remorse.

But it was for her own good, Wayne reassures himself. That's what the man wearing the surgical mask and gloves told me.

Wayne has stared blankly at his reflection for so long now, he doesn't know who he is looking at anymore. The face staring back at him has turned into a collage of blurred ovals —two blue ones and a pink one—plus a mop of hair on top.

"Come on, stupid brain," he says, slapping the side of his head, "work!" Another slap. "Work!" he smacks his head, hard.

I'd be in trouble if Mama saw that. Gently rubbing his head where it stings, the pain reminds him that, by now, his mother must really need pain meds. On the scanner, they said the victim is at St. Michael's. If that's Mama, he thinks, they probably gave her pain meds.

The hospital! He took her to Saint Michael's for chemo every week. Their number is on his speed dial.

Racing to his phone, he calls the hospital. When the operator at Saint Michael's answers, Wayne explains that he is looking for his mother and meticulously spells out her first and last name—Ginnie Stuart—because everyone always gets both of those spelled wrong.

There is a clickety click sound as the operator types into a keyboard "Sorry, sir, but we don't have a patient by that name here."

"She might have come through the ER," he says, "in the last ... uh ..." He looks at the time but really can't remember what time he left the cabin or how long ago he heard the police dispatch mention Saint Michael's. "Uh ... sometime this afternoon."

"Hmm ... let me check. Can you hold?"

"Yes. Thank you, ma'am." Wayne listens to the hold music. It's the kind his mother likes, with violins and no words.

"Sir, we haven't had anyone named Ginnie Stuart come through the ER today. I'm sorry."

Now Wayne is paralyzed with confusion. Who did they take from the cabin to Saint Michael's? And where is his mother?

His papa gets up close—so close that Wayne feels his breath on the back of his neck—and yells that he needs to listen to the damn police scanner and check the news.

Frantically, Wayne brushes the back of his neck, as if a spider was crawling up it. "For what? What do I listen for?" He bites on his lip so he won't cry. His papa curses really, really bad when Wayne cries.

Papa says each word slow and loud. *To. Find. Your. Mother.*

"Don't treat me like I'm stupid!" Wayne yells. Raging inside, he wants to punch and kick and shove his papa.

Except his father is never there when Wayne turns to face him.

In his mother's bedroom—Wayne likes it in there because it still smells like her—he plugs his laptop into a charger and plops onto her bed to check for any news and listen to the police scanner. He still isn't exactly sure what he is listening for but has pen and paper ready in case he gets any clues about his mother's location.

After an hour, his stomach growls, reminding him that he

never ate lunch. His computer is fully charged now, so he unplugs it and carries it to the kitchen.

When the microwave dings, he slides out the mac and cheese, peels back the plastic and sets it on the table next to his phone and the pen and paper. Wayne is blowing on a steaming forkful of mac and cheese when someone says something over the scanner about the cabin.

Scarfing down that bite, Wayne grabs the pen and scribbles, trying to keep up with all the staticky words bombarding him. There is talk, back and forth between multiple deputies and the dispatcher. They haven't found any suspects in the vicinity of the cabin. Coordinates and various road names are given for where they are searching.

Hey, that's Mama's cabin, Wayne thinks.

More chatter about road blocks and perimeters. Wayne doesn't know how to spell some of the words and can't write as fast as they are talking and can't make out some of the garbled voices. Already, Wayne is overwhelmed.

Plus, Wayne is starving. The mac and cheese smells so good and that first bite has his mouth watering like crazy. Scooping up another bite, he chews quickly and swallows, then takes a few more bites, all the while listening intently to the conversation on the scanner.

From the scanner: "What is the victim's status?"

Wayne perks up at the mention of the victim, though he is still confused if that is his mother. Picking up his pen, he leans in close to his phone.

A flurry of questions and answers come fast now, too fast for Wayne.

"Victim is at the hospital."

"Has victim ID'd the suspect?"

"No."

"Did the witness see a suspect?"

"No suspects were seen by witness."

At the mention of a witness and a suspect, Wayne becomes thoroughly confused. He doesn't understand, or can't keep straight, who is the victim, the suspect and, now, the witness. There are three people? Which one is his mother —the witness or the victim?

There is only crackling silence from the scanner broadcast. Secretly, he wishes the broadcast would end. He peeks over his shoulder to see if Papa is watching. Nowhere in sight.

Wayne hits the pause button on the Sheriff broadcast then scrolls to the King County news website and clicks WATCH LIVE.

A pretty lady on the news speaks into a microphone and looks right at Wayne. "We have breaking news on the missing person case of Alicia Meyers." The image of Alicia Meyers flashes on the screen. Wayne recognizes her from the posters all around town. The police also talked to him at Bucatini about Alicia Meyers, but he couldn't help them because he wasn't at work the night she went missing.

The news lady continues. "Late this morning, Alicia Meyers was found, alive, in a remote cabin near Ada Creek Campground. Again, Alicia Meyers, who has been missing for two weeks has been found, alive, and taken to the hospital."

"We don't have all the details but will be reporting to you live as more information emerges. What we do know is that no suspect has been arrested yet, but there is an active investigation underway at that campground and the surrounding area. Now, this is a heavily forested area, with numerous trails so, a suspect could be difficult to find."

Watching video footage on the computer screen, Wayne takes a sharp inhale. "That's Mama's cabin." He leans in close and watches as deputies crawl around the cabin and through the woods, like an army of ants. There is even a helicopter flying overhead.

"We also know," the news lady says, "that Alicia Meyers was found by a Ms. Rachel Sharpe, who was hiking in the woods with her dog when she, somehow, came upon Alicia."

That's her, Papa says. *That lady knows where your mother is.*

Wayne has no idea who this Rachel person is, but if his papa says this is the lady, then Wayne will find her. He scribbles down her name, feeling very proud.

After gobbling down the rest of the mac and cheese, he starts an internet search, smiling as he remembers his mother always telling him how smart he is when it comes to finding things on that darn computer.

———

Turns out the search for Rachel Sharpe isn't so easy to find because there are two ways to spell that last name: with and without the letter "E" on the end. And there are lots of people with that last name. Searching in only Franklin County for that name with both spellings still provides a few results. But the one spelling, "Rachel Sharpe," shows up several times in documents with long, businessy-looking words that Wayne doesn't understand.

Wayne pieces together that Rachel Sharpe is always

listed on these documents with the letters "J.D." after her name. Digging deeper, he discovers that "J.D." means the person is an attorney.

Wayne's eyes sting from staring at the computer for so long. In the search field, he types: RACHEL SHARPE FRANKLIN COUNTY ATTORNEY. At the top of the search results is a website at RACHELSHARPELAW.COM. Pressing his fingertips against his eyelids for a few seconds, he hopes this is the right lady because he is exhausted.

Opening his eyes and blinking, Wayne clicks on the website. Right there in front of him, almost as big as life, is the face of a woman he saw at Bucatini last week. *Maybe she followed me to the cabin*, he thinks. *I have to call the pol—*

I said no police! Papa booms. *Just find that woman, you imbecile.*

42

DAY THIRTEEN, 4:00 PM

PATRICK SAT in Derby Park and talked to a man on the sex offender hotline for over an hour. He tried to be honest enough to get some relief from his shame and rage but not so honest that he risked going back to prison. After the call, though he still didn't fully trust himself, Patrick agreed to a plan that could keep him from sabotaging everything he has worked for.

It was a simple plan: go get something to eat; go to the gym and workout; go to the Alano Club and hang out until the five p.m. men's A.A. meeting; go home and eat dinner; and call the hotline to check in before crashing (earlier, if he needs to talk again). A very simple plan.

All went well until he walks into the Alano Club. The TV is on and several people are clustered around it, talking excitedly. Pouring himself a cup of coffee, Patrick nods and says hi to a couple of men. It doesn't take long before he figures out what all the buzz is about: Alicia Meyers was found.

Patrick goes cold. This is too much. Several hours ago, he

fucked Alicia's face, and now she has been found. He turns to leave then remembers that he has nowhere else to go.

Just relax, he tells himself, you never hurt Alicia. That was just a poster.

Someone in the group around the TV looks up from his phone and says, "This report here says she's alive."

Sitting at a table with his back to the TV, he takes a sip of coffee and wonders if he should stay or go, but alone in his apartment doesn't sound safe. He decides to stay and try not to listen to the news. He definitely isn't going to watch it. If he gets triggered, he will step outside for a smoke or call the hotline.

"Okay, shush everyone," the woman behind the counter says. "Here it comes."

The Alano Club goes quiet. An anchorwoman warns that the coming report involves descriptions of abduction of the victim, Alicia Meyers, which some viewers may find triggering.

You have no fuckin' idea, Patrick thinks. Tuning out the newscaster, Patrick recites his mantra in his head. One is a gun: Two: is it true? Three: re-see.

The anchorwoman describes breaking news in the case of Alicia Meyers, who has been missing for thirteen days. "According to our investigations, we have learned that a woman named Rachel Sharpe was hiking around Ada Creek Campground and heard a woman's voice coming from inside an abandoned cabin."

This gives Patrick a jolt of fear. He keeps his eyes and hands locked onto his coffee mug. He doesn't dare risk seeing Alicia's face again. This morning's trigger almost cost him his freedom; he can't afford another one. A single misstep and his world will be crushed.

The newscast continues. "Apparently, Ms. Sharpe broke into the cabin and found Alicia Meyers inside, unable to escape. We aren't clear yet if she was tied up or, exactly, how she was being held captive there."

Refocus. Refocus. You get to see the horses tomorrow.

The anchorwoman states that they expect to have a statement from Sheriff Garcia soon and will provide updates as more information becomes available. She repeats that Alicia Meyers has been found, alive, and is in the hospital in stable condition.

With his back still to the TV, Patrick takes another sip of coffee. *Two: it ain't true that she liked what that sick fuck did to her.*

43

DAY FOURTEEN, 7:30 AM

THE FIRST THING Wayne does this morning is call in sick. He tells Adriana that he isn't feeling too well and would like to take a sick day. He doesn't like to lie, but he really does feel sick with all the jitters in his belly.

In the bathroom, he checks his reflection and notices his hair is getting greasy. Sprinkling dry shampoo powder along the part in his hair, he massages it in. His mother tries to make him shampoo his hair every day, but he likes the powder. It's quicker than a shower.

Next, he microwaves two breakfast sandwiches, slips his binoculars over his neck and enters 367 ADAMS ST., the address he found on RACHELSHARPELAW.COM, into his phone's mapping app.

Wayne drives by the building where Rachel Sharpe is supposed to work, but he needs to pull over, out of sight, to double-check the address. This isn't a small building like he was expecting; it's a big, two-story, brick building, one of the old ones that is plain and boxy but restored so it looks pretty now. It's too big for an office with one attorney, he knows that. This is the correct address, but on her website, he notices "Ste. A" is listed after the street address.

He doesn't know what "Ste. A" means. Some other part of Adams Street? Another section of town? Or maybe South to East, but then what does the A stand for?

Wayne wants to go back home. He starts rocking, anxiously, forward and back.

Look it up you idiot, Papa says from behind him.

Instantly, he stops rocking. His papa hates when he rocks; says it makes him look like a big baby. Wayne does as he is told and searches the internet for the meaning of "Ste." The first result says this is an abbreviation for "suite," which is an office or apartment within a larger building.

"I get it!" Wayne says, chuckling nervously. "Papa—her office is somewhere *inside* that big building." Silence from the back seat.

Wayne circles the block three times, scoping out a spot where he won't be visible. In one corner of the building's parking lot, there is a big fountain, with no water running through it, and a cluster of trees. He can't park on that side because the trees and fountain block his view.

Finally, he finds a spot where he can see most of the parking lot and has a clear view of the entrance. He parks behind another car and next to a bush that provides his car with some cover, even though all the leaves have already fallen.

With the engine off, he turns the volume on the scanner broadcast down low and focuses his binoculars on the entrance of the building, so, if he sees her, the binoculars will already be in focus. At this level of magnification, things move through the binocular's view so fast. He hates it when the view is all blurry, and he misses whatever he is watching for.

All settled in, Wayne unwraps his first breakfast sandwich. The sandwich is still warm, and he inhales the sausage aroma.

Dozens of people go into the building before he finally sees Rachel Sharpe. She has a cute brown and white dog with her. His mother isn't with her though. Maybe she will come out of the building with his mother.

Wayne sits there for a long, long time without any more sightings of Rachel or his mother. He wants to go home because he has to pee, bad, and is getting hungry. But he is afraid she will come out while he is gone.

Glancing down at this phone, it's a little past eleven a.m. He could race home, pee, make a sandwich, and race back. Counting on his fingers, he figures he can be back in twenty-eight minutes. What could happen in twenty-eight minutes?

When he looks back up at the brick building, a Sheriff's cruiser is heading right towards him.

Instantly, Wayne ducks way down, leaning over into the passenger seat. His armpits break out in sweat. Unmoving, he crouches down there, listening. He is sure that he hears the *thump, thump, thump* of footsteps. They're getting louder, coming closer. Louder. He holds his breath and clenches his eyes shut.

Finally, unable to hold his breath any longer, he exhales in a gush. His neck is throbbing from being hunched over so long. Slowly, he rolls his head so he can see out the driver's window. No one. Rolling his head the other direction, there is no one looking in through the passenger window either.

Inch-by-inch, he creeps his head up until he can peek over the dashboard. No one. Wayne can see the cruiser is in the parking lot, but there is no deputy inside the car.

Get out of here, Papa orders.

Wayne always follows his father's orders.

44

DAY FOURTEEN, 9:00 AM

AFTER HER NAME WAS RELEASED, Rachel couldn't tolerate sitting alone in her house waiting to hear when they made an arrest, so she crashed at her dad's house.

This morning, she and her father watch the news while having coffee. The Sheriff's Office still hasn't made an arrest, which is crushingly disappointing. Rachel's phone keeps buzzing with calls from unknown numbers, which she assumes are regional media outlets.

So, as if it's a normal Monday morning and she didn't just rescue a woman who was missing for two weeks, Rachel sticks to her routine. She takes Ruby for a run, albeit a short one because she is constantly checking over her shoulder and scanning for red Corollas. Then she heads into the office, which feels safe given all the other people in the building. Not wanting to leave Ruby at home alone, she brings her into the office.

Late that morning, her phone pings with a text, and she feels a wash of relief to see a message from Chris. He promised to contact her when there was any kind of an update.

His text says: You at home? Time for quick chat?

She replies that she is at work and gives a thumbs-up emoji, though she has a sinking, thumbs-down feeling that he doesn't have good news. If they arrested the busser, he would have just texted that. Even so, she scrolls through the latest news feed. Again.

Chris asks Rachel how she is doing after yesterday's events—she lies and says that she is doing fine—then he gets down to business.

"I only have a few minutes because I need to brief the Sheriff in—" he glances at his watch "—thirty, forty minutes. The Sheriff and the FBI are talking to the press at five."

"The FBI?"

"She was being held on Federal land."

Held? That's putting it mildly. Did he see that cabin? "Is that better or worse? For the busser?"

He shrugs. "If a suspect is convicted, federal kidnapping is a pretty serious charge."

"The FBI will need a statement from you," Chris says, handing her a business card. "Agent Ramiro—Andrea Ramiro —should be contacting you soon. If you want, you can meet with her at the Sheriff's Office."

Chris sits down then and pops open his laptop. "Can you look at this map and show me, exactly, the route you took out of the cabin? There are two roads that lead up to that area, and I want to make sure I got it straight."

Rachel points to Forest Service Road 2068 on the *Google Map.* "The gate where I parked is right here, where Forest Service land starts. I walked up this way, through the campground to the cabin. It was on the right. The cabin doesn't show on the map, but I'd say it's"—she indicates a general area on the map—"right here. Approximately."

"You brought Alicia out the same way?"

She nods. "Yeah, why?"

"You didn't get turned around, maybe go down this way at all?" He points behind the cabin to a trail leading towards the horse camp. "Down this trail?"

She shakes her head.

"You're sure?"

"Positive. What's this all about?"

Chris hesitates. "Did you notice when you found Alicia ... was she ... was she missing—"

"A shoe!" She slaps her hands on her head. "Shit, I forgot that yesterday ... I don't know how ... Yes, when I found her, she only had on one shoe. The left one was missing. The sock on that foot was already dirty with ... well, I don't what, it looked like dried mud or dirt. I'm sure it got dirtier when we walked out of there, but it *was* already dirty."

Chris starts typing into his laptop.

Quietly, so as not to disturb Chris, and because she isn't sure she wants to know the answer, Rachel says, "You find her shoe back there?"

He flashes her a look of exasperation, or maybe resignation, then goes back to typing but gives her a slight nod.

Contemplating what happened to make Alicia lose a shoe in the woods gives Rachel a shudder.

After a couple of minutes, he closes his laptop and says, "Okay, that's what I needed to know."

Checking his watch again, he continues. "The other thing is, I want you to hear the latest from me and not a press conference. I can't say anything that isn't public information, but I *can* tell you ... Alicia couldn't identify the perpetrator." He pauses for a few seconds, waiting for that to sink in.

Chris explains how the perpetrator came from behind, covered Alicia's mouth and nose with something that knocked her out. "She came to, alone, in the cabin, handcuffed to that rail," he says, pausing for a moment. "She isn't sure what time that was, but it was still dark. The next morning, the perp showed up with blankets, food, water. Started drugging her so she was out of it most of the time. He always wore surgical masks and caps. The only thing Alicia can tell us, for sure, is he had blue eyes and was six-foot tall and thin."

"That's the guy!" Rachel says. "The busser. That fits his description."

"And millions of other guys out there," Chris says.

Rachel's brain is whirring. This psycho is still out there? She came in contact with this predator, touched his hand. He probably saw her sitting in Chris' cruiser that night, knows what she looks like. And her name is all over the news.

Afraid to hear the answer that she already knows, she says haltingly, "So, you're telling me ... the busser ... wasn't arrested?"

Chris hesitates. "I'm saying, no suspects have been arrested yet."

"What about fingerprints and DNA? All the evidence in the cabin? The stuff I had in my jacket and car?"

"Nothing conclusive."

Rachel can feel her blood pressure rising. "What, exactly, does that mean?" She risked her life or, at least, her sanity, certainly her privacy—revealed a part of herself she *never* tells anyone about. And her poor father, oh god, she dragged him into the restaurant to stand by and watch as she went face-to-face with that predator. Basically, Rachel tipped her entire safe little world upside down to catch this guy and rescue his victim. Yet he remains free?

"There were no prints anywhere," Chris says. "The victim said he always wore medical gloves. We got very little DNA and, so far ... no match."

"The doorknobs? The handcuffs? The handrail? There was no DNA that matched the busser's DNA?"

He runs his hands through his hair. "That's not how it works." *How does it fucking work?* "There are databases of people with prior convictions who had DNA samples drawn. But a lot of offenders don't have DNA collected, for various reasons. Or, it isn't entered in the database. Anyway, when we find DNA at a crime scene, we check it against that database. The DNA from the crime scene—which could be from someone who was in the cabin years ago—doesn't match anything."

"So, the busser has no priors or—"

"That's not what I said. The person whose DNA is in that cabin doesn't match any DNA in the federal database."

"You sound like an attorney," Rachel scoffs. "And let me guess, you can't get a DNA sample from the busser because you have no probable cause?"

"Exactly. Having blue eyes and being six-foot tall isn't enough. We're working closely with the FBI, interrogating people, scouring everything for evidence ... We *do* have suspects, but I can't demand a cheek swab from someone because you have a hunch tha—"

"It wasn't a *hunch*. It was a premonition. The same kind that led me to that cabin." Rachel scowls, wanting to remind him that her premonitions always come true, except this is the first one of this type: where someone is harming another. So "always" seems to be a bold statement.

Chris glances away, shakes his head. "Still ... as far as your—premonition—I can't use it to get a DNA sample. Sorry. My hands are tied."

Well, at least Alicia's hands aren't tied—or cuffed—anymore, Rachel thinks. That is what matters.

Sometimes, you *can* stop a person from dying.

45

DAY FOURTEEN, 11:00 AM

WHEN WAYNE HURRIES into the house, Papa is close on his heels and barking at him like a drill sergeant: *Get back to that office building. Take your mother's minivan this time. Make sure the cop is gone. Follow that lady home.*

"My bladder is about to burst," Wayne says, shutting the bathroom door on Papa's voice. He pees with a sigh of relief, about emptying his bladder but, mostly, because he is getting a break from being bossed around.

Peeking out the bathroom door—Papa is nowhere to be seen—Wayne scampers into the kitchen, checking over his shoulder, waiting for the next order. The house is silent.

Wayne gobbles down a few pieces of cold pizza—no time to waste heating it up. He has been gone from Rachel's office building for sixteen minutes.

Grabbing the pizza box with two more slices in it, Wayne does as his father said and climbs into his mother's minivan. The smell of her is so strong in there that a terrible sadness washes over Wayne, making him want to cry.

"It's okay, it's okay. I'll find her."

Don't start blubbering, Papa says, tsking with disgust.

Back at the office building, the Sheriff's cruiser is no longer in the parking lot. Wayne wants to park in the same spot as before, but the car he parked behind earlier won't conceal his mother's van. Instead, he backs the minivan up so it is mostly hidden behind a building, leaving only a narrow view of the front door of Rachel Sharpe's building.

Nervously, he waits and waits and waits, all the while listening to the Sheriff's scanner. There is no chatter about the suspect or the victim. Eventually, Wayne gets thirsty but doesn't drink anything since there is nowhere to pee. When his eyes get heavy and he feels drowsy, he pinches his arm to keep from falling asleep. Bored, he starts scanning the building's windows through his binoculars. He can see some people, but none are Rachel or his mother.

Finally, after what seems like hours, Rachel comes out of the building, the dog at her side. Through the binoculars, he watches them walk among the trees along the side of the parking lot. The dog squats and pees. Wayne snickers.

When they move out of his sights, Wayne panics because he doesn't know what kind of car she drives.

With the binoculars aimed at the parking lot exit, Wayne holds them steady so the exit stays in focus. A million questions bounce around in his head. Was there another entrance to the parking lot? Maybe I won't see her leave? How can I follow her if—

Then, like a miracle, a dark blue SUV, a small one, pulls up to the parking lot exit and stops. He can clearly see Rachel in the driver's seat. She looks left then starts to look right—

He drops down low, out of sight, waits a few seconds, then sticks his head up just enough to keep the blue SUV in his view as it drives away.

46

DAY FOURTEEN 1:15 PM

AS SHE LEAVES THE OFFICE, Rachel has a sensation, like a blade of heat at her back, that she is being watched. Unnerved, she checks all around for the busser or anyone lurking in the shadows. She spots a few red cars but none with a person inside and none are Corollas.

Pulling out of the parking lot, she checks her mirrors constantly but sees nothing suspicious. She considers going to a hotel instead of her house but wonders if a hotel is safer. Not if she is followed there. Rachel checks her mirrors again. Plus, the nicer hotels won't let her bring Ruby, and binge-watching news in a cheap motel that smells like air freshener sounds depressing. Also, at home, at least deputies will be cruising by the house. Supposedly.

Rachel decides her best strategy is to hole up at home for the next day or two and wait for the Sheriff's office to make an arrest. *If* they make an arrest. With the doors and windows locked, she will binge read the news and binge eat tiramisu.

To stock up on supplies, Rachel stops at the hardware

store and buys wireless home security cameras for her front and back doors; the kind with a continuous video feed.

On the way to her car, Rachel has that feeling, again, that someone is following her. Quickly, she peers over her shoulder. No busser in sight. She scans the parking lot for a red sedan. Nothing. At the far end of the parking lot, she notices a small, white van and vaguely recalls seeing one in her rearview mirror when she left the office.

When she pulls out, she drives by the van. It doesn't appear that anyone is in the van.

Next, she heads to the Third Avenue Food Co-Op to get something from the deli for dinner. Something in addition to tiramisu. The Co-Op's tiramisu isn't as good as Bucatini's, but it will have to do.

Loading her groceries into cloth bags at the self-checkout, a string of tension crawls from Rachel's scalp straight down her back.

Someone is fucking watching me.

Lugging her bags off the counter, she spins around as if she forgot something and scans the people in the checkout lines. He isn't anywhere, unless he ducked down in a line, which is absurd. People would be staring down at him. Maybe he sidestepped behind a display at the end of an aisle.

No one has moved into her self-checkout lane yet, so she sets her bags back on the counter and digs through her purse, pulling things out as if looking for something, all the while looking at everyone out of the corners of her eyes. Pulling her phone out, she pretends to check something, swiping and tapping on her phone, while stealing more looks around her. The busser isn't there.

This isn't a premonition. There is no darkness

descending over her. No tunneling vision. No impending doom. No dreadful images. This is paranoia or anxiety or, maybe as Glen said, her radar for danger is super sensitive.

Trying to relax, she shoves everything back in her purse, double checking that her taser is in there. Hoisting a grocery bag over each shoulder, Rachel leaves the store.

Rachel can't help but check the parking lot. Behind one of those monster pickup trucks with lifts and huge tires, she catches a glimpse of a white van. She can't tell if it's the same van she saw at the hardware store. Unnerved, she curses Chris for planting that seed in her already overactive brain about the busser possibly tracking her. Then she curses him for not being able to keep her name from the media.

Reassuring herself that she isn't being followed but is just paranoid after yesterday's rescue, she considers how many vans are around. And how practically every delivery van is white.

Still, by the time she gets to her car, she is holding the taser.

———

Back inside the store, a Co-Op employee saunters over to the self-checkout registers. He can't believe how lucky he was to see that woman again, *the* woman, with the tousled, flaxen-colored hair. It was a like a sign. She actually looked over at him, even left a piece of paper. For him, he thinks.

What the fuck is wrong with you? With all that happened yesterday?

He can't help it. Since he first saw this woman in the store a couple weeks ago, he has wanted so badly to get to know her. Nothing wrong with that, he tells himself. One quick peek at that scrap of paper, and he might learn something about her, a tidbit, like maybe her name.

Acting as if he is straightening things and picking up trash around the self-checkout area, the man looks around to see if his boss or any co-workers are watching. As he comes closer to the piece of paper, he can tell it is a business card.

The card is face down. *Don't do it, man!*

His heart races as he reaches for it.

The business card, only a few inches long and practically weightless, might as well be searing his hand. It is torturing him.

Don't look at it! Throw it in the trash. One is a fuckin' gun, man! Two: she ain't interested in you.

He imagines flicking the card out of his hand like a burning ember. But that thin piece of paper could hold precious information.

Just one innocent glance.

Turning the card over, his gaze flashes down to card at the exact moment his boss calls his name.

Quickly, he tosses the business card in the trash.

DAY FOURTEEN, 2:00 PM

PATRICK FORCES his feet to keep moving as he walks over to his boss, Giselle. He tells himself to calm the fuck down, that it was just a piece of trash he picked up. Another part of his brain is telling him he should've left the goddamn business card alone. Keeping his face relaxed, physically loosening his jaw, he rehearses his excuse. *Was just cleanin' up the self-checkout lanes …*

But Patrick knows trouble when he sees it, and the look on Giselle's face is trouble.

Giselle isn't a cheerful person, but she is usually easygoing. But, as Patrick walks up to her, she has two creases between her eyebrows in the shape of an hourglass, like a tiny nuclear power plant. A meltdown is underway.

All because of that damned woman, Patrick thinks, with her bedroom eyes and her sexy, golden mane. All because she paused over there at the register, tried to taunt me. Dropped her business card. What a dick tease.

Despite knowing that he is about to get fired, or worse,

Patrick smiles at Giselle. That comes from being in prison for years—don't let anyone know you're scared. Ever.

"You got visitors," Giselle practically barks at Patrick.

He blinks. *This isn't about the business card? Wait a sec— who would visit me at work?* The only person who would visit him at work is his parole officer, Daniel, but he has never come to his work. Patrick's body goes stone cold.

"They're in my office," she says, motioning for him to follow.

They? This isn't good. Not good at all. Forget losin' this job, I'm about to lose my freedom.

As Giselle pushes through her office door, beyond her Patrick can see the bulk of a cop's belt: gun, taser, cuffs, billy club. Daniel is sitting to the side. Patrick senses physical fear like he hasn't felt since he was in prison, like a white-hot streak of fire down his back. His gaze moves up to the cop's name tag—Sergeant Hagen—then to the cop's face.

Same pig that questioned me about Alicia. They're gonna try to pin this on me.

He has been listening to a regional news podcast—he can't bear to *watch* or read the news, can't bear to see any visuals—so he knows they haven't made an arrest. Yet.

"Patrick, I'm Sergeant Hagen. We talked the other d—"

"I remember. What's goin' on here?" Patrick crosses his arms over his chest, unable to keep the sneer off his face. He should stay relaxed and act cool, but he is pretty sure that he is about to get arrested.

Sergeant Hagen splays his fingers out on a piece of paper on Giselle's desk, turning it so Patrick can read it. At the top are the words: Conditions of parole. "We just want to ask your boss, Ms. Bryant, to confirm you were working on the evening of October twenty-seventh, like you told me. And what time you clocked out."

Patrick is stunned, physically, like the wind has been knocked out of him. He can't breathe. His mind is reeling. *They think I snatched Alicia Meyers? How? That cunt never laid eyes on me. Not once.*

Daniel says, "Since you're on parole, this doesn't require a search warrant"—*Shit! What if they searched my apartment? The poster. It's shredded all over and the*—"but Ms. Bryant wanted you to be present."

"I wanted his *permission*," Giselle clarifies, looking at Daniel. "I got labor laws, privacy laws, I have to follow. I don't know about these"—she flutters her hand over the paper —"parole conditions."

Daniel motions toward Giselle, conceding to her statement, then looks at Patrick. "Got this, Patrick? Ms. Bryant is gonna share your timesheet records with us." Then Daniel looks around at everyone: Giselle, Hagen, back to Patrick. "All good here?"

Patrick is taking short breaths now, trying to stay calm, trying to figure out what to do, what to say. Mostly, he is frantic to get to his apartment and sweep it of anything they might use to link him to Alicia. If they haven't already been there. Sweat beads at his temples and under his mustache. He strokes his mustache and goatee, pretending like he is being thoughtful and considering his options. But Patrick has no options. Felony sex offenders on parole have no options. And everyone in the room knows it.

48

DAY FOURTEEN, 2:30 PM

WITH HIS EYES locked onto her vehicle, Wayne waits until Rachel's car is almost out of sight before using the binoculars to get her license plate number. On the empty pizza box, he scribbles the plate number and the make and model, a Honda CR-V, in case he loses sight of her car and needs to re-find it.

Slowly, he pulls out and follows her, staying as far away as possible. Every time she turns a corner, he is frantic that he won't be able to find her car once he makes the turn.

From the backseat, Papa coaches him. *Steady now, not too close, stay way back. Okay, she's at a stop sign. You might have to pull over and wait. Okay, go now.*

When she pulls into a couple of stores, he parks far away the first time, then behind a big pickup truck at the second store.

Eventually, she drives out of the commercial area into an area with more houses than businesses. She passes a Thai restaurant, then drives into a residential area.

Papa tells Wayne to pull over in the parking lot of the restaurant—*This one! Right here.*

Wayne takes a sharp turn into the parking lot of the Thai restaurant. His palms are slippery on the steering wheel, and he wipes them on his pants. He blows out a big gush of air, then says, "Now what?"

Nothing from the backseat.

Wayne can barely see the blue car up ahead so tries to look through the binoculars.

Put those damn things down, Papa yells. *You're parked in front of a restaurant. Somebody'll see you looking through those.*

Wayne drops the binoculars and scrunches his shoulders up, waiting to be slapped upside the head. No slap. His papa doesn't say anything either. Not this time. But Wayne knows.

"I can't do *anything* right," Wayne scolds himself.

The blue roof of her Honda CR-V is almost out of sight when it turns right. Slowly, Wayne drives in that direction, fretting that there is no way he will find her now, she is too far ahead of him. He is wondering why he ever listens to his papa. He takes the right turn, scanning the street. Looking at each house he passes, left and right, nothing, nothing, nothing.

Then, up ahead on the left, a garage door is just closing. He can't see inside, but that had to be her. It's a small, tan colored house with a midnight blue door and trim. Turning his head slightly the other direction, he drives past the house, his heart pounding in his chest.

At the next intersection, he looks both ways then turns left. At the next street, he turns left again. Glancing between the houses, he finally sees the back of Rachel's house.

There is a five-foot high, wooden privacy fence around her small backyard. Above the fence he can make out the top of a sliding glass door that leads into her house and a window on either side of it. Right through that door, or through one of the windows, his mother could be waiting for him, waiting to be rescued.

For almost an hour, Wayne drives the nearby streets, never the same one twice, scheming how to get into her house. All the while, his father yells at him to do this, do that, go there, go here.

No longer able to stay respectful, Wayne says through clenched, "Shut—up! I—can't—think."

Papa keeps ranting. Overwhelmed, Wayne slaps his forehead, one, two, three times.

His papa still won't shut up, so Wayne pulls in behind the Thai restaurant—there are no houses there, just the backs of a few stores, dumpsters, a loading dock. Wayne scoots forward, up against the steering wheel and out of his papa's reach, and puts on his noise-cancelling headset. He plays his mother's calm music, the kind with only instruments.

Sitting there in his mother's minivan, listening to music composed by long-dead men whose names he can never pronounce, Wayne devises a plan. The best plan ever.

Even Papa will like this plan, he thinks, driving back home.

49

DAY FOURTEEN, 3:00 PM

THE FIRST THING Rachel does when she gets home, with the taser in one hand and her phone in the other, is walk through every room. Ruby tags along, curiously watching Rachel, which should be assuring because if someone was in the house, Ruby would be growling. Still, with her finger on the taser trigger, she slides open each closet. She checks for feet sticking out from the bottom of curtains before checking behind them. Before leaving her bedroom, she looks over at the bed. The red comforter drapes over the edges to within a few inches from the floor. She can't see underneath the bed.

An image of the busser stretched out under there—silent and unmoving, his head rolled to one side, watching her feet move around the room—fills her with dread. Standing back as far as she can, taser aimed under the bed, she holds her breath and lifts the comforter.

"Phewww," she says, letting out a gush of air.

In the bathroom, she can barely bring herself to slide open the shower curtain, fully expecting him to be crouched in the tub.

There is no one in her house. For once, Rachel is grateful for such a small house. Ruby, done with this boring game, noses through the dog door and runs circles in the backyard.

That dog needs a good, long run, Rachel thinks, guiltily. Maybe tomorrow. Or after they make an arrest.

Clipping the taser onto her belt loop, Rachel goes around and checks, again, that every window is still locked. She even jams into the window frames the wood two-by-fours that her father cut to fit into each window as added security. Until now, those two-by-fours have been collecting dust on the windowsills.

"This is crazy. I'm slinking around my own home with a taser." Rolling her shoulders to try to relax, she hears the tight tendons in her neck and shoulders stretching and creaking.

After installing the wi-fi security cameras, Rachel leans against the kitchen counter wondering if she wants to stay here. Not in the kitchen but in the house. Well, maybe the kitchen. She gravitated to the kitchen because it's the one room, besides the bathroom, that isn't in view of a window. This is absurd since all the curtains and blinds are pulled shut.

Only she keeps thinking of how, yesterday, she shattered a window and crawled through it in a matter of seconds.

She imagines someone trying to peer through *her* curtains, lurking on the other side of a thin pane of glass.

Shaking her head to get that creepy visual out of her mind, Rachel cracks open a beer and takes a long swallow. She could take one of those hydroxyzine tablets, or half of one. Glen says they not only help with insomnia but, in smaller doses, reduce anxiety. Or maybe take two pills and conk out. Instantly, she rules that option out; sleeping heavily sounds vulnerable. Reducing her anxiety sounds vulnerable.

When her phone rings, she snatches it up, hoping for news from Chris. Rachel groans to see Lorena's name on the caller ID. She missed several calls from her already but kept hoping the Sheriff would make an arrest before she talked to her. She should have called yesterday to tell Lorena everything.

"What the actual fuck is going on? You're all over the news." Lorena is agitated. "You found that missing woman?"

"Yeah..." Rachel stalls, quickly checking a few news feeds. Still no arrests. "Uh ... here's the thing—" She blows out a lungful of air.

"Why didn't you tell me?"

"I'm uh ... I'm a witness, and ... they haven't arrested anyone—"

"Yeah, I saw that."

"Well, I didn't want to blow the chance of them making an arrest, so ... I didn't think I should talk about it."

There are several very long seconds of silence.

"You mean, like, you think I'm going to say something ... to talk about it, if you told me?" Lorena asks.

"I don't know ... no. No, you wouldn't. I think it's just ... it was ... a lot. I'm kind of in shock."

"Where are you?" Lorena asks.

"I just got home. From work, actually."

"Are you serious?" Lorena is incredulous.

Only a few beats of silence now, during which it starts to sink in for Rachel just how bizarre this all sounds. Some wonderful anesthetic, probably shock, kept her rather numb all day, but it seems to be wearing off. Rachel isn't ready for full awareness. She is feeling unstable and isolated and exposed, and regrets that she ever got involved in this whole shit show. Except ... she did rescue Alicia.

"Rachel? Are you okay?"

Never worse. "Uh ... I think so. The Sheriff's office was trying not to release my name, but the media was all over this. And being a witness ...." She pauses for a moment. "It's public information. My name. So ..."

"Are you safe or what?"

"Hell if I know. I bought a taser a couple of days ago. And just installed those continuous feed security cameras." She checks the video feed. There is no one outside her house, not even a Sheriff's car. Then she wonders if someone could tamper with the camera feed, make it so the images she sees are fake feeds of her front and back porches. Maybe, in reality, the lenses have been covered up or ... spray painted. Her skin grows clammy.

With the phone still to her ear, Rachel peeks through the front curtains to make sure no one is on her porch. "And the police are supposed to be cruising by my house regularly ..." she mutters, while sticking her head out the door and physically inspecting the camera. "I should've just minded my own business, you know?"

"But you saved that woman's life. How'd you find her?"

"I had another premonition. About a cabin." Rachel physically examines the camera facing the backyard for any spray paint. "It's a long story."

"I'm stunned, really. It's incredible. You saved her life."

Yeah. Sometimes you can *save a person's life.*

"Why don't you come and stay with us until—for however long you want?" Lorena says.

Rachel hadn't thought of this option. When she left her dad's house this morning, he insisted she come back after work, but Margaret will be there this evening. Another situation that would require getting honest about her ESP or lying to Margaret about how she found Alicia Meyers. Both options require more concentration and energy than Rachel can muster. Also, going to her dad's house might put him at risk, if the busser *is* following her ...

She tries to push away that fear, rolls her tense, creaking shoulders again.

Lorena says, "Me and Fletch will come get—"

"No," Rachel blurts out. "Please don't. I don't want you guys within miles of my house. I'm ju—"

"What the hell? You don't want us within miles of your house, but you're going to stay there? All alone?"

"It's not like I'm some key witness in a mob case and have a price on my head."

"Then why can't Fletch and I come over?"

Rachel has no response. What can she say? That she really is uncomfortable in her own home but if some psycho is coming after her, she doesn't want Lorena to get hurt. And that the last thing she wants to do, in her current state of mind, is sit around with Fletcher.

Before Rachel can respond, Ruby blasts from the backyard through the dog door, barking all the way to the front door. A split second later, the security camera app on Rachel's phone dings that movement has been detected in front of the house. Before she can view the camera feed, there is a rapping on her front door.

Rachel flinches, then her hand flies to her chest. *Jeezus!*

Over the barking, Rachel tells Lorena she will call her back.

Checking the video feed, it's only a UPS delivery. Of course. Predators don't knock. Still, Rachel waits until the UPS man gets back in his truck before snatching the package off the porch and relocking the front door.

50

DAY FOURTEEN, 3:15 PM

DRIVING AS FAST as he can without going too far over the speed limit, Patrick heads to his apartment to see if it looks like cops already searched his place. He finished his shift without getting put in handcuffs, but he knows that wasn't the end of Sergeant Hagen.

That pig is after me, Patrick thinks, gripping the steering wheel so tight his knuckles are white. They're gonna try to send me back—

He shakes his head, trying to keep thoughts about prison from taking over. Still, his mind runs wild with defenses. I got an alibi—I worked that night. They don't have anything to link me to her or that cabin.

Some whiskey is what Patrick needs to calm his mind down so he can think straight. But with the cops breathing down his neck, he figures this is would be the perfect time for his PO to piss test him. The last thing he needs is a parole violation.

Getting laid would calm me down.

"God dammit!" He slams his fist against the dashboard.

"Your freedom is hangin' by a fuckin' thread here. Get your shit together, man."

Patrick doesn't even bother reciting his mantra in his head, he rehashes internal orders. Get rid of anything that makes me look guilty. Go to the ranch. Go to an AA meeting. Go back home. Get rid of anything incriminating. To the ranch. To a meeting. Back home. Sweep apartment. Ranch. Meeting. Home.

51

DAY FOURTEEN, 5:30 PM

RACHEL EATS DINNER standing at her breakfast bar, which is now her enclave. Or her cave. Unnerved by notifications pinging from the app every time a vehicle drives by—this camera is too easily triggered; it could use an EMDR session with Glen—she reviews how to change the settings to only be notified if someone is in her yard or on the porch. She doesn't live on a busy street, but dozens of cars passed by as neighbors came home from work and deliveries were made to other houses. She *was* relieved, however, to see a Sheriff's cruiser drive by once and tried to discern if it was Chris, but the video was too grainy to make out the deputy's face.

Ping. Another one. "Gimme a break," she groans and considers ignoring this drive-by while she tweaks the settings, then thinks better of it. Tapping the video, her mouth drops open to see a white van—a fucking white van!—just passed her house. A shockwave of adrenaline blazes from her chest to her arms and legs, settling there in her legs, which are taut and ready to bolt.

Rachel grabs her keys. With that sound, Ruby skitters into the kitchen and is on Rachel's heels.

The garage door couldn't open any slower; it's like molasses. With the car already in reverse, Rachel has the urge to back out now, smashing right through the garage door. She wants to get as far from her house as possible.

Heading down the road, she considers calling Chris. He will know quicker than she can explain to any dispatcher why a Sheriff needs to get to her house. Immediately. Checking her rearview mirror, she thinks that through. What would she say? Come quickly, a white van drove past my house! Chris isn't going to race over, or send another cruiser, for that. Maybe he could cross-check the busser's Toyota Corolla plates and see if owns a—

Fuck! A white van is parked at the curb in front of her neighbor, Heidi's, house. Rachel grips the steering wheel. As she drives by, she turns her head to read the orange and blue logo on the side of the van. It's a heating and air conditioning company.

Remembering that Heidi was going to have her heating vents cleaned before winter, Rachel releases a scoffing grunt. *What did I expect—a Bucatini delivery van?*

Turning at the next intersection, Rachel pulls over, out of view of the van, and drops her head back, staring at the ceiling for a minute. After her pulse slows, she rewatches the video, in slow motion, of the van that passed her house. The slow-motion part was unnecessary. It is the same work van; she can make out the orange and blue logo.

Back home, Rachel opens another beer and sets up the laptop in her breakfast bar cave. Scrolling through the news, she is now, it would seem, a "hero." And there it is, her photo is now out. It's the headshot from her website.

Damn it! I should've taken that photo down. Taking a swig of beer, she stares at her image. She reasons that having her face in the news is no worse than having her name out there. *Well, at least it's a good photo.*

She is glad to live in a small enough town that there is no local TV station, or the media might be camped outside her house. With that thought, she checks her security camera feed, yet again.

Turning back to the news, the Sheriff still hasn't made an arrest. Even though intellectually—and legally—Rachel understands all the constraints to them arresting the busser, she is angry.

After a third beer, she is fuming.

A fourth beer, and she is ranting.

"How do they think I found Alicia if my premonition wasn't accurate? They think I *stumbled* onto a missing person being held captive? In a remote cabin? In a closed campground in November? Really? What the fuck is wrong with Chris—I mean, the Sheriff's Office? And the FBI, they're no better!"

By the time she takes her allergy pill, she realizes that fourth beer might have been one too many. *At least I'll fall asleep quickly.*

Lying in bed, though, she hears every creak in her tiny, old house. Outside her bedroom window, a rustling causes her to lie perfectly still, listening for the snap of a twig underfoot or a jiggle of the window.

Eventually, Rachel falls asleep with her phone next to the pillow and the taser in her hand.

52

DAY FIFTEEN, 10:00 AM

PAPA IS BOSSING Wayne around worse than ever, and Wayne's mind is swimming with all the instructions and orders and details. Desperately, Wayne is trying to keep track of everything because one misstep, one slip, and he might not be able to rescue his mother.

For the tenth time, Papa says, *you gotta take care of that dog. First thing. Get rid of the dog.*

When he hears this demand again, Wayne's back goes stiff. He clears his throat and, with his back to his papa, mumbles, "I'm not killing the doggie."

Papa yells, his hot breath and spittle up and down Wayne's neck. *Do you want to save your mama or not?*

That makes Wayne's heart feel like it skipped a beat. She hasn't had any medication for two days. She is supposed to have it twice a day. The thought of her suffering, her eyes closed and her jaw clenched in pain, is too much. But the thought of killing a dog ... that makes his belly crinkle into knots.

Stomping to the kitchen, Wayne says more firmly, "I'm

not killing the doggie. I won't do it." Then he slides on his noise-cancelling headset and gets to work before his father starts in on him again.

Wayne examines the row of his mother's pill bottles, reading each bottle carefully. He decides that ketamine, a small piece, should be enough to knock out the dog, just make it go to sleep. That way, Wayne can slip through the backyard and into Rachel Sharpe's house without the dog warning her.

Staring into the fridge, Wayne figures all dogs love cheese, so he pulls out a slice and unwraps it. He breaks it into four pieces and starts to roll each piece into a ball but ends up eating half the slice. Unwrapping a second slice, he makes four balls of cheese. Using the pill cutter, he carefully splits one of the ketamine tablets into fourths then pushes a piece into each cheese ball, sealing the cheese around them.

Inspecting all four cheese balls, there isn't one speck of pill showing. He smiles proudly. Placing the cheese balls in a baggie, he zips it shut and slides it into his jacket pocket.

This should work, he thinks, unwrapping another slice of cheese for himself. His plan is to go to Rachel's house while she is at work. And if she takes her dog to work, like she did yesterday, he won't need the cheese balls. If the dog is in her house or the backyard, he will call the dog over and give it a cheese ball, or two, however many it takes to make it go all limp and conk out. Then he will slip through the gate. If it's locked, he will climb over the fence; it wasn't that high. Then tiptoe through the sliding door. If it's locked, he will check the windows, breaking one if he needs to. Then, quick like, find his mother and hurry her out to his car.

53

DAY FIFTEEN, 12:00 NOON

RACHEL WAKES to her phone buzzing and sits bolt upright, keenly aware of another reason she should've skipped that fourth beer: her temples are throbbing. It isn't Chris, as she hoped, but Lorena checking on her and inviting her, again, to come and stay at her house.

"I'll think about it," Rachel says.

"Liar."

Before slinking to her kitchen enclave to make a pot of very strong coffee, Rachel checks for any missed calls from Chris, though she left her phone on all night—then reviews the latest news. No arrest. She is still a hero. No mention of her premonition. She wonders if that made it into Chris' reports. Must not have because the media would be all over that woo-woo shit.

Next, Rachel calls her dad to assure him that she is safe, that cruisers are patrolling her neighborhood regularly and that she is supposed to talk with the FBI soon. A lie and two truths. As if she doesn't have enough to deal with, her father wants to know if he can tell Margaret the full story, about her premonitions.

Really? Can't she just get the same news everyone else is getting? "It's fine if you want to tell her."

After two and half cups of coffee, Rachel takes a long, hot shower—her phone and taser within reach.

Finally, Chris calls in the early afternoon.

Oh, finally, they arrested that fucker.

"Rachel, I'm here with FBI Agent Ramiro. Can you come in this afternoon to provide your statement to the FBI ... or would you rather she comes to your house? Or meet somewhere ..."

Rachel tries to tone down any excitement in her voice. "Wait ... did you make an arrest or—"

"Oh, no," he says. "Sorry, I should've said that. No arrest yet." The letdown Rachel feels is physical. Slumping down at the counter, she drops her head into her palm. "The FBI needs a statement from you—I mentioned that yesterday—to help with their investigation ... so they can make an arrest."

"Ah ... when do you need me to come in?"

A woman's voice comes over the line. "Anytime that works for you."

Getting out of this cave sounds good to Rachel, though so does having an armed FBI agent at her house. *Agent Ramiro and I can have a little sleepover. The kind where she stands guard while I sleep.*

"I'll come to the Sheriff's office," Rachel says. "Be there around one thirty."

Chris introduces Rachel to Agent Ramiro, who isn't at all what Rachel expected from an FBI agent. No black blazer or ear piece or sunglasses; she wears gray cargo pants and a black fleece jacket over a shirt. There is, at least, an FBI insignia on the chest of the jacket. If she has a gun, it isn't visible.

Lot of good she'd do at a sleepover.

Chris shows them to an empty office where Rachel can give her statement then leaves. Rachel finds herself wishing he would stay. Since he knows all about her premonitions—though he isn't doing squat with them—he is sort of an ally, or at least not an adversary.

Flashing her identification for Rachel to view, Andrea Ramiro is to-the-point and all business, which Rachel imagines is necessary for a woman in the FBI. Especially one this short. Rachel is only five foot, six inches tall, but she has a few inches on this woman.

With seemingly as few words as possible, Agent Ramiro describes the FBI CID's role in the Alicia Meyers kidnapping case. Rachel couldn't even get a word in to ask what the CID is. The gist of it is that Alicia Meyers was held captive on federal land, so the CID—*whatever the hell that is*—is partnering with the US Forest Service and the Franklin County Sheriff to investigate the crime and, ultimately, arrest and prosecute the perpetrator. They don't have a lot of boots on the ground in such a rural area so rely on the Sheriff's deputies.

Turning on a recording device, Agent Ramiro says that she has read the Sheriff's report but asks Rachel to describe exactly how and when she found Alicia Meyers. No detail is too small, she says, encouragingly.

The words "exactly" and in "detail" make Rachel's throat go dry. Maybe the FBI can go after the busser in a way the Sheriff can't, she wonders.

"How about premonitions?" Rachel says. "Is that level of detail okay?" This came out sounding more contemptuous than she intended.

Agent Ramiro blinks. "What's that?"

Hah! I'll tell you what a premonition is if you tell me what CID is. "Extrasensory perception ..."

Agent Ramiro's all-business facial expression droops in disappointment. "Oh yeah, Sergeant Hagen mentioned that in his report. So—you're like what—a psychic?"

"I don't call myself that. Let me explain how we—me and my dog—found Alicia ..."

Rachel lays it all out, describing in exacting detail everything that she can recall. All the way up to the present and the recent feeling that she is being watched. *What the hell ...* she even tells her about the white van that was way behind her when she left work yesterday and one at the hardware store where she stopped on her way home.

Clearing her throat, Agent Ramiro clicks off the recorder. For several moments, the room becomes quiet as she leafs through reports and documents.

Clicking the recorder back on, Agent Ramiro asks, "You happen to get a license plate number on the van? Or make and model?"

Don't even know if they were the same van or two different ones. "No, but I told you the plate number on the busser's Corolla. C-A-U-one-eight-six-three. Maybe you can check to see if he also owns a van."

Agent Ramiro cocks up an eyebrow, seemingly disinterested in taking direction from a "psychic." Agent Ramiro scribbles on a notepad. Hopefully the plate number, Rachel thinks.

"I'll let Sergeant Hagen know about the vans. They've got a detail on your place, so ... they can keep an eye out for any suspicious vehicles."

Guess the crazies are handled by the local law enforcement, Rachel thinks.

Standing, Agent Ramiro extends a business card to Rachel. "If you think of anything else, don't hesitate to call."

What is wrong with these people? How do they think I found a missing person in the middle of the forest if my premonition wasn't real?

DAY FIFTEEN, 1:30 PM

PATRICK DIDN'T GET a text or call from Giselle telling him not to bother coming in, so he shows up at work like everything is normal, like he isn't a suspect in Alicia Meyers' abduction. When he walks past Giselle's office to clock in, her door is open, as usual, and dread spikes through Patrick's body in expectation of seeing another cop.

"Morning," she says, and Patrick returns the greeting, trying to keep his voice steady. Neither one of them say a word about the cops who visited yesterday.

Patrick behaves perfectly throughout the day, doing everything he is asked and jumping on every task with a forced smile. Every time he catches a glimpse of someone entering the store in dark clothes, he thinks it's a cop and freaks out inside. He doesn't so much as look at a woman, even when he helps one find something in the store. The only thing he dares say to a woman today is, "Thank you," or "Have a nice day," or "Can I get someone to help you out with those bags?" No way he is even walking into the parking lot with a woman today.

To make matters worse, everyone—all his co-workers, practically every customer—is talking about Alicia Meyers being found alive. Patrick mumbles in reply that the whole thing makes him sick, which isn't a lie.

Halfway through his shift, Patrick is wrecked. Giselle still hasn't said anything about Hagen's visit, which is unnerving, like a hammer is about to fall, to smash into his head, any minute. Patrick would just as soon know if a hammer is coming.

He starts watching the clock, counting the minutes before he can get the hell out of there. With an hour left, Giselle goes home for the day. Patrick hasn't been fired and hasn't seen one single cop, not even one getting lunch at the deli.

Still, unexpected hammers to the head can be deadly.

Forty-five minutes to go. Patrick tries to refocus on something good. There is the offender support group this evening, then the gym, then home. He wishes this was his evening with the horses.

Thirty minutes left. Support group. Gym. Home.

Fifteen minutes. Group. Gym. Home. Patrick is smiling for real, thinking all that panicking was for nothing. Giselle probly showed the pigs my timesheet, they saw I *did* work the night Alicia went missin' and they crossed me off their list.

He is high with relief, like he just had a couple shots of whiskey. Everything is going to be okay.

That is when Patrick's co-worker, Nayeli, hurries through the front door looking around wildly, and he realizes that he let his guard down too soon. Nayeli just went out the door a minute ago with a couple of bags for a home delivery. He can think of only one reason for her to hustle back inside with fear in her eyes—there are a bunch of cops out front.

Here comes the hammer.

His body hums with tension. His instinct is to split. But to where? The place will be surrounded by cops. No, he thinks, why would they surround the place? It's not like there's an armed robbery und—

"Do me a favor?" Nayeli says, out of breath and skidding to a stop in front of Patrick.

Patrick, confused, shakes his head a little. Are the cops after her? "Uh ... I guess. What's go—"

"My son broke his arm. Or they think it's broken. The school called an ambulance. They're taking him to the ER. I gotta get over there. I was supposed to deliver these." She shoves two bags into Patrick's arms. "It's all one order. Nothing chilled. Take them for me. Please?"

Without waiting for a response, Nayeli spins around and heads for the door.

Clutching the bags, Patrick watches Nayeli race out the door and wonders if he could have a heart attack from stress.

He checks the clock. Ten minutes left. Checking the address stapled to the bags, it isn't too far out of his way. He will deliver them on his way home.

Deliver groceries. Support group. Gym. Home.

55

DAY FIFTEEN, 1:45 PM

WAYNE FINDS out it isn't as easy as he thought to get into Rachel's house because he doesn't know where she is. And he can't break into her house if she is inside there. He drove by the big brick building at 367 Adams Street to make sure she was at work before going to her house, but her blue Honda CR-V wasn't in the parking lot. Driving along all the roads in a six-block radius of the building, he couldn't find her car. Then he drove by her house, but all the curtains were drawn so he couldn't tell if she was inside or not. He even drove by the hardware goods store and the little grocery store where she stopped yesterday. Her car was nowhere to be found.

Now he is full of anxiety and fear, doubting that the tan house with the dark blue trim is Rachel Sharpe's house. After all, he didn't see her car pull into that garage yesterday.

Not sure what to do—even Papa is stumped and not saying much—Wayne drives back home to regroup.

Rummaging through the medicine cabinet, there are some pills he can take when he feels jumpy and upset, but the bottle is empty. The label reads: 0 REFILLS. His mother always ordered his meds when they ran out, and he doesn't know how to get more.

Wayne lights up a cigarette, mumbling, "Sorry, Mama" because she won't let him smoke those nasty things in the house, but, at times like this, a cigarette calms him down.

Pacing in circles, Wayne smokes and talks through the situation. "Rachel isn't at work. Unless she took a bus. Or maybe she's out doing something else, shopping at another store."

Wayne practically jumps out of his skin when Papa says, *Hey, Dufus. Check her garage.*

There *was* a side window in that garage, he recalls. He could peek in to see if her car is in there. Then, if it isn't, he can go around back like planned. "But ... if her car is in—"

Then try again tomorrow, Papa says.

Wayne recalls that yesterday, Rachel left work around this time. His stomach gets jittery. If I'm going to do this, he thinks, I better go.

PART 4

A SUSPECT

56

DAY FIFTEEN, 2:30 PM

BEFORE LEAVING the Sheriff's parking lot, Rachel places an online order for home delivery of groceries and some deli food from the Co-Op.

By the time Rachel hears her doorbell, she is already checking the video image that pinged on her phone. It's not the busser; this man is in his late thirties with a well-trimmed goatee and stylish, rectangular wire-rim glasses. At least he isn't driving a white van. Or a red Corolla.

Just to be safe, Rachel says through the door, "Who is it?"

"Third Avenue Food Co-Op. Got a delivery for, uh—" he looks at the tag on one grocery bag then on the other bag. He lifts the tag up and looks at the paper underneath it. He stares at it for a few seconds. "It's, uh ... it's for ... it's for Rachel. Don't got a last name."

Opening the door, she can tell from the stunned look on his face that he has been watching the news. Thumbing through her billfold for a tip, she feels him staring at her, feels his attention drilling into her. Must be her new status as a hero.

As she pulls a few dollars from her wallet, something niggles at the back of her brain that she didn't hear the usual *thwop* of the dog door, and Ruby isn't at her side. That dog never misses a chance to greet a visitor. Never.

Rachel's senses prickle. With a split-second glance, she notices the man's head is tilted, creepily, as if he is intrigued by her. As if she is being assessed.

A visceral fear blooms in her chest.

Rachel knows that her nerves are fried, that she is on edge, but there is no way she is going to stand there, in her own home, and feel like some kind of prey, like she is being hunted.

In fact, for the past two days, that is *exactly* how she has felt in her own home.

As Rachel presses her hand against the door to shut it—she couldn't care less if that is rude—Ruby begins barking.

The barking is coming from the backyard.

57

DAY FIFTEEN, 3:05 PM

PATRICK CAN'T TAKE his eyes off her. Standing a few inches away, with her door yawning wide open, is the woman from work. *The* woman. But is it *the* Rachel they've been talking about on the news? The one that found Alicia Meyers? Can't be. That would be too bizarre. Must be a different Rachel.

He can barely focus on that possibility because he is consumed with how beautiful this woman is up close and personal. She is take-his-breath-away beautiful. Those jade green eyes are mesmerizing. On the right side of her nose there is a small, tan mole that he wants so badly to kiss. Her golden hair is pulled back but several thick strands dangle loosely, as usual, which makes him want to smile and gently brush them from her face.

Patrick blinks. Once. Twice.

Rachel. Her name is Rachel ... I wonder what that name means.

This woman triggered him the first time he laid eyes on

her, and when he saw her at work again yesterday. He marvels to think that only yesterday. It seems like an eternity.

She is triggering him at this very moment.

One is a gun. Leave. Skedaddle. Now!

Without looking at him, she extends to him a few dollars. Patrick is aware of the grocery bags hanging at his sides. His fingers ache because he is clutching onto the bags with tight fists.

Give her the bags, he tells himself. And maybe, ever so slightly, brush against—

No! Set the bags down and go.

Only he can't move. He is frozen, not even breathing, unable to take his eyes off her. If he passes the bags to her, this moment will be over. Gone. Forever. Why would he do that when, in two steps, he could be inside her home? Inside. He could lock the door behind him and wrap his arms around her. She would like that.

Fuck no, she don't want you. And the cops are already on your ass.

Patrick is about to pry his fingers off the bags when a dog starts barking, frantically. In a flash, Rachel's face pales and she slams the door. Right in his face.

And just like that, his moment with her is gone. He stands on the porch, food bags dangling, staring dumbly at the door for several seconds, then he hears her shouting. The dog's barking grows wilder and more ferocious.

Patrick hesitates, wondering what is going on, but one misstep and he could lose his job. Hell, a big misstep and he could lose his parole. His freedom.

Setting the food bags on the porch, he heads for the car.

In the driveway, he can tell the commotion is coming

from behind Rachel's house. He could walk around the outside.

Rachel screams that she is calling the police.

That's it. Get in your car. Drive away.

With his hand on the car door handle, Patrick hears a man blubbering.

Probly some pathetic ex tryin' to get her back, he thinks. She *is* smokin' hot, but still … a grown man cryin'?

Patrick pauses and listens.

Now, loud and clear, the man lashes out, hostile and screeching. "What did you do to her? Where is she?"

With that, Patrick's body goes rigid. *No—fuckin'—way.*

Worming around in the deep recesses of his brain is the fear that this *is* the Rachel who found the missing woman, and that he is, somehow, being set up. A much larger portion of his brain, however, is directing him—against his better judgement—to see what is happening in her backyard.

Peering over the fence, Patrick watches in disbelief as the tall, skinny punk moves, step by slow step, closer to Rachel.

What the hell is this idiot gonna do?

Don't matter, he tells himself. Cops are probly on their way. You need to split.

As Patrick turns to high-tail it out of there, that punk lunges at Rachel, flings her around until he is behind her, then covers her mouth with his hand.

Patrick lights up with adrenaline. Seeing Rachel jerked around by her hair, being suffocated, causes something inside him to snap.

58

DAY FIFTEEN, 3:10 PM

THROUGH THE SLIDING GLASS DOOR, Rachel recognizes the man in her backyard. It is the busser. He is in her yard, holding something out to Ruby and coaxing her to eat it. Ruby is uninterested and barks at him savagely.

On the back porch and whipping out her phone to call nine-one-one, Rachel yells, "Hey, get the hell away from my dog! Get out of my yard. Now! Ruby, come. Come here, girl. Ruby, come!"

Ruby is in territorial, defense mode and barely moves toward Rachel, positioning herself instead between Rachel and the man, growling and baring her teeth. Those usually smiling, pearly whites are now menacing. The busser takes a few steps closer to Rachel.

"I'm calling the police," Rachel screams.

In the few seconds that she looks down to call nine-one-one, he lurches to Rachel's side, grabs her ponytail, and swings her around until he is behind her, the phone flying out of her hand.

Ruby leaps at his arm, falls to the ground and leaps again.

296

This time, Ruby locks her jaw onto the elbow of his jacket, catching some of his flesh. The busser yelps in pain and tries to fling Ruby off his arm. Ruby is growling and thrashing, her feet scrambling against his leg to keep her grip on him. As he is flailing to get Ruby off his arm, he still has a hold of Rachel's hair and is yanking her head around.

"Let go of me," Rachel shouts, reaching back to try and free herself from his grip.

The busser manages to fling Ruby off his arm, then tries to shove into Rachel's mouth whatever he was trying to feed to Ruby. It smells like cheese and is being smeared all over Rachel's lips. Thrashing her head left and right, clamping her mouth shut, she tries to pull his hand away from her face.

Now Ruby locks onto his leg.

"Stop it," the busser yells, kicking and shaking at Ruby but with his hand still pressed against Rachel's mouth. As hard as she can, Rachel bites his hand.

He yelps and yanks his hand away from Rachel's mouth.

The metallic taste of blood, his blood, is in Rachel's mouth. She spits out his blood then shouts as loud as she can. "Help! Someone, call the po—"

Clamping his arm around Rachel's neck, he instantly silences her. Her hands fly to his arm, clawing at it, trying to free her airway, trying to relieve the searing pressure against her throat. Ruby is snarling, leaping and biting at his arm but unable to jump high enough to latch on. Rachel kicks backwards, slamming her foot against his shins. Desperately, she jams her elbows behind her.

The busser is unaffected. Through clenched teeth, he says into Rachel's ear, "You—took—Mama. Where—is—she?"

Unable to pull his arm away from her throat and unable

to breathe, Rachel gropes for her taser. Her fingers find the taser. She fumbles to release it from her belt loop, but suddenly her brain can't get her hands to move the right way. It feels like her eyeballs are bulging out of their sockets, and her head is going to explode.

There is some kind of motion, a blur, something moving fast by the gate. Inside Rachel's mind, she shouts, *Help!* But no sound escapes her vocal cords. Her vision grows blurry and a roaring thrum begins in her ears.

Rachel feels a sharp tug then ... her neck is free.

With a loud, guttural, *"Kuuuh!"* Rachel sucks air into her lungs, coughing and gasping uncontrollably. As blood rushes back to her brain, Rachel's vision starts to clear, though dozens of specks of light are flickering in and out of her vision. The pain in her throat is excruciating, like a ring of fire. She gulps in air, sputters, gags, tries to swallow.

Someone grunts and shoves the busser away but still he holds Rachel by the hair. The three of them stumble backwards, forcing Rachel's head back, pain shooting deeper into her windpipe. Ruby drops to the ground from somewhere, from someone's arm. The roaring sound in Rachel's ears dissipates, and she hears Ruby barking vicious circles around the three of them.

Blinking, Rachel can see more clearly. The delivery man is struggling to free her from the busser's grip.

Rachel reaches again for her taser, feels it hard under her fingers, releases the clip. Squeezing tightly onto the taser, her index finger finds the trigger.

The delivery man pulls back his fist to punch the busser. At the same moment, Rachel twists around—he is still clutching onto her hair—and jams the taser into the busser's gut.

Squeezing the taser as hard as she can, a sustained buzzing, like an electrical current, pierces the air. *Zzzzss!* Still, Rachel squeezes, holding the trigger down with all her might.

"Aaahh!" The busser shrieks and releases her hair, finally, then falls to his knees.

Still coughing and gulping air, Rachel stares down at him, taser in hand. He is buckled over, clutching his gut and rocking back and forth, back and forth, whimpering, "Mama. Where are you?"

Scrambling to pick up her phone without taking her eyes off the busser, Rachel shakily punches the nine-one-one buttons.

59

DAY FIFTEEN, 3:20 PM

PATRICK IS STUNNED, but his senses are on high alert, his eyes locked onto this nutcase crumpled at his feet. Meanwhile, his brain is screaming wildly for him to get the hell out of there. But something inside him has been set into motion or knocked loose. He felt this before, sometime ... somewhere ... he can't put a finger on it. All he knows, for sure, is that he isn't budging until he knows Rachel is safe.

"I need to report—" Rachel lets out a cough "—an intruder in my yard." Her voice is hoarse as she states her name and address. "Yes, he's still here." A beat of silence. "On the ground." More silence, during which Rachel rubs her throat where the skin is angry and red.

Patrick notices how gorgeous her neck is, so creamy and soft.

"I hit him with a taser," she says. "He tried to hurt—"

"Kill," Patrick interrupts. "He tried to kill you."

That is when he recognizes this new sensation. This is how he feels when he is with the horses, especially brushing them. This is protectiveness; he protected this woman. An almost hysterical laughter builds inside his gut, but he holds it in, doesn't even smile. I just saved this woman's life, he marvels to himself. Nah, she woulda gotten that taser out, zapped his arm. That woulda stopped him. Or would it?

Glancing at Patrick, Rachel says, "No. The uh ... a grocery delivery man is here."

When she acknowledges his existence, he feels disoriented, as if the world tipped, ever so slightly. *She isn't alone because I'm here. Me! As if I'm keepin' her safe.*

Rachel extends her phone to Patrick. "They want your name too ..."

That jolts Patrick back to the present, like time stopped for one, magical moment and is moving again, zooming glaringly into focus. A whisper in his head says, Get. The. Fuck. Out.

His next thought is, Too late. An intruder was reported. Cops are on the way. A man runnin' from the scene—that's a good way to get shot in the back.

Patrick takes Rachel's phone and shuffles a few steps away from the punk, but still within reach in case he grabs for her again. Dropping the tone of his voice as low as he can, he mutters, "Name's Patrick Staite." With a quick glance over his shoulder, Patrick sees the nutcase blinking, looking around, but not at him. He seems to be looking for the source of the sirens in the distance.

As the sirens grow close, Patrick's instinct to run buzzes through his entire body, like an internal taser. *Don't even think about it. These cops will come in hot, guns drawn.*

Keeping the punk mostly behind him but , Patrick

stiffens his leg muscles, planting himself firmly where he stands, moving his hands away from his body, in plain sight, so some trigger-happy cop doesn't mistake him for the perpetrator.

60

DAY FIFTEEN, 3:25 PM

FIVE DEPUTIES DESCEND on the backyard, guns drawn, and the first one through the gate is Chris. Rachel has never felt so relieved in all her life. While the deputies are demanding everyone to get their hands up where they can see them, the busser is screaming again about his mother. In the chaos, Rachel raises her hands and says loudly, so all the deputies can hear, "This is my house. I made the nine-one-one call. I'm Rachel Sharpe."

At that moment, the busser jumps up and makes a mad dash for the fence. Chris turns and chases after him.

Deputy Juarez by the gate screams, "Stop and put your hands up. Stop now!" He doesn't stop. Juarez quickly holsters her gun and whips out a taser gun, while screaming again, "Stop, or I'm tasing you!"

Juarez aims her taser at the busser and, as he reaches for the top of the fence, darts shoot out of the taser gun with a *Zzzap!* His back arches, and he drops to the ground.

Seconds later, Chris is on top of the busser, who is flat on his face and stomach. Chris handcuffs him then pulls the taser darts out of his back.

"Drop it," Deputy Kreisel yells at Rachel. "In your hand —drop it now!"

Rachel releases the grip on her little taser, letting it flop to the ground.

"I live here," she repeats. "I'm the one who made the nine-one-one call." She ticks her chin at Patrick. "And this man ... uh, he ran back here and helped. That guy was choking me and he pulled him off."

Deputy Kreisel frisks Rachel and Patrick.

By the fence, Chris mirandizes the busser, who is groaning. Deputies Ostrem and Williams help Chris lift him off the ground, but he begins to flop around like a fish out of water, wailing now for his father.

His behavior is so incongruent with what Rachel expected—except for the part where he tried to choke her— that she can't make sense of what is happening. Maybe it's from the lack of oxygen to her brain for a few seconds. *This is the stalking predator? Pleading for his mother and father? Sobbing like a child?*

Another siren grows closer to Rachel's house, the ambulance she insisted that she didn't need. The sirens get the busser kicking and writhing even harder, yelling something about a man from the hospital.

Kneeling, Chris holds the busser's feet firmly to the ground, while Williams and Ostrem pin him on his side at the shoulders and hips.

"Juarez, go get the wrap," Chris hollers. Then he looks down and says, "Wayne, if you can't calm down, we're going to restrain you. Can you do that? Can you take a couple of deep breaths?"

When Rachel hears Chris call him Wayne, she shakes her head a little in disbelief, then realizes that, of course, Chris knows who this man is. He would've questioned him weeks ago when Alicia went missing. And Rachel has been harping on Chris about the busser—Wayne—being the person who abducted Alicia.

Bet Chris believes me now, Rachel thinks.

Wayne begins bashing his head against the ground, pleading with Chris to find the man from the hospital, that maybe *he* came back and took Mama.

Chris keeps talking to Wayne, calmly, then mumbles something to Deputies Ostrem and Williams.

Deputy Kreisel, standing near Rachel and Patrick, radios back and forth with dispatch about the suspect being tased and needing to be restrained. When he releases the mic on his radio, he reaches down and reengages the safety hood on his holster, clicking it over his gun. Patrick watches him do this, and Kreisel shoots him a warning glare.

Carrying a long black bag, Juarez jogs over to where the deputies have the still-flailing Wayne pinned on the ground. She kneels at Wayne's back and zips open the bag. Pulling out a bulky, rigid black and yellow restraint pad, she wraps it around his lower legs, cinching it tightly.

"Help!" Wayne hollers, twisting his torso, thrusting his hips and nipping at Deputy Ostrem, who is still pinning his shoulders to the ground. "You're hurting me!"

Chris says, "Wayne, we're rolling you onto your stomach, so you need to turn your head ... turn your head to the side ... there you go."

Juarez puts another restraint pad on Wayne's back and

threads a strap under each of his arms, which are handcuffed behind him. Then, Williams and Ostrem hoist Wayne into a seated position while another part of the torso pad is flipped over Wayne's shoulders. Juarez quickly cinches the pad around Wayne's torso and snaps together a strap between the torso and leg restraints.

Wayne is immobilized in a seated position with his hands cuffed behind him. This seems to have calmed him down. Rachel recalls the horror of how he had Alicia handcuffed so she could only move a short distance around that handrail.

Chris directs deputies Williams, Ostrem and Juarez to step back and check their gear, but Rachel senses he wants everyone to de-escalate. It can't be any fun to physically restrain someone when they are trying to kick and bite you.

After a few moments, Chris leans forward, hands on his knees, and looks at Wayne. "In a few minutes, we're carrying you to a patrol car. You going to keep banging your head?"

Wayne appears comatose, staring blankly into the distance.

Chris steps over to Deputy Juarez and the two confer and nod. Chris takes a padded helmet from the restraint bag and leans down to Wayne again.

"I'm putting this helmet on your head so you don't hurt yourself. I don't want you biting at me. You understand? If you do, I'm putting a spit shield over your face, too."

At that, Rachel turns away—and Patrick instantly averts his gaze from her. This scene is nauseating Rachel, bringing to mind how Alicia was cuffed to a wall. The musty smell of Wayne's hand still lingers on Rachel's face, making her want to puke. She leans over and spits, realizing the salty, metallic taste of his blood is still in her mouth.

61

DAY FIFTEEN, 4:00 PM

WHEN THE PARAMEDICS SURROUND RACHEL, Hagen pulls Patrick aside to get his statement. Patrick tenses up so bad that he feels like a robot, like he is walking stiff and rigid. Walking like a guilty man.

Of all the cops that could have shown up, Patrick thinks. His body is more wired than when he was pulling that punk off Rachel, like he is bracing himself for … for what? For Hagen to poke his finger at him and say, Registered sex offender here, cuff him! Having flashbacks to his arrest twelve years ago, Patrick berates himself for getting involved. He should have just left her damned groceries on the front porch and split. Should have just let the cops handle this.

But then, Rachel might be … dead.

"So, Patrick, explain how you ended up in her backyard," Hagen says.

"I was delivering stuff from the co-op. Was at her front door when she ran out back to check on her dog. It was barkin' like crazy. I was headed to my car when I heard her and some guy screamin' at each other. So, I come around the outside of the house"—he points at the fence—"and see this guy behind her, got ahold of her hair, hand over her mouth. Then he gets her in a chokehold, so I come through the gate, pull the guy off her, then she tased the fucker. He went down, and she called nine-one-one."

It takes almost two hours before Hagen gets enough information from Patrick—and from Rachel, though they are questioned separately—to confirm that Patrick was simply a bystander.

During that interrogation, Patrick is careful to not look at Rachel. Not once. Not even a peek.

Before he releases Patrick, Hagen asks him one more question. "Are home deliveries a regular part of your job?"

"What d'you mean?"

"With your record," Hagen says, "I'm surprised they have you doing home deliveries." He locks eyes with Patrick.

Patrick knows cops are trained to watch a person's eyes to see if they are lying.

"Hmmh," Patrick scoffs, shaking his head. *Unbelievable. I save this lady's life, and this pig still don't trust me.* "I do lots of business deliveries. Ain't been asked to do a home one before, but the boss never said I couldn't. A co-worker had to go to the ER cuz her kid broke his arm. She asked me to make this delivery. That's it. You can ask her—name's Nayeli. I was just doin' her a favor."

62

THE NEXT DAY

AS SOON AS Patrick opens his eyes, he is full of dread about yesterday's encounter with Rachel, the cops and that nutcase. The whole scene was too bizarre and seems like a message, and not a good one. That cop, Hagen, isn't done trying to connect him with Alicia Meyers' abduction.

To make matters worse, it's another day off; he didn't do so well on his last day off.

But today, he has a plan: eat a late breakfast, catch a noon meeting at the Alano Club, go to the gym then go to the ranch early. He might go back to the Alano Club for an evening meeting given the way his mind is spinning about being watched by the cops and possibly being sent back to prison.

While taking a quick shower, Patrick plays the news podcast he has been listening to, non-stop, for the past three days. As he gives his goatee a final scrub, he hears an update about Alicia Meyers.

Quickly, Patrick shuts off the water and grabs a towel, listening intently.

Sheriff Garcia is talking. "... suspect, Wayne Middleton, who worked at Bucatini where Alicia Meyers was last seen, has been arrested and charged with her kidnapping—"

"Hell yeah!" Patrick shouts, fumbling to put on his glasses. Scrolling through his phone to find the latest news and finally sees it.

"Mother fuck ..." Right there on his phone is the face of the man he pulled off Rachel yesterday. He reads on: WAYNE MIDDLETON WAS ARRESTED AFTER ASSAULTING RACHEL SHARPE YESTERDAY EVENING NEAR HER HOME. MS. SHARPE IS A WITNESS IN THE KIDNAPPING CASE OF ALICIA MEYERS, WHO SHE RESCUED FROM THE ADA CREEK CAMPGROUND ON SUNDAY, NOVEMBER 9TH. MR. MIDDLETON IS BEING CHARGED WITH KIDNAPPING AND MULTIPLE COUNTS OF ASSAULT. HE IS CURRENTLY BEING HELD IN THE FRANKLIN COUNTY JAIL.

Patrick scrolls through several news feeds, all with the same basic information and none that mention him. He lets out a huge sigh of relief.

For several wonderful moments, Patrick dances around the room, laughing and punching the air and saying, "Yeah-hhh! I'm a free fuckin' man. Free. I'm free."

Never has Patrick been so happy to hear about someone being arrested.

63

____

TWO DAYS LATER

PENDING HIS ARRAIGNMENT, Wayne is held in a specialized unit at the jail for inmates with behavioral issues. He has been alternately weeping, screaming at the guards to release him, crying out for his mother and pleading for his father to leave him alone. Without his noise-cancelling head-set, Wayne can't block out his papa's voice.

The public defender, Brandon Dougherty, talks to the County's psychiatrist before meeting with Wayne. The psychiatrist describes Wayne as being in a state of extreme distress and likely delusional. He has been given a sedating medication but is still easily agitated. The doctor suspects Wayne is likely schizophrenic but explains that further evaluation will be necessary.

Sounds like a nut case or a meth addict to Brandon, neither of which he wants to deal with three days before his vacation. What he needed was a simple, cut and dried case, like a DUI. Brandon has been a public defender for five years, and already he is burnt out. He loved law school, all the history and the legal analyses and debating, but criminal law has soured Brandon to the point that he is seriously considering something easy and more lucrative, like real estate law.

After reviewing the police report in detail, Brandon is pleasantly surprised to find that Wayne Middleton is also being charged with kidnapping Alicia Meyers. His interest in Wayne shoots up a few notches because a high visibility case like this recent abduction is always good for an attorney's reputation. Getting his name more widely known could open some doors for Brandon.

Peeking through the window before entering the interview room, Brandon is elated that Wayne looks rather ... child-like. He is a tall man, but his posture—shoulders rolled forward, gaze down at the floor—makes Wayne look meek and harmless. That will have a positive influence on a jury.

Brandon introduces himself then says, "Wayne, do you understand that you're being charged with assaulting Rachel Sharpe."

Wayne stares at Brandon with a completely blank look on his face.

"The day before yesterday? In her backyard? The police report says you tried to choke—"

"No, no. That's wrong. No. Rachel ... *she* should be arrested. *She* is the suspect that took Mama. And she bit me." He holds up a bandaged hand.

"Hmm," Brandon scribbles on his legal pad then skims the police report. "It says here your mother—" he looks up at Wayne "—died recently?"

Wayne's eyes go wide with disbelief and anger. "Who

told you that? Who? They're lying. That woman, that Rachel, she has my mama."

"You're also being charged with kidnapping. Are you aware of this?"

Chewing on his lower lip, Wayne is rocking back and forth.

"You're being charged with kidnapping Alicia Meyers ..."

"I don't ... don't know her. Don't know who she is."

"Alicia was missing for two weeks. She was found in a cabin that belonged to someone in your family. Near Ada Creek Campground."

Wayne shakes his head, vehemently. "The man from the hospital, he brought Mama to the cabin ... he must've taken this ... Alicia lady there, too."

Wayne looks over his shoulder then and hisses. "Shhh. I don't care! Stop telling me what to do."

"Uh ... who're you talking to there?"

Cupping his hands around his mouth, Wayne whispers, "That's Papa. He's *always* bossing me around."

"Right ... hmm. Listen, I'm going to file some paperwork for the judge to look at tomorrow. It's called a competency evaluation. That means someone, a mental health professional, can talk to you and see if you're able to go to a hearing right now and ... understand what you're being charged with, what this trial would be about ... Does that sound okay with you?"

"Will they let me out? Cuz I have to go to work. What day is it? I think I missed ... two ... maybe three days."

"Well, you'll probably get out of here, but you'll go to a hospit—"

Wayne explodes, jumping up, pounding the door to get out and screaming. "No hospitals! I don't want to go to a hospital. No! No hospitals."

Okaaay, Brandon thinks. No need for a jury any time soon.

64

THREE DAYS LATER

AS RACHEL DRIVES over to meet with Chris and the prosecuting attorney to discuss the attack, she is uneasy on many levels. The Franklin County Prosecutor's Office is right across the street from the three-story, brick building that houses the County jail where Wayne is being held. Rachel clearly has a titch of PTSD from this predator. She isn't looking forward to talking about the attack again. And, as a witness to the kidnapping case, Rachel will also need to talk to the prosecutor in detail about Alicia's rescue, including her premonitions. She still can't believe with all the media coverage, Rachel's image, along with Alicia's, splashed all over the news, that her clairvoyance hasn't been mentioned. Not yet.

This isn't the Salem witch trials, Rachel reminds herself again, as she walks through the county building's security check.

The prosecuting attorney, Erika Terrell, is in her mid-thirties with bleached hair and wearing so much powdered make-up her skin looks cakey. She is also very pregnant, waddling to the table and easing herself into a chair. This is the first time Rachel has met Erika, but she has heard from other attorneys about her reputation: hard-ass, stubborn to the point of being unreasonable, seldom willing to plea bargain. The perfect qualities for prosecuting a predator.

Erika gets right down to business. "Mr. Wayne Middleton's arraignment is tomorrow at nine thirty. The public defender is requesting a competency evaluation and anticipates, at some point, a plea of not guilty by reason of insanity. It appears he has some level of developmental disability."

Rachel struggles to wrap her mind around this information. Is this predator faking that he is mentally delayed? The man who abducted Alicia without a trace—except for that earring—who held her captive in a cabin for two weeks is delayed? Then a mortifying thought comes to her. Did she falsely accuse a developmentally disabled man of being a predator? All this time, her premonition was wrong? Did they arrest an innocent man? Her cheeks burn with embarrassment. She can't even look at Chris.

Wait a minute—this man tried to choke me. Why would he do that if it wasn't because I found his victim?

Erika continues, "His primary caregiver or—" she flips through papers in a folder "—his primary support was his mother. It's unclear what level of dependency he had on her, but she died two months ago. He thinks she's still alive." She pauses to catch her breath. "Keeps asking for his father, too. Also dead."

Erika is practically panting. Rachel guesses that is from the baby pressing up against her diaphragm. This woman looks like she could go into labor any minute. *Hope that isn't a premonition.*

"It all jives with the victim's statement," Chris says. "He

called her 'Mama' and talked about her being 'brought home' from the hospital ..."

An image flits into Rachel's mind: Wayne in her back-yard, weeping and calling out for his mother. At the time, it didn't make any sense because Alicia didn't look old enough to be his mother, and why would someone abduct his own mother? Rachel had assumed he was crazy or whacked out on drugs.

"I'm really confused," Rachel says. "Did he abduct Alicia Meyers?"

"Like I said the other day, the victim can't make a positive ID. And he kept her doped up every day, so ... things are hazy for her, she can't—"

"He *is* being charged with first degree kidnapping." Erika shifts a little in her seat and rubs her very large abdomen. "We've got a good case."

Chris says, "That was a family cabin, where she was being held—owned by his great uncle. Sits on a small, private inholding on Forest Service land."

"My best guess," Erika says, "is he'll end up being committed to the state hospital's forensic unit. Doubt if he'll ever get out."

65

SIX DAYS LATER

GISELLE SAID she had no choice but to let Patrick go. It wasn't the deputies showing up at the Co-Op that got him fired, it was that home delivery, which wasn't in his job description. He can't prove it, but Patrick is pretty sure that cop, Hagen, said something to Giselle about having a sex offender make home deliveries. This is the thanks he gets for saving a woman's life: the cops got him fired.

And now that he is on Hagen's radar, Patrick is afraid he will never have a normal life. The cops will be watching his every move. Every time a woman is assaulted, is Hagen going to show up at Patrick's work, or the ranch—that would be devastating—asking for proof that he worked on such-and-such day? And for the next two years, while he is on parole, cops will never need a warrant to talk to his boss or search his property.

Every time Patrick thinks about it, he becomes furious and feels trapped, which makes him want to escape. And that can trigger old behaviors. If he knows anything, he knows how to escape, at least in his mind. Dr. Levitsky is trying to help him break that cycle, but for now, Patrick tries not to think about Hagen or any cops so he can avoid the explosive anger.

Patrick is no longer sweating bullets about going back to prison, though he doubts if he will ever stop looking over his shoulder for cops. Now, he is sweating bullets about not finding another job and ending up homeless. One good thing coming his way is that a room at the Mountain Home Ranch is supposed to be available next month. If he can just hold it together that long, he will be living there full-time.

Occasionally, a nice thought pops into his mind, like maybe Rachel Sharpe *would* go out with him some day. After all, he did save her life.

The only time his brain completely shuts up is when he is at the ranch where there are no cops, no triggers, no news, no women, no booze, just him and eight carefree, powerful horses. He tries to let go of any hostility when he is around the horses because they are intuitive animals, and anger bubbles close to the surface for Patrick. If he made the horses skittish, he would never forgive himself.

Today, his favorite horse, Buster, a dark brown horse with a shiny black mane and tail, nuzzles his hand with its velvety lips, and Patrick can't help but relax. When Scout sniffs at Patrick's neck, tickling him with soft, flicking whiskers, Patrick figures he can't be too horrible of a person if these animal like him.

Raking fresh straw around the final stall, Tilly bumps up against Patrick's shoulder and whinnies. "Hey there, girl," he says, scratching behind her ears. She lowers her head and pushes against his hands. Chuckling, he says, "You wanna be brushed, don't you?"

He leads Tilly into a stall and brushes her back and flanks, breathing in the faint musky smell mingled with the scent of grass and dirt and fresh straw. Smiling, he says, "You've been rollin' in the field, haven't you?" The thought of being so free that you could roll around in a sunny field brings a lump to Patrick's throat.

Tilly's neck is warm under his hand as he moves up to brush her coarse, silky mane. He is super gentle, knowing that he must never, ever tug or pull on a tangle in a horse's mane. The stable manager explained to Patrick that if he yanks on their manes, not only does it hurt them, it destroys their trust.

66

___

THREE WEEKS LATER

RACHEL HAS BEEN KEEPING busy at work, taking Ruby to scent training, spending more time with Lorena and, grudgingly, with Fletcher, and hanging out some, but less than before, with her dad and Margaret. With Wayne in the state hospital, she even went back to Bucatini for dinner once, on a date with Fletcher's friend, Brett. It was a bad idea—the date and the restaurant.

Figuring she has seen the last of Chris, Rachel initially thought, Good riddance! She was angry that he never acknowledged that her premonitions were spot-on. He didn't even thank her or invite her to continue volunteering. After a couple of weeks, she softened and decided he may have his reasons, professional ones, no doubt, for his oversight.

Maybe he isn't allowed to thank a volunteer without clear, probable cause.

Despite her better senses, however, Rachel has begun to wonder how Chris is doing, with his brooding eyes and long legs. She wonders if those sumptuous lips of his have finally broken into a smile.

In her weekly counseling, Glen and Rachel have been using EMDR to reduce her anxiety from Wayne's attack, as well as to curtail her ESP. Her last premonition was of the old variety—impending doom radiating from a woman who works at the Third Avenue Food Co-Op. Rachel was able to ignore it or, at least, bypass it and not stew over it. Her clairvoyant brain hasn't been rewired, but it does seem to be getting short-circuited.

Today, Rachel has been discussing with Glen her mixed feelings about Chris.

"And you know what's really weird?" she says. "When I think about him lately, I just want to ... hug him. *That* is what I fantasize about." She shakes her head in dismay. "Not about having sex ... well, I've thought of that, too ..."

"Oh yeah, lots of women want that—a big old bear hug." He motions his arms as if enveloping someone.

She stares at him for a few beats then blinks. "They do?"

"Sure. Comes up a lot in couples' therapy. Makes women feel loved."

"Then I've been cheated. All this time, women are out there getting hugs and being held? Are they ... asking to be held?"

"Some are."

Disheartened, she lets out a scoff. "I never even let myself *want* to be hugged. Except by Dad or Lorena. And Margaret, she's a real hugger. I'm trying to get used to her hugs."

"Well, you need a strong connection ... and a lot of trust ... to let someone hold you."

"Nooo," Rachel says. "You have to *not* have premonitions."

"Ahh." Slowly nodding his head, Glen looks towards the

ceiling for a moment, apparently, thinking that one through. Hopefully, he is also coming up with a solution, Rachel thinks.

"But Chris knows you have premonitions," he says.

"Right ..."

"And you trust him?"

"Strangely, yes."

"Maybe you can talk to him about it ..." He holds his hands out, palms up, like this is a perfectly reasonable suggestion.

Rachel gives Glen a skeptical look, eyebrows raised.

"Maybe he isn't afraid of your premonitions," Glen continues. "But you'll never know unless you ask. Then you two can agree on how to handle it if you do have one."

Rachel rolls her eyes and lets out a groan. "Oh, that sounds like a healthy start to a relationship. I *hate* this ESP."

"Is it possible ... you won't have one about him? Aren't there some people who remain blank to you?"

"My parents—well, Mom until the accident—and Lorena. My aunt and uncle."

"I wonder if that's because you were close to them. You were bonded with your relatives long before you had premonitions."

"Maybe. I did have one about my grandma—my dad's mother—but we weren't close ... I mean ... we didn't see her that often. She lived back east."

Rachel furrows her brow in concentration, considering Glen's suggestion. She recollects her early friendship with Lorena and how their connection was almost instant. Rachel felt like she had known Lorena for her entire life. In fact, they had only been friends a few months when she told Lorena about her premonitions. And a few boyfriends, except Aaron, about whom she never had premonitions. Those were men she warmed to fairly quickly.

Tentatively, Rachel says, "So ... what you're saying is ... getting close, connecting with people—the thing I've been avoiding my whole life—could actually help me *not* have premonitions about them?"

"It kind of make sense, doesn't it? Because when you're close to someone, you can relax around them and—"

"Oh, I wasn't relaxed around Aaron at first ... I liked him too much." She recalls how afraid she was to have a premonition and blow it all to hell. "Took me a couple of months to start letting my guard down with him ... Lot of good that did me."

"Hmm. Well, it's only a theory. The more you can let your guard down, not be hypervigilant, maybe the less likely your—ESP or, your premonitions, will be, uh—" he struggles to find the right word "—triggered or activated." He gives an unassuming little shrug but Rachel suspects Glen has had this theory since learning of her clairvoyance; he was just waiting for her to be ready to hear it.

A bubble of excitement rises from Rachel's gut and spreads to her chest. She isn't sure, but it feels like hope.

67

———————

FOUR WEEKS LATER

EVEN THOUGH PATRICK got fired from the Co-Op, Giselle gave him a good reference letter. Between the reference letter and the parolee second chance program, Patrick finally gets a new job, which he likes better anyway.

Most days, he is done by three thirty, so he has more time to spend with the horses. Plus, including tips, Patrick makes more money at Black Bird Café. The only problem is that if Rachel is looking for Patrick at the Co-Op, he will never know. He imagines she might want to hand him her number and say, Thanks for saving my life. Gimme a call sometime.

Patrick thinks about sending Rachel a simple note but isn't sure if she would like that or be creeped out by it. He might run the note idea by Dr. Levitsky so jotted down what it would say: I HOPE YOU ARE RECOVERY FROM THAT ATTACK. I'M GLAD YOU & YOUR DOG WERE OKAY. GOOD THING YOU HAD THAT TASER & I'M GLAD I COULD HELP. IF YOU NEED TO REACH ME SINCE I WAS A WITNESS MY # IS 360-305-7012.

If he ever mails the note, Patrick painted a handmade card to send with it, which turned out beautiful. He likes looking at the painting and has it propped in his bedroom windowsill where he sees it each night before he climbs in bed and first thing each morning. The painting is a landscape scene with tall, green grasses waving in the foreground and two horses galloping towards mountains in the far-off distance. One of the horses is dark brown with a glossy, black mane and tail, and the other is chestnut with a flaxen mane and tail, just like Tilly at the ranch. Patrick had to mix the paint to get the exact color for the mane and tail: a light golden brown, like honey. The same color as Rachel's hair.

Seeing as how they went through such an intense experience together, Patrick thinks about Rachel more than ever. Mostly, he has friendly, nondeviant thoughts. They would *really* have something to talk about now. Though he is dying to find out what Rachel does for a living, where she works, maybe even stumble on her phone number, he has resisted doing any "research" on her. So far. When his thoughts about Rachel get dark, he goes for a run or a workout or rides one of the horses. Patrick won't risk any more triggers; he has too much to lose.

A room finally opened up at Mountain Home Ranch, so Patrick lives there now and can work with the horses and ride whenever he wants. For the first time in decades, things are finally going his way. He is starting to feel like a new man, like a human again.

Today, while riding Buster, Patrick stops at the bottom of a valley, deep in the woods, and climbs off the horse. Digging a hole several inches deep, he buries the last piece of his former self, tapping the dirt over the hole with his new cowboy boots. It feels like a tiny funeral.

Scattering some dead leaves over the area, he can't even tell the ground was ever disturbed. There isn't one shred of evidence of the man he used to be.

Or of the handcuff key buried there.

68

———————————

SIX WEEKS LATER

RACHEL WAITS until eight p.m. on a Tuesday to call Chris, figuring he will be off duty by then, not yet asleep and, hopefully, not on a date.

After some casual chit-chat, Rachel finally gets to the point.

"Sooo ... I was wondering ... since it doesn't look like I'll be testifying in a case anytime soon ... if you'd like to go out. You know, on a date." She doesn't want any crossed wires. "We could go out for dinner or ... for a trail run."

"A trail run?" he says, sounding amused, which Rachel thinks is a good sign.

"Do you run?"

"I do run. Usually *on a road*. Sometimes my treadmill."

"Well, it's much more fun in the woods. And I can let Ruby off leash there, too. Of course, I haven't done a trail run since ... you know ... Alicia and all that."

"I bet," he says. The phone line hums with a few seconds of silence. Then he adds, "And now you're stuck asking cops out just so you can run in the woods again."

"Basically," she says smiling. "I'm starting with you, then working my way through all the single deputies. And I've already been background checked, so that should be a plus."

He chuckles.

Wow, Rachel thinks, he is really cutting loose here.

"Yeah, us cops have a real high bar for who we date—no criminal record."

"Ahh! Are you saying that's all I have to offer the single deputies of Franklin County?"

At this, he genuinely laughs. Rachel realizes she has never heard him laugh and likes the sound of it. Being a cop might be harder than being a clairvoyant, she thinks.

"Noo, you've ..." Chris stammers, "you've got ... more than that." Rachel enjoys this seemingly unflappable man sounding a bit awkward. "But, technically, you *are* a witness," he continues. "Of course, this case might never go to trial. Or not for years, so ..."

Chris hesitates for a few beats, long enough that Rachel thinks his professionalism is going to win this one.

"I'm off this Thursday," he says. "How about we do one of these trail runs then?"

"Okay! Say around three?"

"Can't wait," he says. "Then let's go out for dinner."

Now we're really getting somewhere. "Sounds good. Have you been to Black Bird Café?"

ACKNOWLEDGMENTS

After writing two memoirs and a biography, writing a novel was a huge shift—telling the truth is *so* much easier than making stuff up. I couldn't have created this story without the help of a weekly writers' critique group, two great editors and several beta readers. Thank you all for helping me bring this story to life: Adam, Carol Guesno, Linda Herzog, Kitty Hogan, Sarah Horowitz, Kay Kenyon, Connie Mehmel, Carol Ann Seaman and Steve Wiser.